By the same author

FICTION

A Cobra's Bite Doesn't Hurt

The Bengal Tiger's Silent Roar

The Bengal Tiger's Silent Roar

Published by The Conrad Press Ltd. in the United Kingdom 2022

Tel: +44(0)1227 472 874
www.theconradpress.com
info@theconradpress.com

ISBN 978-1-915494-13-9

Copyright © Anil Nijhawan, 2022

The moral right of Anil Nijhawan to be identified as author of this work has been asserted in accordance with the Copyright, Designs and Patents Act 1988.

All rights reserved.

This is a work of fiction. Any resemblance to actual persons, either living or dead, or to actual events or locales, is entirely coincidental.

Printed and bound in Great Britain by Clays Ltd, Elcograf S.p.A

Typesetting and cover design by The Book Typesetters
www.thebooktypesetters.com

The Conrad Press logo was designed by Maria Priestley.

The Bengal Tiger's Silent Roar

ANIL NIJHAWAN

My inspiration, my sons, Kavin and Rohit

1

Malvya Nagar, New Delhi, 1953

Tarun pulled out his Atlas bicycle from under the tarpaulin, gave the chrome hub dynamo a quick shine with a handkerchief, and clipped the grease guards to his trouser legs. Earlier that morning his brother had insulted him, calling him a station coolie. What girl will want to marry someone who looks like a coolie, he had said. Burning with anger and hurt he was going to the tailor to order a new shirt and trouser. I will show him who is a station coolie. He whacked the bell with the palm of his rugged hand, making it ring out riotously and began pedalling towards the market.

Pali, his nephew, hollered from the front steps, 'uncle, are you going past the bus stop, may I have a pillion ride.'

'You can very well walk to the bus stop,' Tarun replied with a dismissive wave of a hand, 'you have legs.'

In the lane past the bus stop, the cobbler with a grey moustache looked up at him expectantly. A refugee from Lahore. He had set up the shoe mending trade under a mature banyan tree and was keeping Tarun's ageing Bata shoes in wearable condition. At the scooter repair shop someone was throttling an old Lambretta engine, making it cough repeatedly. It reminded Tarun of old men with chronic bronchitis. At the crossroad, tinkling the bell furiously at the shoppers crossing his path, he felt a sudden drag on his bicycle as if an invisible force had taken control. He stepped up on the pedals, the effort forcing him off the seat. The bike wobbled. Fearing flat tyres or some other failing he applied the brake and whacked the bell again. More bloody expense, he thought. As he was dismounting, a cry resonated in his ear, '*ha, ha*, got you.'

He turned around sharply.

'Salim, you, you had me there for a moment,' Tarun cried, pleased to see his former workmate grinning roguishly and flicking his eyebrows. 'I thought there was something wrong with my bicycle.'

'Bicycle is all right, it is the rider who needs fixing,' Salim said, releasing the hold on the frame and laughing, exposing his *paan* stained teeth. The moustache was the same, as was his confident manner. He was wearing a silk shirt fashionably unbuttoned at the chest.

'Come on let us have something to eat,' Salim said, placing an arm on Tarun's shoulder.

Tarun's joy rapidly turned to anxiety. He would have to pay for the food since he owed Salim a favour for the gift of a portable Pye radio. 'But I – I have to do some urgent shopping,' Tarun said.

'Shopping? To buy vegetables *alu baingan gobi*?' Salim said, 'that's a woman's job. Haven't you got someone at home, a wife?'

Tarun hesitated. Does he think there is something wrong with me? 'Not vegetables, I am going to buy some clothes.'

'What's the urgency about clothes *yaar*? Are you going to a wedding?'

'Wedding? No, no, no,' Tarun said with an exaggerated shake of the head, conscious of his own unwedded status. Twenty-eight years old and still a bachelor. What must people think? 'Let us go home, my mother will cook us a good dinner,' he said and instantly wanted to retract the invitation as it came to his mind Salim was not a Hindu. 'You are asking me to cook for a Muslim?' mother would hiss sternly in Tarun's ears. The memory of the Hindu family in Lyallpur, who lived three doors away, being set upon by a Muslim mob yelling slogans, *Pakistan zindabad, Pakistan zindabad*, was still fresh in her head. She often talked of the terrifying screams of three young children whom she had known from birth, going silent one by one, and of the torching of the house. She never tired of reliving the past when in company of her friends in the neighbourhood, and the neighbours had their own tales of the horror of the partition of 1947.

'Home? Who wants to go home?' shouted Salim, 'we are going to eat out.'

'All right, let us go to Moti Mahal,' Tarun said, feeling guilty at his lapse in hospitality, 'it's the biggest restaurant in Malviya Nagar. Their *kulfi falooda* is famous.'

'Oh good.' Salim said, rubbing his hands together.

Tarun pressed his hand to the shirt pocket where he kept the money. There was little money to feel though. It was the end of the month. Why should Salim not pay for the food? He is not short of money. He has a well-paid job as head electrical technician, and the lucrative side business he has going with his father-in-law, a merchant of electrical goods.

'Are you still with Mohindra Pal?' Salim asked.

'Yes, I am. Where else will I go?' Tarun said impassively with a shake of the shoulders and then recalled the early days at Mohindra Pal & Co. Salim was the senior technician working on complicated installations. Tarun's duties initially were to carry tools, ladders and be useful. He was grateful to Salim for going out of his way to show him the intricacies of the job. A year later when Salim had announced he was leaving, Tarun was disappointed. The disappointment had turned to jealousy when Salim said his contract was with a luxurious hotel at double the pay.

'Is he looking after you?' Salim said.

Tarun nodded. What else could he say? He was grateful to even have a job. In fact, Tarun was astonished that Mohindra Pal had agreed to take him on. The heart leaping like a mad frog, he had promised the boss he would work diligently and learn on the job. That was eighteen months ago. It was his first proper job. Like everyone else, he had taken to wake early, bathe, dress-up and cycle to work to arrive at a predetermined hour.

Tarun was too embarrassed to tell Salim the whole truth, that he had landed this job through his older sister, Savitri's sagacity. A strange chain of events had taken place in the summer month, which led to a chance encounter with Mohindra Pal. And the businessman offered him a job without even an interview or a meeting.

❁

Up at six, Savitri took off for the half hour brisk walk to the Ganesh temple, to offer a prayer for Tarun. Dear God, please help my brother find a job, anything that will give him purpose in life. All his older brothers are educated and settled with good jobs and families. Tarun is the only one left behind. Why must that be?

She stood under blue, fluorescent tube lights and prayed with bowed head to the life size marble statue of Lord Ganesh decked with garlands of jasmines and marigolds while the head priest in flimsy dhoti chanted *shlokas* in Sanskrit. Beside him another priest, naked from waist up, was clanging a brass bell with mechanical dexterity and keeping an eye on the coins that fell on the donation mat. After she had finished praying, she unknotted a corner of her white sari, released a coin from its folds, dropped it on the mat and turned back. Outside, as she was slipping her foot into the sandal her friend Kanta, also in white sari, was withdrawing her from a green slip-on.

'Oh Kanta,' she said, 'go on, go on, say your prayer. I will wait for you outside.'

Kanta returned five minutes later, and they started the walk back home, matching strides, comfortable in each other's company.

While they were chatting, a dog crossed their path, and then came back to lick Kanta's feet.

'*Yaeek*, shoo, shoo,' Kanta yelped and pulled her foot

away. The animal, a black and white mutt, looked up at Kanta with its round eyes, as if hurt by the rejection. Behind them, Savitri heard the temple bell ring out with sudden violence – dong, dong, dong – on the dying note of the priest's last shloka. In the conspicuously loud racket, she heard a thud. It was louder, as if a cymbal crash of an oompah band. Savitri stopped and turned around. What she saw horrified her. A little girl was lying in the middle of the road. An arm cranked under the body and legs splayed. Four or five yards away was a black Morris Minor, embedded into roadside boulders, its engine still running. The driver was beating his head to the steering wheel, making the car horn beep with each strike as if in accompaniment to the ding, dong of the temple bell.

Savitri rushed to the scene and picked up the girl, who was howling and beating her arms and legs. She asked people in the rapidly building crowd if they knew the girl. No one came forward. 'We should take her to the hospital,' Savitri said to Kanta.

'Let us take her to Dr Mallick. He is not far,' Kanta suggested.

They extricated themselves from the crowd, which was now threatening to beat up the driver. 'Have you no shame you son of a donkey, drinking alcohol this time of the morning, when the world is praying to their Gods.'

At the end of the lane, they saw a parked auto-rickshaw and clambered onto it. 'Dr Mallick's surgery, quick, quick,' Savitri yelled at the confused rickshaw driver puffing on a cigarette, 'what are you gaping at, come on move.'

The surgery was already packed. Savitri rushed in with

the girl and demanded to see Dr Mallick.

'Madam, the doctor is with a patient. You wait for your turn,' snapped the compounder busily scribbling something on a label attached to a cobalt glass bottle, his white coat stained yellow and orange.

'There has been an accident. This child needs attention instantly. Tell him I am Savitri Sehgal.'

'But you must wait, *na*,' the compounder mumbled irritably, 'they all want to see him first… no patience.'

'Don't you understand, you fool, this is an emergency,' Savitri screamed, making heads turn in the waiting room and on hearing the commotion Dr Mallick lifted the curtain to his office and put his head out. 'What's the matter?'

'Doctor *sahib*, a car hit this child. You must examine her straight away.'

'*Arre* Sunita, what are you doing here?' the doctor exclaimed seeing the pale, frightened face of the child in Savitri's arms.

'You know her?'

'Yes, yes, I know the family well. I have been to their house.'

'Then you must inform them immediately because I don't know who she is or where she lives.'

❁

A month later Savitri was hopping from foot to foot on the sun scorched concrete while hanging washing on the clothesline. A radio in someone's house came on with a deafening blast. She recognised the song from the film Baazi – *aaj ki raat piya dil na todo* – and began humming under her breath. Presently she heard a knock on the door and someone calling, 'is anyone home.'

She threw the last of the garments on the line and hurried to the front. A stranger with hands joined reverentially, broad-shouldered, greasy hair neatly combed with side parting, was standing at the door.

Savitri shrank. Oh no, not another volunteer asking for donations for the Malviya Nagar Dussehra festival. It will be the biggest and the best this year, they always say, sisters give generously.

She was about to ask him to go away, but the man spoke first. 'Are you Savitri *behan*?' he asked.

'Yes, I am,' she said, adjusting her sari.

'Savitri Sehgal?'

'Yes, yes.'

'Then I must thank you for saving the girl.'

'*Achha*, you mean little Sunita.'

He bowed his head a little deeper. 'I have had a word with her, forbidden her to run around on the streets alone.'

'How are you connected to Sunita?' Savitri asked.

Humbly, the man replied, 'she is my daughter; my wife's daughter and I hope yours too. Without your prompt action, who knows what would have happened to her. We are most grateful to you.'

She saw the resemblance then. The shape of his nose and cheek bones were like Sunita's. She noticed his immaculately pressed shirt, no loose threads or stains, shoes shining like a trooper's. 'Come inside. It is hot. Would you like a drink of lemonade?'

'No, no, no thank you. I just came by to let you know Sunita is fine, shaken but no broken bones, thank God. Doctor *Sahib* took loving care of her. I went to the police station, had the case against the car owner dropped. He was not to blame; my girl had foolishly dashed into the road without looking. You know what children are like. She was chasing her dog. Foolish girl.'

'A black and white puppy?'

'Yes, she calls him Spotty.'

'Hmm. Does she have any brothers and sisters?'

'A brother and an older sister. She is of marriageable age,' he said.

'How old is she?'

'Sangeeta is twenty-six.' He did not elaborate, did not say if she was working, or sitting idle at home, or in higher education, nor did he say she was a *ladli kuri*, a pampered daughter. Twenty-six, still without a husband, there had to be something wrong with her, Savitri concluded.

'Now I must get back to work, the men are waiting for me.'

'Where are you from?' she asked, now keen to learn a little more about the family and the daughter, Sangeeta.

'My family is from Sargodha, but I was born in Delhi,' he said and looked impatiently at his watch.

'What line of work are you in?' Savitri asked.

'I am an electrical contractor, Savitriji. Our work is with businesses and shops. If I can do anything for you, you must let me know.'

'There is something you could do,' she said, 'my young

brother is looking for work. He is not very educated but strong and hard working. Could you find him something to do? I will be grateful.'

'It will be done Savitriji,' he said without hesitation, 'ask him to see me. My name is Mohindra Pal.'

That is how Tarun entered the world of the employed, a wage for a day's work, of give and take, understanding how the wheel of commerce turned on its axis. It was a shock to his system, but he persevered.

❁

Moti Mahal was buzzing. Laughter, animated conversations, spoons scraping plates, clatter of tin dishes, a radio tuned to popular music periodically breaking into crude commercials. Smell of cooked food drifted from the kitchen into the main hall. They took a corner table facing each other.

'I thought you were taking me to some place air-conditioned, like Gaylord,' Salim said, eyeing the surroundings with disdain.

'It's not so bad here,' Tarun pointed at the ceiling fans above their heads and pushed a plate of cucumber and onion salad towards him, 'here try this.' He gazed at the mirror on the wall behind Salim's head and watched the customers' reflections move in and out of the roses and vines engraved along its edges.

Salim dived into the food as soon as it was set on the table, tearing pieces of roti, scooping up yellow dhal or pieces of meat. 'Wah, what tasty,' he said, looking up and gesturing with his hand, making a circle with forefinger and thumb, 'first class. But why aren't you eating?'

'*Baas*, I am full now,' Tarun replied, shaking his head.

'Eat like a man, have a *paratha*... waiter.' He raised a dhal stained finger to catch the waiter's attention.

'No, no paratha.' Tarun pulled Salim's hand back down to the table.

He had been keeping a tally of the bill; making sure it did not exceed the amount of money in his shirt pocket. 'I am full, *bilkul*,' he said, patting the stomach.

'Why do you keep looking this way and that way. Is something bothering you?'

Tarun feigned surprise, 'bothering me? No, nothing is bothering me.'

'*Abe saale*, you can talk to Uncle Salim. Didn't I teach you how to strip a cable and solder, and a hundred other things? Didn't I?' Salim said, acting like an older brother, though both were of the same age.

'Yes, you did.'

'How many brothers and sisters do you have?'

'Seven.'

'Married?'

'Yes, all of them.' He waited for the inevitable next question: so why are you not married. How could he explain the tyranny of his family, that they considered him unqualified for marriage? As if one must first sit an exam, obtain a certificate, and then face a panel of judges. In his case the judges were the family members, each with their own prejudices and vested interests.

But Salim surprised him. He glanced slyly to his left and

right and did a hand gesture. 'Doesn't that thing stand up?'

'Shh, keep your voice down.' Tarun blushed. Twenty-eight years old. He had never tried to befriend a girl, never touched anyone in an intimate manner, fearing they would rebuff him. When in company of young girls, he busied himself with mundane tasks. Even on the street, in public places, he deliberately kept his gaze away from attractive girls, in case they accused him of ogling, 'you dirty old man, have you no shame?' All through his childhood, he had known only one way to deal with life, which was to lie low and remain invisible. When he was eighteen years old, he used to watch his younger sister, Usha, confident and bubbly, flirting with boys who came to the house. He used to wonder why no girl showed similar interest in him. Now aged twenty-eight he had stopped wondering. He often looked without emotion at the courting couples on park benches or those coming out of cinema halls holding hands. Gone was the hope that he could be one of those lucky ones on the bench leaning into a beautiful female.

'You want to do it? Eh?' Salim said suggestively, 'come with me, I know girls. They are so beautiful; *bachoo*, you will start drooling when you see them.'

Tarun looked around him and then picking up a tumbler of *lassi* took it to his lips. It was empty. He peered inside the tumbler, puzzled, and then brought it back down to the table, a bit too hard, with a crack. His hand began trembling. He clasped the tumbler as though it would give him support. The other hand searched for something to latch on to. He knew what was coming but could not articulate. The mouth opened and shut. The knees buckled and he sank to the floor. The chair screeched. He saw a fleeting image of Salim springing up, and people stepping away from him, disgust showing on their faces. A plate crashed to the floor. 'He is a drunkard, throw him out,' someone said.

And then nothing.

The words he heard next were: what happened to you? He forced his eyes to focus. Saw Salim's face. It was peering into him. Too close. And then he realised Salim was on his hands and knees. It came to Tarun that he had not taken the medicine. He slid his hand in the pocket, searching frantically for the small glass bottle.

Salim repeated, 'what happened to you?'

Tarun nodded. 'Epilepsy fit. I forgot my medicine, left it at home. How long was I gone?'

'Too long,' Salim said, 'what a frightening sight.'

'I am all right now,' Tarun said, 'feeling better.'

'You don't look all right.'

A big man in *white kurta* came over waving his arms as if herding a flock of goats. 'Take him outside, take him outside, give him fresh air... come, come, come,' he said.

'*Abe saale*, you gave me such a shock, I have lost my appetite now. At least you could have warned me beforehand.'

'How could I have known? I have not had one... in eighteen months... I am telling the truth... believe me.'

They walked to Tarun's bicycle and before parting company Salim advised him to eat butter parathas, chicken, and mutton. 'It will make you strong, like me.' He gave his bulging biceps a hefty pat. 'All this epileptic business will go away, and your penis will become strong and stiff like this.' This time he swung his fist like a boxer demonstrating an uppercut.

Tarun smiled. 'No chance, my mother is a strict vegetarian. She doesn't cook meat and will not let me eat either.'

'So, you don't have to tell her. You come with me to Khans in Paharganj. He makes the best mutton biryani in Delhi. *Hanh* let us go there on Sunday. Afterwards we will go to meet the girls. What do you say?'

Unable to bring himself to say yes, he just nodded and instantly felt a stab of guilt in the chest as if he had already done something immoral and dirty.

'Good, meet me at Ajmeri Gate.' Salim slapped Tarun on the shoulder. 'And give the penis a good spit and polish. Get it ready for action.'

Tarun walked home feeling weak and yet exhilarated for agreeing to meet the girls, a strange kind of sensation, one he had not experienced before. Later he reflected on the fits he had had over the years. When he was young, his friends used to tease him, 'a *bhooth*, ghost has possessed Tarun,' and then run away fearing they too would catch the 'ghost,' as if it were contagious. The most embarrassing, yet memorable was at his younger sister, Usha's wedding. It came without a warning. Momentary disorientation and then he was flat on the floor. His brother described it to him later, 'you were thrashing about like a landed fish.'

Usha's wedding was a lavish affair lasting three days. At her insistence, the reception took place in the lobby of the newly opened Manor Hotel. Instead of a brass band from the bazaar she had booked a six-piece orchestra to play dance music. Even at the *ladies sangeet* she had hired musicians with suitable repertoire to entertain the guests. A cocktail party was organised to welcome the bridegroom and his family. The guests arrived attired in the most elegant chiffon saris, sherwanis and three-piece suits. The air was thick with small talk, laughter, and shouted greetings. Aroma of rose petals and imported whiskey hung in the air. Friends who had been away for months fell upon each other with loud cries. Relatives who met only at weddings or funerals embraced tearfully and exchanged the latest news of distant cousins. One or two Tarun had met before; others were vaguely familiar faces on fading photographs tucked in the family album. Servants in white livery were serving canape. The tables were laden with food of exquisite varieties. Tarun in a navy-blue suit borrowed from his brother Krishan, with instruction to keep the platters topped up, was moving around the tables. Sister-in-law Pushpa, who he disliked and feared equally, handed him an empty platter, and whispered instructions in his ear. Tarun nodded vacantly, making out he was listening while staring at Mrs Verma's rolls of fat bulging around her bra strap. She was Usha's former schoolteacher. 'Don't embarrass us you fool, now go,' Pushpa hissed. In response Tarun simply keeled over as if cut down with an axe. He fell heavily on guests' feet, the platter smashing into pieces and began rolling on the ground, jerking his shoulders, feet thrashing wildly. The news travelled to Dr Mallick, who was cracking jokes, surrounded by an all-male cluster of guests, a rose bud in the jacket's buttonhole and glass of whiskey in hand. He supervised Tarun's removal to a hotel room. This bit Tarun remembered clearly for he had come around by then. His face washed, a wet napkin on his forehead, doctor forced medication down his throat.

Next morning Tarun tried to picture the appalling scene. He could vaguely remember Pushpa whispering in his ear. 'What did I do?' he asked.

'What did you do?' Usha lashed at him, 'I will tell you what you did. You spoiled the cocktail party, made a mess of it, after so much planning had gone into it. What must Prakash's family think of us, that Usha has a brother who is an idiot, a hysteric. They should put you away, lock you up.'

'Yes, lock me up, Usha, lock me up,' Tarun cried and lay face down on the ground with legs tucked under him and began knocking his head against the solid floor.

Seeing Tarun on the floor, Usha began howling. When Suraj, the elder brother from Calcutta, came to investigate, Tarun bawled, '*bharaji*, take me away, lock me up, lock me up.'

'What is going on here? Stop it, stop it, both of you. Tonight, of all nights, we don't need any more hassles.' Suraj pulled Tarun off the floor and yelled at a servant, 'bring him some icy water, now.'

'And you,' he said to Usha, 'go to your room, not another word.'

Usha hissed at Tarun, 'don't you dare do that at the wedding. Don't you dare.'

2

Malviya Nagar 1927

'Oh, Manju, come and open the door, the smoke is choking me,' Dadima yelled in her usual thin but lively voice. She was sitting hunched on the threshold of the bed set in the front veranda converted into a room by boarding the openings with sheets of advertisement hoardings taken from the roadside. The walls had turned charcoal grey over time as if to blend in with the colour of the smoke which flowed out of the kitchen twice a day. Now the smoke was whirling around Dadima in small circles like mini tornadoes.

Manju walked to the front door and flung it open. The smoke instantly stopped swirling and gushed into the lane like prisoners released from a crowded jail.

'Who has opened the door?' Manju's mother yelled from the kitchen.

Dadima launched into a fit of coughs, slapping her chest, exaggerating the discomfort. Manju looked at her. Why is she being so melodramatic?

'Why don't you speak?' mother said.

Manju did not answer. She knew mother knew who had opened the door.

'Why are you shouting at her? Talk to me, I asked her to open the door,' Dadima replied, scratching her head with fingers of both hands, the rumpled hair like a thatch of grass after a storm.

'Yes, yes, and invite all the rats, mosquitoes, and creatures of the street into the house? And why did you ask her? Is she your servant?'

As if rats were not already in the house, and if they wanted to come in, they would dutifully only use the front entrance, Manju was thinking. She often heard them scuttling in and out from cracks and gutters. The boys in the street said rats were God Ganesh's soldiers. Their job is to protect Ganesh. Why do they come to our house? Ganesh doesn't reside with us, she thought.

'Am I to die of coughing in this house, an old woman like me?' Dadima moaned.

Mother came out of the kitchen mopping sweat from the face with the loose end of the sari. 'If there is anyone doing the dying in this house, it is me,' she said cuttingly and then drawing Manju closer, 'you come with me.'

Manju felt comforted by the familiar coarse smell of mother's sari. But she did not go with her to the kitchen, fearing mother would ask her to chop vegetables. The last time she had tried, her finger received a nip, releasing tiny blobs of blood. Instead of consoling, mother had scolded her for not learning to hold the knife correctly. 'What will you do when you are married and have your own home?'

'God help me,' Dadima croaked, and shook her head

after mother had retreated to the kitchen. It seemed to Manju, Dadima and God were never far apart, as if they were on speaking terms.

'Go and call Phooldevi, go now,' Dadima said, whispering, 'my head is hurting so much. She will give me medicine to cure the ache.' And then she gestured at Manju to come for a hug. Manju went over and pushed her face into Dadima's chest. She liked Dadima when she was this way, but not when quarrelling with mother.

Once mother had caught her sitting on Dadima's lap. 'Come with me.' She had dragged her away to the kitchen, mother's headquarters. 'God knows what charm she has cast on my girl. Does her lap grow sweets?' she said waving a ladle, her narrow face appearing even more intense, 'I forbid you to sit with her and listen to the nonsense that comes out of that mouth.'

Phooldevi was an herbalist. 'I know cures for all ailments known to humankind,' she often boasted. Then why don't you cure your own rotten teeth, Manju would chuckle to herself. A severe looking woman with long teeth set wide apart, she rarely smiled. Father had a theory that Phooldevi was a witch in disguise. How did she get the name Phooldevi, which meant Goddess of flowers?

On the way to Phooldevi's house she stopped under the peepal tree to look for fallen leaves. It was difficult to find a good untrampled specimen. She spotted one which was still green and fresh and ran to pick it up. Ants were crawling over it. She held up the leaf and watched the little insects run around in panic. They were the small red ants. She had seen boys in the street catch the bigger black ones and hold them to candle flames. The insects burn with crackle and snap like mini fireworks. It amused the boys, but she thought it was cruel. She blew the ants off the leaf and held it like a delicate flower. She intended to place the leaf in a book and leave it pressed for ten days. When completely dry she would paint flowers on it, the way her friend had shown her.

At the tailor's shop she saw Ramu smiling at her. He often gave her little offcuts of fabric which were of no use to him. She already had a small collection of pretty patterns and intended to ask mother to make a patchwork tablecloth. She often stood and watched Ramu work, fascinated how he cranked the handle of the sewing machine with the right hand and guided the fabric through the needle with the other, twisting and turning here and there, and the ease with which he could thread a needle. She did not like the owner of the shop, Bhagwan Das, a tall man with a heavy moustache and permanently angry looks. 'He is a friend of your father,' mother had said, warning her to stay clear of him, 'shameless both, drinking and gambling till the middle of the night.'

Dadima perked up when Phooldevi arrived. 'May you and your family prosper and have decent daughter-in-laws,' she said with a raised hand as if blessing Phooldevi, 'as for me it is not in the stars. I do not know what bad deeds I must have committed in my previous life for God to punish me like this. That too in my old age.'

Manju was surprised Dadima had forgotten she had a headache and was busy complaining about mother. Phooldevi's long teeth clacking, adding spice to her grumbles. 'Look at me,' she was saying, 'I have worked hard all my life, never had anything, never had a chance, never knew what a chance was, but I am not complaining, not going on like her, shamelessly.'

Manju alternated her glances between the two, feeling irritated, the pulses of her body throbbing. If mother heard all this there would be an almighty row.

'Come, sit with me,' Dadima said to Manju and began stroking and massaging her head in her unique way. Manju found it pleasurable and relaxing.

Like Dadima, mother also frequently hugged and kissed her and stroked the forehead, usually after she had finished the day's work. They would sit under the night sky with millions of stars and the moon overhead. She would often talk of her past as though Manju had asked her a question. 'You want to know, then I will tell you. I got married at fifteen. I was only a girl. What did I know about the world? Nothing. Your father was a loafer, always out with the boys. Even after we were married, he did not stop. I had to cook for the family and wash clothes. Your grandmother would start cursing if the food preparations were not the way she wanted. Did not your mother teach you anything, she would shout and curse, what a mistake I have made, marrying my son to you. I was so unhappy, I used to cry all night. My mother did not support me either, she said I must do what he says, as I am a married woman. WOMAN! I was only a girl.'

One day she told Manju, 'I was not much older than what you are now when I got married.' Manju stiffened up, alarmed. 'Does that mean I will be married soon?' Mother looked at her with pity. 'Not if I can help it, but your father is a stubborn man, and your grandmother too. She says it's a family tradition.' Manju imagined herself married to someone like father. It was an unpleasant thought, and she began dreading getting older. I will run away from home before I am fifteen. But where will I go? She thought of Ramu. He is always so nice and kind, and so well dressed, unlike father whose shirts have holes at the armpits, darned pockets, scruffy shoes with heels worn at an angle.

One day she went to the shop and stood outside staring at Ramu, studying him from all angles.

He offered her pieces of fabric. 'Take this.'

She shook her head, 'I don't want it.'

'Then why are you here?'

'Nothing,' she said and ran back home.

❁

They had not eaten all day. In the kitchen mother was throwing pots and pans about. When she could not express her emotions any other way, she took it out on the pots or anything else at hand. Sometimes she cursed and slapped her own face, as if punishing herself. It made Manju go cold with fear, and if she went to father or Dadima, they showed no interest.

Not daring to ask mother for dinner, she fetched her bag of offcut fabrics, emptied it on the floor and began piecing them together, trying various positions, like a complicated jigsaw puzzle. It was a conundrum for there were odd-shaped pieces too, which did not fit anywhere. Her concentration faltered when she heard the door fly open. A wave of stink surged in from street gutters. She heard father cursing and making guttural noises, like someone trying to hold back hiccups. He staggered into the centre of the veranda and fell on his back like a wrestler slam-dunked.

'Bring me food,' he yelled. A crude harsh voice, like someone grating a stone on tin roof. 'Bring me food, I said.'

Mother came out of the kitchen. Her eyes were like two fireballs. As if to stoke the fire, Dadima said, 'you can see for yourself son, I don't get even two rotis to eat on time. The devil has turned this house into a mad people's home.'

'The only mad person in this house is you,' mother screeched, 'where am I to produce rotis from. From my head. There is not an inch of flour in the house, even coal is running out. Why don't you ask your son to give me money to buy these things?'

'Why couldn't you borrow from neighbours. I told you I will give you money tomorrow,' father said.

'Fine, then you can eat tomorrow.'

'Shut up – shut up – or I will shut it for you,' father yelled making a fist.

'You want to hit me. Go on, do it, do it. See if that produces food.'

'Shut your mouth. I am warning you…' His head swayed as if the neck had lost the strength to hold anything upright.

After a short silence he turned to Manju, 'go to Banya's shop and get some flour. Tell him I will pay tomorrow.'

Manju jumped to her feet, willing to do anything to defuse the situation. Her cold heart palpated for this madness to end.

'I have already been to Banya,' mother said, stopping Manju from leaving. 'He laughed at me. I cannot have anything more until the old debt is clear, he said in front of all the customers. I felt so ashamed.'

'I am warning you…' father said as if accusing mother of lying. His fiery expression reminded Manju of a story father had told her once when he was in a playful mood. In school plays teachers invariably gave him the role of demon God Ravana. The teachers said he was particularly good for the part and praised him for the skilful acting. But there were others who said he did not have to act; he was born a Ravana, look at those eyes and the hooked nose.

Manju went over and tugged at father's trouser leg. 'Dada, dada I want to show you something, come this way.' She took his hand and tried to cox him towards the patchwork of fabric pieces which lay spread on the floor.

'You keep out of this,' father yelled.

She withdrew as if she had received a stunning slap. Her first instinct was to run out into the street. But she could not bring herself to leave. Please God stop them, please God stop them from fighting, she was praying. Dadima began wailing, 'oh God, send me death now. Death is better than this torture.'

Dadima's pathetic cry appeared to push father further into an inferno of rage. With the suddenness of a prancing bear, he caught his wife and slapped her across the face.

Manju placed her hands on the ears hearing her mother's scream.

'Beat me, beat me, beat me to your heart's desire,' mother was saying, offering no resistance. And she said taunting the mother-in-law, 'proud of your son, the wife beater?'

The next blow sent her tottering towards Dadima's bed. She fell. As she sat up with hands above her head to ward off further blows, Manju saw the red stain on her lips. 'Ma,' Manju screamed and as she ran to throw herself on mother, she caught father's full fist blow on the chest. She too went sprawling to the floor.

He stopped abruptly and stared at Manju lying on the floor, as if he could not understand how she got there. He looked at his hands, turning them over, scrutinising them intently. The fiery rage on the face now replaced with horror and extreme anguish.

Mother touched her lips. She saw the blood-stained fingers and began howling again. Her cries mingled with Dadima's, who was calling on God to take her away.

Father covered his ears as if he couldn't bear it any longer and dashed into the back room, slamming the door shut behind him.

Nothing happened for several moments. Then they heard the latch click into lock position.

As if there was a meaning to the metallic click, mother stopped howling. She came up off the floor and stared at the door. Her eyes wide, every crease and fold on her face screaming fear and agony. It was a different kind of expression, one that terrified Manju even more.

Mother flung herself at the door and beat it with her fists while weeping like a child.

Manju ran and swung the front door open. The neighbours had already come out of their homes and were listening in and whispering aloud.

'He is beating her again,' someone was saying.

'Maybe she deserves it.'

'You can't clap with one hand,' someone else said.

'I saw him drinking in the *daaru* hut earlier.'

Next day someone found father's body in the nearby goshala, hanging from the rafters with a rope tied to the neck, while cows sat under him chewing cud in the midday heat.

3

1953

'Pabiji when are you going to arrange a marriage for me?' Tarun asked his mother, peering into her eyes with an anxious half smile.

They were sitting under a corrugated roofing erected in the backyard of the house in the town of Malviya Nagar. A dining table sat pushed against the wall on the covered veranda. Beside it stood a metal Godrej almirah, which complained of its years of ill treatment in a rash of rusty patches and livid scars. Sounds of morning rituals were drifting in from neighbouring houses. In the lane Tarun heard Satish Babu, a neighbour, coughing and clearing the throat before setting off on his morning walk. A bank employee, and of advanced age, he was a meticulous time-keeper. Taking cue from the neighbour Tarun readied himself to head off to the market to collect milk and grocery. But first he wanted to extract a response from Pabiji, a positive response.

'Are you going to arrange a marriage for me?' he asked again.

'The boy wants a wife,' Pabiji cried theatrically to the dusty corrugated roofing, 'and he wants one today.' Sitting cross-legged on a stool, an earthenware pot in her white sari-clad lap, she was churning yogurt with a wooden spindle held between the palms. This early morning ritual of extracting butter from yogurt was not a necessity but she saw it as an obligation to maintain family tradition. 'In our time we did not go to the market for our milk or butter, the milkman came to our house with his cow and milked her right in front of us, fresh and wholesome, the whole family drank glasses of it. Still there was so much left over we used to share with all the neighbours.' She would say with monotonous regularity, wallow in nostalgia with glazed eyes. It bored Tarun and others around her, but no one had the heart to ask her to stop.

'Pabiji, can you hear me?' Tarun said, a little louder, bringing his face level with hers.

'Yes, I can hear you. No need to shout,' she replied, 'have I not said I will think about it.'

'But you have been saying it for so many months now. How much do you need to think?'

'I will think as much as I need to think. I have told you a hundred times.'

'Everything that you say is for the hundredth time,' Tarun said in a mocking tone.

She gave him a hard look. 'All right, now fetch the milk. Make sure that Ram Lal has not diluted it with water again. Such a dishonest man,' Pabiji said and ran a finger along the rim of the pot gathering up overspilling yogurt.

'What can I do about that? He doesn't do it in front of

me, does he?' Tarun replied.

'*Achha, achha*, now go, I must prepare breakfast, also bring half a seer of okra and peas from the market. Pick only the tender ones, you hear, not like the last time.'

Tarun dragged the stool closer. 'But mother you have married off all my brothers and sisters, even Usha who is younger than me is married. I am twenty-eight years old now. I want to be married like them. Is that not my right?'

Pabiji raised her hand as if to quieten a noisy gathering. 'Kaka, listen to me…are you able to provide for a wife… and *nikkey*, the little ones, when they come. Will you be able to look after them?' Her habit of addressing him as *kaka*, irritated him. I am not a schoolboy anymore mother, he wanted to scream, I am an adult, just like my four brothers.

'You know I am a working man now. I have money. I can look after them.' He clicked his tongue, making a sucking sound.

'Don't *che, che* me. I know what is best. Do you think it has been easy for me these past six years since your father passed away?' Though she did not often talk about him – she could hardly mention his name without threatening to break into tears. Mindful of Pabiji's feelings, children rarely talked about their father openly. But father was everywhere still. His eccentric ways, the loud guttural growl, *hmmmph*, and impatient tapping of the walking cane. And his preference to eat dinner sitting on the front porch by himself, or in company of the neighbour friend, who like him was an educationalist, assistant principal of a government school. Or the awkward silences and impatient tapping of fingers on tabletops when in the company of ladies.

Her nose reddened as she glanced at her wrist which used to sparkle with chunky gold bangles of twenty-four carat purity. Crafted by the family jeweller, a pot bellied man with a happy face, who had the habit of saying yes to everything, even when he meant no. He would make Tarun sit with him while they discussed jewellery tessellations. Pabiji shaking her head, appearing dissatisfied, 'no, no you must show me better designs', and the man repeatedly enquiring if there were any engagements or weddings coming up in the family.

The earrings she wore were so heavy her earlobes had permanently stretched an inch; the holes elongated as well. Not that she had minded the deformity, for it signified wealth and social status.

He had been with his brother Mohan, when they had negotiated the sale of mother's jewellery and silver, to a man in the back street of Lal Masjid, who himself was wearing gold earrings under long tassels of hair and reeking of attar perfume. That it was a bad deal, Tarun knew from Mohan's expression.

Pammi came out of the bathroom in fresh *salwar kameez*, slapping wet slippers on the floor. Two pigeons on the clothesline took off and settled on the back wall. She slung a damp towel over the line and on way to her room deliberately kept her gaze averted from Tarun uncle as if to show she wasn't listening in to mother and son's conversation.

Pali, in flimsy pyjamas and flip-flops, chewing the thick end of a neem tree stick, strolled in from the back alley. At twenty-four he was three years older than his sister Pammi. Pammi was a student at a teacher-training college, but gossiping, banter and dissertation of latest Bombay movies seemed her true vocation. Pali, with a recently obtained engineering degree, was job hunting. The degree was the easy bit, it is getting employment, which is proving formidable, like dislodging the British raj from India, he would complain and then take out his frustration on Dharmu the postman, who was known to have worked for the postal service all his life. First for Her Majesty Postal Service, and then for All India Post. 'Why do you keep bringing these rejection letters? For once bring me good news,' he would say to Dharmu in English, safe in the knowledge he would not understand a word. Dharmu in response always produced a toothless grin, believing they were commending him for excellent work.

'Go now before the milk runs out. Do I always have to tell you a hundred times?' Pabiji said.

Tarun's myopic eyes glared from under the bushy eyebrows as he stood up, hitched his pyjama high up the waist, and stormed out with long sturdy strides. A robust walker, he could traverse long distances on foot, even under midday sun in the middle of summer, a habit formed out of necessity to save bus fares. Pabiji often harangued him. 'Kaka why do you walk the streets in the sun. Take a rickshaw or bus. Or you will get sunstroke.' He ignored her warnings, or that of his sister, Savitri, who said exposure to direct sunlight can tan the skin. 'Look how dark you are already,' she would say, as if to a lowly creature, 'and why don't you dress properly.'

He possessed no more than two or three pairs of trousers and shirts. When compelled to purchase a new garment he was slow and deliberate, selecting items for their durability rather than finesse or fashion.

After a cold shower at the end of the day, with generous puffs of Lakme talcum powder in the armpits, topless but for an old saggy vest, he would lower himself on a stool and gaze longingly at the steaming pots on the stove. 'Is dinner ready?' His nephews and nieces teased him, 'uncle ji, when are you going to retire that vest of yours… pointless wearing it with so many holes… did you make the holes on purpose for ventilation.' He would ignore them or emit guttural '*hums*' and '*hahhs*.' 'I know what I must do. Now let me eat dinner in peace.'

●

In the front room Tarun was dusting his Pye radio, lovingly, with a piece of cloth set aside for this purpose. A recent acquisition, he rarely switched the contraption on or let anyone near it. Padma and Pammi often pleaded with him, 'uncle just once, can we listen to music on your radio, after all that's what it is for.' His reply, accompanied with a terse shake of the head, was always, 'no, it is too valuable to mess around with; I don't want it breaking down.' That it could relay music, news of the day or cricket commentary at the turn of the dial, was enough for him. He had no interest in listening to any of it.

A compulsive hoarder, he had drawers full of old watches, clocks, fountain pens, family photographs and picture books of wild animals. Someone had given him a book titled, The Man-Eating Tigers of Kumaon. Flicking through it and reading in fits and starts, the fascination for the majestic Bengal tigers had taken root. The Pye radio was from a work colleague who had gone upscale to a new-fangled gramophone-cum-radio, an imported model. 'I am going to throw away my old Pye,' Salim had said while boasting about his new acquisition. Tarun was shocked. 'You are going to throw it away?' he said and then grinned coyly, 'give it to me.'

A noise at the front gate alerted him to visitors; he replaced the radio carefully in the cabinet and went out to investigate.

'Oh, Balraj *bharaji*, what a surprise,' Tarun cried and rushed to take the black leather suitcase from Balraj, his older brother's fingers. 'Give it to me, I will carry it in.'

Sister Savitri, widowed at an early age, four years older than Balraj, came out from a back room. Her children, Dev, Pali, Pammi, and Padma followed behind. Single parent, a tiny pension, she had moved into the recently acquired family home in Malviya Nagar.

Pabiji came hurrying, adjusting her white sari. 'Why didn't you write to let us know you were coming,' she cried, and flung her arms out to give Balraj a hug. She regarded him up and down. 'Wah, you look like a big boss,' she said, caressing his shirt collar as if dusting fluff.

'I was busy, didn't have time to write. In any case it is good to give a surprise.' Balraj laughed and made his eyebrows jump up and down.

Dressed in a starched shirt, Parker fountain pen in the

breast pocket, beige gabardine trousers, brown shoes, he was radiating an air of a no-nonsense senior executive. With a doctorate in study of metals from Sheffield University, he had landed a job with a metallurgical research laboratory in Jamshedpur and risen rapidly in ranks.

'Huh, busy, big boss.' Pabiji said with a wave of a finger. 'You may be boss to your underlings, but for me you are the same Bali who used to run around in short pants playing in the dirt outside our *kothi* in Lyallpur.' Her eyes mellowed and lips quivered, and everyone could see she was about to delve into the past and a lengthy tirade against politicians of the day, who she was convinced were responsible for all her problems.

Balraj did the clown act to try and distract her. It was futile.

'Remember the *kothi*, *kaka*? What a big house it was. Now see what we have.' She looked around her solemnly, at the four bare walls, no decorations or ornaments, a calendar hanging from a nail Tarun had hammered into the wall (a gift from the local sari shop, Banarasi Sari Bhandar). 'What comfortable life we had back then. And your father was so well respected. All lost now, gone forever.' Her eyes fired up. 'I tell you it is the doing of that half-naked *dhotiwala* Gandhi and his friend Nehru. They want to take us back to the dark ages. Mark my words.' Her finger moved like a windscreen wiper. 'They divided the country and forced us to leave Lyallpur, our home. Gross injustice....'

'Yes, Pabiji, what was to happen has happened.' Savitri cut in, 'leave the past now...'

Pabiji brushed Savitri's hand away. 'Only I know how I

endured the four-day train journey crammed in that windowless mail train without food and water. It was so overcrowded, there were people hanging on by railings outside, others crouching like monkeys on top of the carriages too, and Muslim boys hurling stones from the embankment.'

Tarun nodded vaguely, as if in agreement. As the only male in a group of a dozen ladies and children of the family, he had felt the yoke of responsibility on his shoulders, though there was nothing he could do other than be with them. In Delhi they had sheltered in a tented refugee colony on Pusa Road. There was little food or clean water. Tarun would wake to whirling hunger and lie in the dark with his heart in his ears and the mouth running as if something within was eating him up. Pabiji rationing the food. When he asked for more, she would say, 'have you got worms in the stomach?' As if accusing him of wilfully harbouring the gluttonous organisms. After a month they had moved to a one room apartment in the centre of old Delhi, Darya Ganj.

Pabiji often recounted this horror story to women she had befriended in the neighbourhood. It took my son Mohan two years of head banging from one government department to another to receive our reparation. What did we get in exchange for the big six-room mansion? A tiny house in Malviya Nagar outside Delhi. You call that justice?

Pammi threw her arms around Pabiji. 'Don't worry grandmother, at least we are safe now. Tell me this, did Uncle Tarun also run around in short pants when he was little?'

Pabiji appeared distracted at first and then she looked up at her son, his fraying singlet vest with holes wide enough to push a finger through; two bruises on his chin resembling bloated bed bugs, caused by a blunt razor blade. Her mouth opened and shut, and then she said, 'he was different.'

❂

'Tarun, oh Tarun, where are you? Tell everyone the breakfast is ready,' Pabiji called.

'Why can't you tell them yourself, Pabiji?' The anger was still simmering in him over the way they had made him look small the previous night. 'They can hear you as well as I can,' Tarun said. He was lathering his chin with a brush. Shaving paraphernalia lay around him in a semicircle, soap stick, an aluminium mug with warm water, a hand towel, a portable mirror, a packet of double-sided safety blades.

'Don't you answer me back. Fetch a chair for Balraj,' Pabiji yelled back.

The family drifted in, in ones and twos, and sat dawn, squatting on the floor around Pabiji, who was now turning over sizzling parathas on the hotplate, releasing wisps of smoke and a strong odour of scorched ghee.

Balraj pulled the chair up to the table. As a man and a breadwinner, it was customary, indeed expected, he should sit at the top of the table. Dev and Pali chose to sit with their uncle. No one asked Tarun to join him. He sat at the back listening to the conversation which had turned to politics.

'So, what is this election about?' Balraj said.

'For the president of Delhi University Students Union, uncle. Again, they are discussing issues that have no relevance,' Padma replied promptly, 'they are calling for solidarity with primary school teachers in their wage bargaining. What has the student's union got to do with all this?'

'Too right.' Pammi threw a hand up in the air, 'teachers need our support, and we are demanding employment opportunities for students when they graduate.'

'I hear they are insisting Nehru sticks with non-aligned foreign policy. Ha, ha. I ask you, is this election for president of the Students Union or for Prime Minister of India?'

Dev butted in. 'You don't understand *baba*, political parties have become part of the campus. You cannot separate the two anymore. I was never in favour. Now they are saying India will progress only if we return to ancient Hindu traditions.'

'What's wrong with our Hindu traditions?' Pammi said.

'Nothing wrong. It's just that they have no place in politics or running the country.'

When the conversation turned to the fighting between Muslims and Hindus Savitri became agitated. '*Baas*, all day long you talk of who killed who, who is to blame. Does that solve anything? Talk about something else.'

'But mother, fact is fact. They are killing Hindus. We must fight back. As it is, they want all of Kashmir. Should we give it to them?' Dev slammed the table top a little too hard.

Tarun worriedly scanned the underside of the table, at the leg intersection, which he had repaired recently.

'It is the fault of the British, I tell you. They have divided the country on purpose so Muslims and Hindus will be at each other's throat while they sit back and laugh. And that Churchill, he was never in favour of independence for India,' Dev said while tearing a paratha fresh off the hotplate, and then blowing on his singed fingers. 'Pabiji your parathas are too hot,' he complained.

'Then don't eat,' Pabiji snapped, 'give it to Padma.'

'Yippee,' Padma yelled, 'give it to me.'

Dev scowled and pulled his plate closer to the chest.

'And I thought you were applying for jobs in Churchill's England,' Pammi said, nudging Padma with a stifled laugh.

'That… that… is not true,' Dev said, appearing embarrassed.

'Then why are you applying for a passport? Is it simply to tease Churchill?' Pammi scoffed and waved an imaginary passport at his face.

'You shut up. Mind your own business,' Dev retorted in English, working his tongue to emulate an upper-class English accent.

The girls burst into laughter. 'Ooo – mind your own business,' Pammi mimicked his accent and Padma added in a low-pitched male voice, 'my dear chap, one must not mind someone else's business.'

The discussion turned to the job market and Pali sat up as though he had been waiting for this moment all along. Hair unruly, faded cotton *kurta*, leather two-strap *chappals* on his feet, he appeared a younger version of Gandhi, lacking only in steel rimmed reading glasses.

'Thousand applications for each job advertised, uncle,

the system is riven with bribery and nepotism, what chance do we stand,' Pali said.

Balraj tapped a spoon to his plate as if contemplating. 'Attitude of mind and appearance is as important as qualifications,' he said.

'But if they do not call me for an interview, how can they know anything about me?'

'Do you enclose a covering letter with the application?'

'Yes uncle, always.'

'Son the way you compose the letter, choice of words, its length, all that is important. It gives them a clue of your personality. My advice is work on the letter. What you must never do is beg for a job, which is what most people do. Do not be flippant or negative either. Make it concise, business like. That's the key.'

A mere letter carefully crafted could land you a job. Tarun was in awe at Balraj's knowledge, the quiet confidence, the ability to get things done. Do they see me? he wondered. He was seeing them all right, larger than life. Balraj's legs were visible under the table, the muscles of right leg just above the ankle appeared shrunk. A sports injury sustained years ago. Tarun remembered the incident well, for he was with mother watching. Balraj, dressed in black vest, standing across the white chalk line on the dirt pitch. The sports master blew the whistle. The boys began running. The parents cheered from the side-lines. Ten yards on, Balraj and another boy collided. Balraj crashed into a railing, his leg caught the lower rung, and he went down somersaulting. They rushed the boy to the hospital, who had passed out by then. When the doctors said his ankle was severely damaged, he may never walk again, doctors had to revive Pabiji for she had fainted too.

Now all he wanted was privacy with Balraj, to seek his approval, ask him to persuade Pabiji to look for a suitable girl for him. His interest in politics was cursory, nor did he understand the intricacy of job markets. He would hear the words employment, iron, steel, construction, and engineering mentioned in the same context and his head would spin. Once he asked Dev what it all meant. Dev laughed. 'Uncle don't strain your brain too much, it might explode.' Instead of the brain, he exploded. 'You people think I am stupid?'

He announced he was not hungry and would eat later. 'Not good to eat when you are not hungry, *na*.' Pammi said sarcastically and relieved too that she would not have to watch him gobble the food and masticate with a frenzy as though this were his last meal. His appetite too was a sore point since he ate more than others. Savitri often scolded the girls for being rude to the uncle and then she would take Tarun aside and reason with him, 'the food isn't running away, why not take your time and eat with composure, then you won't upset anyone around you.'

'You are right, I will do as you say.' Always conceding meekly while convinced all this was a conspiracy to make him feel inadequate and inferior and hence undeserving of a wife.

In the morning Tarun found Balraj sitting on the front porch with an open file on his lap. He shut the front door and sat down opposite, working out how to broach the subject. He didn't know what Balraj's reaction would be.

'What are you reading?' he asked, showing a casual inquisitiveness, a preamble to the serious business he wanted to discuss.

'Just some office files,' Balraj replied without looking up.

Tarun cleared his throat. 'Pabiji is being difficult as usual,' he said, 'I want to get married, but she is not agreeing. Can you have a word with her.'

'You want to do what?' Balraj said and snapped the file shut. Two courting pigeons on the ledge above fluttered their wings. A feather came floating to the ground.

'Brother, I want to get married, just like you,' Tarun said hesitating, and his face blushed in embarrassment.

'So, you have someone in mind.'

'No, no one at all,' he said, 'I have been asking Pabiji to look for a suitable girl for me.'

'How long has this been going on?'

'Many, many months,' Tarun replied with a wave of the hand, 'she keeps saying she will think about it.'

'But Tarun,' Balraj said after a long pause, 'if you want to marry, you will have to smarten yourself for a start, look respectable. What girl will want someone who looks like… I mean… like a station coolie.'

Tarun chuckled, taking it as Balraj's weird sense of humour, like his famous circus clown caricatures.

'You do look like a coolie. Have you ever seen yourself in the mirror?' Balraj said curtly, as if ticking off one of his juniors.

Tarun stiffened up, realising Balraj was serious. Do I look like a coolie? He visualised the army of porters at station platforms. Always in battered uniform, reeking of sweat and poverty. Passengers barking orders at them, throwing a handful of coins on their leathery palms, barely enough to feed a child at the end of the day

'Moreover, you can't stay here with the wife, you understand.'

'Why not?' Tarun said. He meant to sound indignant but managed only a whimper.

'This is a tiny house. Already there are seven people living in three rooms, a total of one thousand two hundred square feet plus the yards, according to the plans I have seen. Add one more, it will heave at the seams. Don't you think?'

'Yes, but…'

'If you are thinking of renting, will you be able to afford one at your salary?'

'I will work it out somehow.' He kept the voice level, so as not to show the exasperation, and hurt he was feeling. He still needed Balraj on his side. 'All I am asking is please speak to Pabiji. Ask her to look for a girl for me. I want to get married. Am I being unreasonable?' His voice cracked and suddenly he felt weak, and the weakness turned to utter exhaustion on hearing Balraj's casual reply. 'I will speak to her when the time is right. Now I must work.'

Ask her now, today, not sometime in the future. Tarun wanted to scream, what does 'when the time is right' mean anyway. A truck roared past the house, adding to his woe, and disturbing the chain of thought. He pulled himself together and started again. Blast of a car horn vaporised his words into thin air. The taxi had arrived to take Balraj to Connaught Place.

Tarun grimaced – more to himself than to register a protest. He carried the root of the unrest with him, a root not the kind that pushed the self on and up to accomplishment but a poisoned thing that wasted its strength. The fact was he wanted love – not something his brothers and sisters could give. He needed a woman's love in which he could see this image he had of himself reflected and thus becoming half true.

Sleep eluded him that night. He lay awake staring at the wall, resentment prickling his skin. Wires from the wall socket trailed downward and disappeared. The porch light outside the window was an eye that watched him. Every nocturnal sound was like a blast of a trumpet. Balraj was asleep on the same bed, facing away from him, breathing deep with contentment.

A thought came to him, why not build a one room extension on the side of the house, like Mr and Ms Kumar have done at number 32? It will solve the accommodation problem. He yanked the sheet off his body and looked around the room, at the walls from ceiling to floor. I will ask all the brothers to share the cost. It will be an investment in the jointly owned property which was sure to rise in value. When they moved here three years ago, it was just an empty shell, but newly built. He recalled the aroma of fresh paint, unlike the foul-smelling tiny flat in Darya Ganj. A hired Tempo loaded with the few belongings, the largest of which was the Godrej steel wardrobe, secured as Bank of India vaults, a gift from the property owner.

Slapping the neck to catch the mosquitos, he slipped off the bed and shuffled out of the room to survey the ground where the extension could stand. He paced up and down, avoiding the buckets and jerry cans, which stood ready for filling as soon as the water supply resumed next morning. He strode a straight line, mentally drawing the boundary wall, already convinced it would work. The tree must go. He gave the trunk a pat and looked up at the sky. The moon above was larger than he had ever seen, an astonishing pale circle of power. It looked as if he could reach out and touch it, that God had pushed it down from the heavens for his human hand to hold.

He sat down on the step, impatient for the day to break, to discuss his brilliant idea with Balraj, then take him to see Mr Kumar's extension which was elaborate with an added upper storey.

'It is not so simple, Tarun,' Balraj said, sipping tea from a steel tumbler and shaking his head, 'not just your brothers, but their wives, your sisters-in-law will have to be in on it. Do they all agree to you getting married?'

Tarun knew the score. Not all of them were in favour, and those who did not oppose had no opinion.

'But it is me. Don't I deserve a married life.'

'Not up to me, if anyone objects to your marriage the extension will be a nonstarter.'

❋

Back from work Tarun padlocked the bicycle, gave the lock a strong tug, and draped the tarpaulin over it.

A cool evening breeze was blowing. A collective noise of thousand rustling leaves mingled with screams of children playing in the green and chatter of *ayahs* by the gate. Pabiji was sitting cross-legged on a charpoy, shelling peas from pods, her face a manifestation of peace and contentment. She said in a mildly excited voice, 'Usha is coming. The letter arrived only today.'

'Oh, good,' Tarun said and clapped, 'when is she coming?'

'Next month.'

He had not spoken to Usha for far too long since she left Delhi for Jamshedpur. Her approach to relationships was unorthodox by Indian standards. Love marriage or arranged marriages, both are fine, she always said. He admired her for it, sought to emulate her, and express those opinions openly. But he dares not, fearing people might look at him askew, take him for a fool.

She had an extensive network of friends, and was bound to know girls from good families. They do not have to be beautiful, as long as they are good at heart and are willing to accept him.

'Here try this,' Pabiji said, pouring a handful of shelled peas on his open palm, 'they are so sweet.'

A familiar voice at the gate rang out. 'N*amaste* Mataji, *namaste*.' Ram Lal, the milkman with a well-oiled moustache twisted into pencil tip sharpness at each end of his upper lip was standing at the gate with hands joined. A man of fifty, he carried a permanently worried expression on his rugged face.

'Oh, Ram Lal, you...?'

'Yes, Mataji, Ram Lal, your humble servant.'

'Have you come to collect last month's due? But we have

already paid. I gave the money to Tarun to pass on to you… Tarun, haven't you paid him?'

Tarun glared at him. 'I paid you. You even counted it, right in front…'

'No, no,' Ram Lal interrupted, his gaze fixed on Pabiji, 'it's not that. I have come to ask for a favour, a humble request.' Here he raised his joined hands above the forehead.

Pabiji continued snapping peapods, appearing unimpressed with Ram Lal's theatrics. 'I know all about your humble requests. If you are thinking of increasing the price of milk yet again, the answer is no we will not accept.'

'No Pabiji. It is not that. All I ask is that you don't send Tarun sahib to collect milk. Because of him my customers are deserting me – as it is, I only have a few.'

'Why, what has he done?'

'He starts shouting as soon as he arrives. Every morning he does the same thing, accusing me of adulterating the milk.'

'But Ram Lal, you listen to me, your milk is not what it used to be,' Pabiji said, wagging a finger, 'you can't fool me.'

'No Mataji, I never adulterate the milk. I swear to God. God is my witness. My other customers have no complaints.'

'If your milk is pure as you say, why do they want to leave you?'

'Because of sahib. Yesterday morning he created such a big racket, accusing me of dishonesty in front of everybody. I explained to Tarun sahib, I do not add water or anything else. This milk is as it comes out of the cows' udders. Tarun sahib would not believe me, saying if you are not doing it then your cow is producing adulterated milk. He picked up a stick and started beating the animal. This is not good Mataji, hitting a holy cow, Lord Krishna's trusted companion – Ram, Ram.' He touched each of his earlobes. 'People in the village saw it all. They wanted to catch *sahib* and beat him with the same stick. If I had not stopped them, God only knows what would have happened, God only knows.'

'I did not hit the cow,' Tarun exploded, 'He is lying. I only tapped it gently with the stick.'

'*Accha*, you go now. I will sort something out,' Pabiji said and bundled the discarded pea shells on a piece of paper and offered it to Ram Lal, 'take these for your cows. How is your wife, Chandni?'

'Don't ask. Work, work, work all day. I tell her to slow down. But she will not listen. What to do.'

Chandni often dropped by to the house for a heart-to-heart with Pabiji, complaining about her husband, about his misogynistic behaviour. A diminutive figure, but fiery in temperament, she ran her own business selling roasted *bhujia* and peanuts. From a rickety cart on the pavement, she had progressed to owning her own lockup premises, equipped with chairs for customers to sit on. She offered newspapers to those who could read, while they ate snacks and drank her tea. She said the secret of her success was to give customers what they wanted.

Padma lauded Chandni, saying she was a modern Indian success story, and should be written about. 'I was right, wasn't I? Give Nehru time he will transform the country. There will be no beggars on the streets, no poor people. Everybody will be rich.'

'Oh yippee,' Pammi yelped, 'ask him to hurry up. I want to buy this beautiful dress I have seen in a shop in Chandni Chowk.'

Padma rolled her eyes and slapped her forehead. 'I can't believe what I am hearing.'

'If we are all going to be rich, then who will clean the toilets and sweep the floors, and do small jobs here and there?' Savitri said.

'You too mother?' Padma cried, throwing the dupatta over her shoulder and walked away.

❁

'That will be foolish,' Dev said and whistled a derisive note when he heard Tarun was going to Moti Mahal to settle a bill.

'Salim and I ordered the food. Even if we could not finish it, we still must pay,' Tarun said self-righteously.

'What they don't know they will not miss,' Dev said, 'when they overcharge you, or claim they use pure Vanaspati ghee when in fact it is Dalda, when they use stale adulterated milk bought from that crook Ram Lal, do they come to your house the next day with an apology. Sir we accidently made a fool of you, here take the money back.'

Tarun brushed past Dev and lifted the tarpaulin off his bicycle.

The fat man was as usual behind the counter, poking the

rubber end of a pencil in his ear while shouting orders to a bare-chested kitchen porter.

'You remember me? I was here the other day with a friend,' Tarun said.

'Yes, yes, what do you want?' the fat man said, tapping the pencil on the counter, as if he had no time for frivolities such as recalling peoples' faces.

'I fell ill over there.' Tarun pointed at a table. 'We left in a hurry without settling the bill. I have come to pay now.'

The man regarded Tarun with narrowed eyes, taking him for a conman, a confidence trickster. 'Ah, you have come to pay, of course,' he said knowingly, as if he had heard those lines before, 'show me the money then.'

Tarun scooped out the pre-counted coins from the trouser pocket and placed them on the marble counter. The coins clattered and rolled before they settled down. 'I was keeping a tag. This is exactly what it added up to.'

The fat man's mouth opened wide and stayed that way as Tarun turned to leave.

'*Arre, arre* you can't leave so quickly, let me offer you something... cold *lassi* to cool you down, it is so hot outside.'

'It's all right,' Tarun said with a wave of the hand.

'No, no, I insist, have a glass of sweet *lassi*, our speciality. Please come back.'

He made Tarun sit at a reserved table beside the counter. 'One large deluxe special *lassi*, sweet, quickly, quickly' he yelled at someone in the kitchen.

Chilled yogurt drink, frothing over the sides of the glass, arrived in no time.

'Drink, drink,' he said, 'our *lassi* is famous. People come from miles, even from Delhi to taste it.'

'It looks delicious.' Tarun took a sip and nodded in appreciation.

'I am grateful to you. You are so honest... so very honest. These days where does one find people like you?' He placed his arms on the table and leaned forward as if to bring Tarun in into his orbit of friends and confidantes.

'I don't like to cheat anyone or keep anything that doesn't belong to me,' Tarun said, feeling a little buoyed by the praise.

'These days everybody is out trying to steal, rob, take what they can get away with, no fear of how they will be judged by the society,' the big man said, slapping the table. A waiter shuffled over promptly. The fat man waved him away and continued, 'no fear of anybody, not even God, I tell you. This business you see, I have built with my own hands, with honesty and hard labour. I did not cheat anyone or ask for help. No sir.'

Tarun made a face to show how impressed he was.

'I was seventeen when my father died. With no money there was no education, so I started selling *aloo-tikki* and *chana* from a stall at the station. I worked hard, shed so much sweat you could have filled an ocean with it. Eventually I was able to take the premises. At first it was so small I could only fit two tables.'

'You have done very well,' Tarun said, warming up to the man. He too was young when father had fallen into a long stretch of ill health. Though the death was not sudden, he was still devastated, taken it as a personal betrayal. When he was younger father had said, more than once, with arms around his shoulders, 'son you do your best, and leave the rest to me. I will look after you for ever and ever.' When father went into a heart attack Tarun felt rudderless. At the same time, he noticed, the family had started treating him as an adult. He wanted desperately to live up to their expectation, to please everyone. He tried. Ended up making a fool of himself. He felt out of his depth, and the feeling of inadequacy, inferiority made him want to hide.

'It was a conundrum,' the fat man was saying, 'with two tables we could only serve so many customers at a time, not enough to make a profit. So, we removed the tables, made it a standing room only. The shop began filling up…'

Across the street someone started playing shehnai with a sudden loud flair. Its long melodious pitches brought back one of his earliest memories with father. Father did not care for music. He baulked at anyone singing or dancing in his presence. Stop that racket, he would say, clicking his fingers. But shehnai? He would never shut his ears to the brass wind instrument played in temples or at weddings. He had kept the love of shehnai a secret. Only Tarun knew. One day father had taken Tarun for an evening walk. They were passing a house where someone was playing this instrument. Father stopped to listen in the fading daylight. 'Do you know what that is?' he said, 'young Bismillah Khan has made it popular now, but it dates back hundreds of years. A barber in a Mogul emperor's court was first to play it.'

There were other things which could unbridle father's soul. Wistful thoughts frequently combed his melancholic spirit. He often sat in the yard brooding, overly critical of things, no place for ironies or satire. One day he saw a bird, a badly plumed sparrow, in the dirt. An injured wing was preventing it from flying. Father's soul cleaved to the bird. He picked it up gently in his hands and called Tarun to fetch a handful of grains and a tumbler of water. For three days he cared for it and when it finally died, he gave it a proper funeral by burning its body to ashes over lit kindling and wood. This is also how father went. His white-shrouded body on a funeral pier. After the priest had said the prayer and the wood set alight, each son took turns in stoking the fire with a log. As the fire took hold, flames licked the air, wood crackling and spitting like sprinkled water in a vat of hot oil. Father raised his upper body with a sudden jerk as if he had changed his mind about dying. Tarun gave a silent shriek and jumped back. Are we burning him alive? Someone placed a reassuring arm on his shoulder. 'These things happen,' he explained, 'due to intense heat the muscles in the body contract, especially in the middle section, it makes the skeleton buckle and distort.'

'...so here we are now after twenty years,' the fat man said leaning back with a self-assured smile, 'more lassi?'

'No more, I have to go now,' Tarun said.

'You must come again, bring your family. I like to entertain families and children in my restaurant. Oh, my name is Manu Bhatia.'

Bring the family? Tarun gave the idea a short shrift. Pabiji and Savitri would be horrified. God knows whose hands touch the food and what rubbish they must put in it, they would say. Why eat out when everything is available at home. The nephews would holler as if at the punch line of a joke. Really, uncle ji you are offering to pay. It did not bother him though. He had learned to compartmentalise people, relegating those he disapproved of in a corner of his psyche. He listened to them without paying too much attention.

'My name is Tarun,' he said before leaving.

4

Tarun was wearing a clean vest, one without holes. Even the boxer shorts were new, without urine stains. He was meeting the girls and did not want to take any chances. The blue shirt he was wearing starched so stiff; one could imagine pressure marks left on the wrists.

On the bus, crammed between two men smoking *bidis*, creating such a haze he had to fan his face to disperse the cloud, worrying the odour might settle on his clothes. The neighbour on the right offered him an extra inch by wriggling his hip. 'Where are you going?' he asked.

'Ajmeri Gate,' Tarun replied and peered out the window to avoid getting into a conversation. They had entered a congested lane lined with colonial houses, the masonry crumbling, rust stains showing from leaking drain pipes. A truck overtook a bullock cart, blasting dust in its wake, clouding the roadside stalls and tiny eating places. Flies were swarming over open drains, men urinating against the wall. It looked so distasteful. He was beginning to vacillate. I should not have agreed to come out. It is going to be a disaster with the girls, a waste of money. What if Salim is late or does not come at all.

At the meeting point outside the teashop on GB Road, a crowd was watching a snake charmer perform tricks with his reptiles. Salim was not in the crowd or in the teashop. He asked the shirtless tea seller, 'have you seen my friend, a big, tall man with a thin moustache?'

'Oh, *babu*, my chai is famous around here. I have tall men, short men, small and big men, good and bad men, coming here all day long to taste my special brew with pure milk, *hanh* pure milk. How am I to know who your friend is? You tell me.' He hit the giant-sized aluminium kettle sitting on charcoal fire with an iron tong, making it ring riotously, 'will you drink some tea or just stand there ogling.'

'No tea,' Tarun said. He paced the pavement like a cat in a zoo cage, occasionally stopping to watch the cobras slithering on the man's arms and shoulders. Abruptly the snake charmer thrust his begging bowl at Tarun's face. Tarun looked helplessly into the bowl. The man rattled the coins in the bowl as if addressing a blind man. A hand came to rest on his left shoulder and a voice on his right said, 'come on, give the poor man some money.' It was Salim, sporting a freshly trimmed moustache and smelling of *attar* essence. 'Let's go,' he said, flashing his eyes as if he had an exciting itinerary lined up for him.

'You are late again. I thought you were not coming,' Tarun said gruffly, half wishing it were true so he could take the next bus home. God knows what it will all cost. Before leaving home, he had placed twenty-five rupees in his shirt pocket and patted it flamboyantly, as if money was no object. But now buyer's remorse had set in even before making the purchase. He dares not ask Salim if twenty-five rupees were enough, fearing ridicule and finger pointing: who is the tight-fisted *banya* then.

'Not coming?' Salim patted his puffed-up chest, 'when Salim makes a promise, he keeps.'

'Yes, yes, you do,' Tarun said, trying to catch up with his friend who had started up GB Road at a brisk pace, ignoring hurrying office workers in white shirts, fountain pens clipped to their breast pockets, dabs of blue ink staining the fabric. School children with bulging cloth satchels were screaming at each other. Tarun passed the sugar cane juice seller cranking the wheels, cows idling or munching the husk nearby. The air took on odours of over-ripe mangoes and diesel fumes. They arrived at a junction. On the left was a dusty brick wall plastered with bills advertising latest movies, potions for curing impotence, skin lightening creams, remnants of *Leave India* slogans directed at the British. Yet the building had been built by the British several decades ago in a belated attack of conscience. Originally intended as tenement for market traders, its construction was so bad even the homeless had refused to move in. So, the building was converted into a jail to house freedom fighters.

They turned right into a wide lane. Tarun gasped as if he had stepped into the epicentre of a fireworks display. The entire lane lit with strings of coloured lights like hustings, blast of music, cacophony of overlapping tunes, as if each house had a party going on. Girls were standing crammed in doorways, on balconies. Yet nore were peering out of open windows. More rouge and red lipstick here than Tarun had seen in a ladies' cosmetic store. A girl dressed as a wedding party guest crooked her finger at Tarun and pouted her lips. Tarun blushed. Even the mannequins in sari shops dressed in Japanese nylon with flowery patterns and gold and silver embroidery, flashed from the windows like gaudy, shimmering ladies propositioning the passers-by. And passers-bye were in numbers, gawking, craning their necks. Occasionally someone made a furtive dash to a door which opened mysteriously and shut as soon as the punter was in, like a piranha's snapping jaw.

Tarun wanted Salim to slow down so he could do some more gawking. They turned into a side lane and suddenly the bright lights, the noise and the bustle were no more. This was a tree lined avenue, orderly, and peaceful. Houses with high outer walls and identical painted wooden doors. None numbered. It was difficult to tell who lived in them, except they had to be rich. Salim strode confidently to a house and beat on the door with the palm of his hand.

Tarun patted his shirt pocket and rubbed his moist hands against the thighs. 'Are you sure we are at the right place?' he whispered, 'this looks like a private house.'

'*Saale* don't worry; I have been here before. And keep your penis under control. I don't want you to start waving it at the first girl you see.'

'I have met girls before if you must know,' Tarun replied indignantly.

'Yes, but not like these girls. *Bachhu* wait till you see them. You will be drooling like a dog in heat with that thing scraping the ground.'

The door opened. A short muscular Nepali in khaki uniform stood barring the way. He studied Salim's face with fixed glare, nodded, and stepped aside. An internal door opened mysteriously revealing a courtyard surrounded on three sides with open balconies, two storeys high. Ornamental palms in ceramic pots positioned for maximum effect, blooming red bougainvillea were trailing up to the first floor. At the centre was a round rattan table with a glass ashtray, easy chairs with cushions around it. On the right were steps leading to a mezzanine section. This too was set with table and chairs, potted plants, Usha fans on pedestal, sighted strategically for maximum air flow. Hooded light fittings of the Mughal period adorned the walls. It seemed to Tarun whoever lived here entertained guests in large numbers.

It felt as if they were in a temple of high priests where everyone had taken an oath of silence, far removed from the jungle of auto rickshaws, taxis, buses, roadside hawkers, and easy girls.

The creak of an inner door opening broke the silence like the explosion of a firecracker. A lady in a green embroidered sari and a short matching blouse appeared, her sandals lightly tapping the marble floor. There was grace in her movements, confident and unapologetic. She saw Salim and her eyes widened in recognition as she raised both her arms in an expansive gesture of greeting. 'Salim *bhai*, welcome, welcome. We have not seen you for so long. Are you well?' She spoke Urdu, the voice rich and cultured, of Begums and Nawabs, and it seemed to Tarun they had stepped into a different era of history, of days gone by.

'I am well Abida Bai, it's just that I have been busy at work. But today I have a friend with me. His name is Tarun.'

'Tarun, what handsome young fellow you are. Come on inside.' She twirled her long fingers in graceful movements of a dancer, 'come, come, you must tell me all about yourself.'

Tarun blushed to the depth of his soul. Never had he received such compliments about his looks – a handsome young fellow – that too by a beautiful lady with such exquisite manners. She led them into another room, furnished with colonial style sofas, chunky carved wood easy chairs. Fans spinning silently from the high ceiling, dispersing a lavender laden air which reminded Tarun of the lobby of the Presidency hotel he had once visited to run an errand for brother Suraj. The hotel's interior, buzzing with a clutch of English travellers, sealed from the outside world, had a brilliant new world feel to it. Tarun's imagination had gone into overdrive. Do houses in England look like this? Do people live in palatial homes with all the comforts, including air-conditioning? Oh, what a luxury to have an endless supply of water for a cooling bath twice a day.

'Sit down, sit down,' she said and looked over her shoulder. A young girl appeared and stood deferentially. 'The guests will like a drink, Pinki. Don't keep them waiting.'

'The usual,' Salim said to the girl, 'rum and bring some ice too.'

'Give me lemonade,' Tarun said.

'So, will you be listening to Saida? She is in excellent form these days, has built up quite a following, you know,' Abida Bai said, taking a seat opposite the boys.

'Yes, yes, we will definitely listen to her ghazals, oh what exquisite voice she has,' Salim said, 'sweeter than a *mynah* bird, even better than Jasmini Devi who is a regular on All India Radio. Which *ghairana* does she belong to?'

'Her *ghairana*? Why this is her *ghairana*. She lives, eats, and sings here. Her father was also a famous singer of the old school, from the court of Maharaja of Alwar. After his death she moved to Delhi.'

'All praise to you Abida Bai, for keeping the tradition alive.'

She waved the compliment away, and addressed Tarun, 'where have you come from today?'

'From Malvyanagar,' Tarun replied and cringed at the sound of his own voice, imagining he was coming across common and provincial.

'Ah, Malvyanagar,' she said, 'I have a friend living there.'

Tarun's eyes twitched, he felt uncomfortable enquiring who the friend might be, in case the person was known to his family.

She pulled a stool over on which lay a tray with a stack of betel leaves and an assortment of jars with *paan* making ingredients. She picked up an already folded *paan*. 'I was making it when you came, how fortunate,' she said and offered it to Salim.

'*Arre wah*,' Salim said and accepted the offering eagerly. His manner astonished Tarun. You pretentious two faced rascal, he wanted to thump his friend, just remember where you have come from.

She set out making another *paan*, her fingers moving expertly, pasting, and sprinkling ingredients like an accomplished *paanwala*. 'There is an art in this you know,' she said folding the green leaf into a triangle, 'I learned from my grandfather. The Banarasi *paan* was his creation only.'

'Try this,' she said to Tarun.

'I don't eat *paans*, never have.' Tarun said apologetically, rubbing his hands together.

'*Wah, wah* Tarun,' she said with a little complimentary clap, 'very virtuous man. You don't drink, don't eat *paan*. Are there any sinful habits you do have?'

Tarun grinned and Salim said gravely, 'he has many, but he doesn't like to talk about them.'

Abida Bai laughed. 'Don't we all? So, tell us Salim *bhai* what are your weaknesses. Or you wish to keep them secret too.'

'Ah, if I start talking about my sins of past and present, we will be here all night. But I will admit to one weakness. When I meet beautiful ladies like you my knees tremble and then one can manipulate me to do anything by the click of a finger.'

Abida Bai chuckled and then sighed audibly. 'I wish it were true. You are such a convincing liar.' She turned to Tarun, 'isn't he a scoundrel?'

Tarun blushed. He had no answer to that question.

'Anyway, I know how busy you men are. I will call the girls.' She conveyed a silent nod to Pinki who was standing beyond the door.

'They will be here shortly,' she said, 'I will have to keep an eye on you Salim bhai, in case you charm my girls away. They are still so young and gullible.'

Salim raised his hands defensively. 'Trust me, I am incapable of doing anything like that.'

They heard shuffling footsteps and faint whispers behind a foldable walnut wood partition, as if a troupe of actors were psyching themselves to walk on to a stage. A girl appeared swinging her hips. No older than Pinki, she was in a Rajasthani traditional costume, provocative, with a low cut blouse and a corsage of ethnic silver jewellery. Another girl followed behind, and then a third and fourth. They were in saris and short blouses, exposed midriff, bracelets on their waists and ankles. Provocative, yet shy, hips gyrating, they came over and stood in a straight line, presenting themselves to the boys.

Tarun gaped wide-eyed. He had only to raise a hand to touch a thigh or an exposed waist, the belly buttons hidden behind silver pendants. Their chests rising and falling, he could almost hear the breathing. He imbibed the perfume of their bodies. Feeling Salim's elbow in the ribs he lowered his gaze, realising he was ogling. And then he saw Salim looking intently, appraising the wares one at a time from head to toe. Finally, his gaze settled on the girl in the traditional costume. She lowered herself beside him. His hand came to rest on her thigh, patting it gently.

The other three girls eyed Tarun, posturing to appear more attractive. He blushed to bright crimson, and then fixed his gaze to the glass of lemonade sitting on the table. His mind was racing, shifting from present to the past in the speed of a rocket, He thought of mother. What if she knew what he was about to do? He continued to stare at the glass, at the beads of moisture on its outer surface drifting slowly downward. Confused memories rose in a clamour. An episode of the past grew on him, carrying him along on its strong current, re-energising the musty, but human and comforting, odour of his father's cotton shirt. He was twelve or thirteen years old, while playing on the street with the servant's daughter, also his age, he had lashed out at her, shouted demeaning insults, for she had dared to defeat him at a game of marbles. Father had witnessed the incident. He dragged the boy indoors for a reprimand. But it never involved slapping, or beating, unlike his school friend fathers who happily resorted to corporal punishment. Father made Tarun sit down and explained the error of his behaviour. Son, it is not right to insult a girl, even if she is from a lower-class family, a servant or washerman's daughter. Treat all females with respect as you would like them to treat you.

Still with his eyes on the glass, Tarun said, 'I don't want any of this.' He did not want to pick one girl and insult the others. He did not want to make them feel they were unattractive, unwanted, inferior.

Salim looked at his friend, astounded. 'Now what's the matter.'

'I have changed my mind. I can't do this,' Tarun said. There was sadness in his voice.

'What do you want to do then.'

'Not this... not this.' His eyes welled up, not of tears but of emotion, of anger that he had listened to Salim, followed him to this place.

Salim looked at the girls, apologetic. 'Give him a moment, he will be alright.'

The girls appeared confused; they had never been in a situation like it. Something we have done to upset him. They were nervous, fearing reproach from Abida Bai for displeasing a customer.

'Come on now, make your choice,' Salim said, 'we haven't got all day.'

'No, I am going home.'

'Are you sure?' Salim asked, irritated.

'Yes.'

'Then please yourself,' Salim said and took the girl's hand, 'let us go darling.'

The girls began dispersing, back to the screen. Tarun's heart began thumping. He did not know why. Was it about not insulting the girls? Or something else. Was it because he was afraid, paralysed with guilt for wanting to do something he knew was immoral? When he looked up, he realised he was not alone. One of the girls was standing in front. He realised she was the last one in, shorter and dark skinned but prettier with intelligent eyes.

'Will you not stay? I will look after you,' she said.

Her voice was not seductive. He realised she was not trying to arouse him by shaking her hips and bosoms.

Tarun shook his head.

'I will do anything you want,' she said.

'I have to go,' he said.

'If you must then go before madam comes out… or you will have to pay,' she said, 'this place is not good for you. It is…'

A commotion drowned out her voice. 'Get out of here, get out, get out.' A woman was screaming. 'Call yourself *ganteelman*, eh, we have seen many *ganteelman, shantelman* like you.' A door crashed open. A man roared with laughter, loud and theatrical, like a stage villain. 'Get out or I will call Bahadur,' the woman yelled.

The laughter stopped. 'Don't you know who I am. I can have you arrested for this, the whole lot of you,' the man roared.

Tarun looked up. A man was leaning over the banister, dangerously close to toppling over, unbuttoned shirt, ruffled hair. 'You too,' the man said to Tarun, 'I will have you arrested.' He locked his eyes on Tarun, ferociously, unblinking. An inexplicable memory from childhood leapt in Tarun's head. He was in a toyshop greedily surveying the gaudy coloured model trains, boats, ships; there were board games and dolls for girls too. His eyes lit up at a ship made of tin, painted blue and green. He knew he could not afford it but picked one up anyway. To his horror the funnel came away from the ship's body. In panic he put it down, hoping no one had noticed. The shopkeeper's big round head, like a pumpkin, reared sharply from behind the counter. He glared with such savagery Tarun wet himself.

The girl saw the panic on Tarun's face. She placed a hand on his arm, guiding him firmly towards the exit. The glass bangles on her wrist tinkled. 'Go, go, go. There is no one at the door,' she whispered urgently and gave him another firm push.

The feel of long sexy fingers and the sound of jingling

bangles stayed with him throughout the bus journey home and long after he had fallen asleep, for he had a lengthy and convoluted dream that night of naked girls jingling and jangling their glass bangles in his face while he is lying on a comfortable four-poster with plush satin bed sheets, arms and legs stretched out in post-coital slumber.

5

Pabiji was sitting on the divan bed, combing her milky white hair. Periodically releasing the loose hair trapped in the teeth of the bakelite comb, she rolled the hair on her finger into a ball and let it fall on the floor by her feet.

In the lane an earthenware water jug seller, with merchandise loaded on a donkey, wailed in a high-pitched voice. 'Su-ra-hi! Su-ra-hi!' She had a half mind of calling him over and negotiating a price for a tall neck pitcher.

'I am here,' someone announced casually at the door. It was Pyari, the cleaner. Without a word she got to work, sweeping the front room in brisk hurried arm movements, running the homemade reed broom in semicircles, making small heaps of dust.

'Pyari, take these as well,' Pabiji said pointing at the balls of hair on the floor, 'how is your daughter, Manju?'

Pyari looked up as though the answer might be on the ceiling. 'Don't ask about that Manju.' She sighed, and the hand that held the broom came to a stop, heavily. 'That wretch, she will see me dead soon. Trouble, trouble, what else to expect from her. The day she was born was a cursed day.'

'Why? What has happened now?' Pabiji asked. She knew Pyari had problems. Three daughters. No husband. Up at dawn she sold onions in the market which she cultivated illegally on government land and then toiled all day as a sweeper in five or six houses.

'Oh, Pabiji, why ask? Do you want to hear what she has done now? Left that man of hers and ran off. To find herself work she says. What work will she find, eh, tell me? She cannot even lift a finger to work. But she thinks she will find work in someone's home; they will feed her, clothe her for nothing, and give her money too. That girl lives in big, big dreams.'

'But Pyari, why do you say that? She will find a good household. Ask her to see me. I will help her.'

'Who will take her. One glance at her is enough. People will know what she is good at. The other day I asked her where you got those expensive bangles from, you keep jingling in my ears. But will she tell? No, not that one, curse of my life...' She slapped her forehead with the heel of the palm and pulled at her tired looking sari. 'This is all I can afford to wear, I spent all my money to bring her up and the other girls, what did I get in return? I am fifty years old.' She repeated, fifty, as if it was a great age. 'Mataji, for you it was easy, you had five boys. Boys are no problem.'

'*Hanh, hanh*, but I had eight children to bring up, five more than yours. Do you think it was easy for me? Don't forget I had three daughters too... three daughters, *hanh*.' Pabiji showed her three fingers of the right hand to stress the point. 'And then we became refugees. We had to leave everything behind and run. Our life was in danger. I had to resettle my family from scratch. What do you know about all that?'

But Pyari knew all about that, the loss of the family home in Lyallpur and three-day train journey without food or water. How could she not know? She had heard the story so many times, sometimes with frivolous added details.

Pabiji kicked the broom in Pyari's hand. 'Are you listening to me?'

'Yes *mataji*, you say you have had a tough time as a refugee? Look at us; my family has lived in this town for generations. Never been refugees. Yet my life is no better....'

'What did you say,' Pabiji said, not as a question but as a reprimand. How dare she, a *chamar dalit*, claim to be at par with an upper caste *kshatriya* family. She was prepared to allow a servant social access into her upper-class status, but only up to a point, so long as she did not take undue liberties, attempt to rise too high above her station.

Pyari did not reply.

'You talk too much, work too little,' Pabiji said, 'pick up the hair on the floor at once.'

❧

Coming off his Atlas bicycle, a leg still in the air, Tarun saw his sister Mita in her trademark white baggy *salwar kameez*. She was lounging on a chair in the front yard under the shade of the jamun tree. She looked so relaxed, as if she had never left home. Looped around her wrist was the familiar red bean rosary.

'See, made with stones of wild berries found only in the foothills of Himalayas,' she said proudly, 'a sanyasi gave it to me. He said so long as it is in my possession, I will remain blessed.'

Tarun gave the beads a cursory glance. 'How long will you be staying this time?' he asked. What favours will she demand of him this time, Tarun wondered. A woman of strong beliefs she had the habit of dragooning people into accepting her needs were more important than theirs. Tarun had not forgotten the day in the winter of 1940 when Mita had arrived home and announced she had changed her mind about being a doctor and was dropping out of university. There was massive furore in the house, shouting, screaming, and weeping. Father was white with rage, while mother wailed as if someone close had died.

Mita said she was going to join the Jain sect and live near the temples in the town of Palitana and climb the thousands of steps with the other pilgrims and devotees to the top of Shatrunjaya hills every day. Overnight she had become a different person. As if she had received a vision instructing her to go forth and exalt God.

When gentle persuasion failed, they tried emotional extortion. 'Look at father's face,' Pabiji said, 'look at him properly. He is so heartbroken. Is this what you want? A tortured, broken-hearted man. At his age. And what will the relatives say?'

But she would have none of it. She gave up all her possessions and took to wearing whites without makeup or jewellery. At the youthful age of twenty-five she had started looking like an old fashion aunty. Her day was ruled by ritual, from the moment she woke to make her salutations to the sun, her ritual bath and morning prayer. Tarun was at first shocked, then amused to see she had started preparing her own meals using separate pots and pans. She would say grace before eating and if there were others with her, she would insist they do so too.

'Days... weeks, I don't know,' Mita replied and unwound the rosary from the wrist and stroked each bead as if taking stock, that none had escaped the twine.

Tarun wondered if she still went to the temple at seven in the morning and again in the evening. Will she spread out a rush mat on the floor, sit cross-legged and chat with family to catch up on the latest news of births, marriages, deaths, illnesses, scandals, gossips, rumours, tittle-tattle.

'Come, let us go to the market, we need some fresh vegetables for the evening meal,' Mita said, rising from the chair and slipping her feet into the chappals.

'Not now, I need to wash.' Tarun kicked the bicycle stand into position.

'You can wash after shopping. I don't want to be late to the temple. You know I always go there at seven.' She was already out of the gate. 'Come, come let's go.'

They had covered half a block. A boy was selling roasted corn-on-the-cob by the roadside. 'How much?' she demanded.

The boy raised four fingers.

'Hoh, four paisa,' she cried, dismissed the kid with a

wave of her hand and started walking.

She said to Tarun, 'so, you want to get married.'

'You – you – have been here only half a day and already my personal affairs have been discussed,' Tarun replied.

'You have someone in mind?' she said

'No, I don't.'

'Then listen carefully to what I have to say. Marriage will give you grief and unhappiness. Who knows what kind of in-laws you will get? All the fighting and quarrelling and backbiting. Do you want all that?'

I have nothing to lose. I get all that already, Tarun thought.

She continued, '... and you must be rich if you want somewhere decent to live. Like these people.' She pointed at the house under construction, a stack of bricks and other building material spilling out on to the pavement. 'These Gopals, real crooked people.'

Tarun closed his eyes to block out the negativity, as if to transport himself to the secret location of the lake across the railway track, a place of safety which Mita did not know existed. Over months and years his relationship with Mita had been weakening, as if it had osteoporosis. She did not just pour acid all over his ideas, hopes and self-esteem, she quarrelled with other male members of the family. She told Dev he was not attractive enough to females, and only the most desperate would consider marrying him. Most annoying was her tendency to peek into the other person's past, the way she did into the future, so that she often dismantled their dreams and lifted shrouds from corpses of buried secrets.

'Look at me,' she said, slapping his wrist. She spread her arms wide like wings, and Tarun felt his own body contract. 'I am so happy. I can go anywhere, do anything without having to answer to anyone. My mind is at rest knowing God is looking after me. You should do the same, become His disciple. Come away with me. I will guide you.'

She had the habit of preaching to all who had ears to hear her. Lord's power can lift the burden of the ignorant, the oppressed, the drunk, the poor, the misguided. Her feet stomping was legendary while she shook with passion from head to toe, chanting bhajans ululating the glory of God. She had the chameleon skill of making herself appear as innocent as a rabbit with big fluffy ears, graceful as a swan, beatitude shining glassily from her brown eyes. But she would not say the loyalty He demanded was absolute, for His engines of retribution were swifter than His engines of mercy.

All this Tarun had seen and understood. So how could he become a disciple of a Godman? Sit for hours listening to lofty philosophies, read teachings of the holy books of Bhagwat Gita, Mahabharata, not aspire to accumulate wealth, give it all to Godman's establishment. It seemed to him the main reason for having a religion was to cheat death and live again. Well, he did not want another life, not if it was going to be like the current one. He did not even go to holy places, at least not voluntarily. Once he accompanied Pali to a temple. What a disaster that turned out.

Savitri had asked her son, Pali, to go to the temple and

pray to God sincerely with devotion. Only then the rejection letters will stop arriving. She released a one-rupee coin from the folds of her sari and handed it to Pali. 'Donate this to the temple.'

Pali was horrified. 'So much to give to that fat pundit?'

'What is one rupee if you get that Civil Service job with free living quarters,' she said and then to Tarun, imploring, 'could you go with him.'

They arrived at the temple just as the sun was setting. Took off the chappals and deposited them on the shelves under the sign FOOTWEAR. Pali manoeuvred himself through the crowd to the front, facing the huge statue of Lord Ganesh draped in finest muslin and silk and marigold flowers.

He bowed his head, hands joined in namaste, stood still for ten minutes, longer than even the most ardent worshippers present, as if to ensure He would take note of his presence and place a tick on the ledger book. Once finished he took out the King George V silver rupee coin from his pocket and with an exaggerated gesture of devotion dropped it on the donation mat. The pundit moved swiftly and placed a foot on it. 'Watch, he is going to pocket it when others are not looking,' he whispered in Tarun's ear.

Finally, they made their way back out to retrieve their chappals. But their footwear was absent. A temple employee conducted a quick search in cubicles and shelves and declared with utmost confidence, 'your chappals are missing.'

'That we have already ascertained Panditji,' Pali said, 'we would not have bothered you if they were not missing. The question is this. Will the temple compensate us for the loss?'

'Are you sure you were wearing them when you arrived,' he said.

Pali laughed in the fool's face, 'how could we have left our footwear accidently at home?'

'You should have been more careful. How can we guard everyone's shoes, slippers, chappals? You tell me?' he said and then appeared outraged, as if they were being unreasonable in their demand. When Pali pointed out the temple had a duty of care for the visitors, he became even more irate and threatened to have them barred from the temple. Not much of a punishment then, thought Tarun, chuckling to himself. But when another visitor confirmed this was a regular occurrence, chappals were going missing, stolen to order, the priest changed his tune. 'Perhaps you have a genuine grievance,' he said in a more accommodating tone, 'anyway it is not a big problem, is it. You look at the sadhus and the learned sanyasis when they emerge from the caves after years of meditation, do they have fancy Bata shoes on their feet? No, they are always barefoot, as nature provided. So, if you went home today barefoot you will surely be in good company.'

Now Mita was glaring at him fixedly as if to hypnotise him into submission.

'I will think about it,' Tarun said.

Mita stamped her foot. 'I know what your thinking about it means.'

'It means only that I will think about it.' A tiny smile dragged the corner of his mouth.

She saw it. 'You are an insolent man. You were born like that,' she said as if referring to his chronic illnesses, 'do you know why? Because God is punishing you.'

God is punishing me. Tarun felt it deep inside him. This was a jibe that gave him no peace. It burned.

At Moti Mahal, Manu Bhatia was standing by the steps. He gave a short cheerful wave to Tarun.

'Who is that horrible man? You should not talk to these low-class people, have self-respect,' Mita said, 'have you seen what kind of people go in there? *Chi, chi.* I hope you don't,' and then she said in the same breath, 'pack your bags, we are going to the mela next week.'

'I go to work; in case you have forgotten. I cannot go anywhere?"

'You can ask for leave, can't you? How can a woman go to a mela alone? Moreover, I need help with luggage.'

'No, I can't. My boss is extremely strict. He won't let me go, not even for a day.'

'Yes, he will if you tell him you are going to meet sanyasis and bathe in holy water of the Ganges. How can he refuse that? If you are scared, I will speak to him, leave it to me,' she said and walked on ahead as if the matter was settled.

6

'Tarun is now twenty-nine years old – soon he will be thirty,' Pabiji said thoughtfully.

Savitri nodded. She guessed Pabiji was thinking of Tarun and marriage, two words rarely uttered in one sentence. She knew the news would ripple through the ranks of the female relatives. Raised eyebrows and cynical laughter. Does he have the maturity to be a husband and father? He wants to bring home a wife. What is he going to feed her? Dry roti?

Pabiji began scraping the rough skin of the karela gourd with a serrated knife. 'I only want to do what is best for the boy. Now if we were back home in Lyallpur none of this would have happened.'

'Will you stop talking about going back home? This is our home now,' Savitri cut her short.

Pabiji shut her mouth, the lips a thin line arching downwards.

'Let us not waste time,' Savitri said.

Pabiji did not reply.

'I have a girl in mind,' Savitri said quietly and sneaked a peak at Pabiji to see her reaction

'Who?' Pabiji cried as if in shock and disapproval.

'That employer of his, Mohindra Pal has a daughter of marriageable age. Twenty-six years old, he had said. But I am sure he was understating her age.'

'Twenty-six?' Pabiji said, and then added as if there was nothing more to discuss, 'she must be married by now.'

'I have made enquiries; she is still unmarried. And I have heard they are struggling to find a match.'

'But Savitri *beti*, if they are not getting any offers, there must be something wrong with her?'

'Oh, nothing to worry about Pabiji. She has a disability with her right leg, the result of an accident when she was young, and she is a little plain looking. I have heard she is a quiet homely type. Just what we need.'

Mother and daughter looked at each other, saying nothing but each aware what the other was thinking.

Pabiji finished peeling the last of the *karela*. 'Is there anything else you want done?'

'*Baas*, nothing else,' Savitri said, 'leave them to one side… The man is Tarun's employer. I will have to manage him deftly. If he says yes, it will be the best news of the year.'

Pabiji glared at her daughter as if to warn her not to have these foolish dreams. 'I am not sure if Tarun is ready for marriage,' she said.

'He will do something foolish if you don't let him,' Savitri said after a long pause.

Pabiji picked up an old fountain pen and an aerogramme letter from the shelf. She flattened the blue and green aerogramme on the desk, pulled the pen cap and began writing. The sentences trailing up or down, sometimes beyond the paper, little blotches of leaking ink here and there.

Usha dear… he wants to get married, but in my heart, I fear no respectable family will give their daughter to us… it is my wish that all brothers and sisters pitch together and find a solution. Unfortunately, your brothers, I will not name them, are not taking it seriously. If your father were alive, he would have taken on the responsibility. Then I would not have to worry myself to death…

❁

Later that evening, lights switched off, the only sound was the neighbours on the left quarrelling. Savitri began massaging coconut oil on her arthritic feet, slowly, moving up the calf, down again. Her face muscles relaxed. She started on the left foot, massaging the toes and the instep. Slowly she drifted back in time, to the days when Tarun had started going to school. She remembered his thin legs emerging sadly from his wide khaki shorts the way his scrawny neck did from his white shirt. Coughing or sniffling from the last round of illness. He carried his bag of books and pencil boxes as a coolie might stagger along under an oversized load. Chalk dust on his clothes, socks slipping down to the canvas shoes which he chalked white every morning.

Sometimes she would overhear aunts talking about him, discussing trivia, like the toys he loved or the clothes he wore, things he liked and disliked. It was only partly accurate, mostly made-up. But if the family chose to agree on a subjective matter it became – automatically and quite irrevocably – the truth, without any of them being aware of the collective alchemy which had made it so.

'Do you remember your school?' she asked Tarun the next evening, while he was slumped on a chair, exhausted from the rigour of going up and down ladders in the midday sun.

'I remember,' Tarun replied, mopping his face with a handkerchief, 'the two Jesuit priests who ran the school.'

'English and religious studies were compulsory subjects. Were they not?' Savitri said.

'Yes,' Tarun replied, 'arithmetic too.'

He shut his eyes, threw the head back and placed the square handkerchief, moist with his sweat, on the face. Slowly a parade of noxious childhood memories which had gone into hiding in a remote corner of the brain began passing before his eyes in vivid three dimensions, complete with sounds and smells which strangely now did not seem as painful as they were at the time.

7

Lyallpur 1920

'I am not sure how a boy can become a mota khota, big hulking thing and yet not be able to read and write,' the teacher bawled at him on the first day in class, 'and your father wants me to give you special tuition, make you intelligent. Can donkeys become intelligent? *Hunh?* Look at me when I am speaking, you will learn nothing by staring at that wall.'

Tarun turned his head to the scowling face with small eyes. Spectacles sitting on the edge of the nose.

'Open the book.'

Tarun fumbled with the book. Before he could open it fully the teacher slammed his hand on top of his and yelled, showering him with specks of spittle, 'why haven't you covered it with brown paper?'

Tarun sat motionless. No one had asked him to do anything to the books.

'Did you not know all books must be bound in paper, and the title printed on the outside?'

Tarun tried to speak, but the words muffled in his throat.

'Never mind, I will send a note to your father. Now open the first page and read aloud the top line so the whole class can hear.'

Tarun did not move. He was like a farm animal in the open field which stands very still while the rain lashes down on its head. He could hear his classmates' titter behind him while he continued to stare at the oversize belt buckle mere three feet from his face as if it were about to spring to life and strike him on the face.

A hand smashed the desk, and a voice boomed in his face, 'READ.'

Tarun burst out crying.

Once, in English class he had felt a need to wee. Scared to ask permission to leave he sat holding the abdomen tight, waiting for the bell to ring. The bell did sound, but he was too slow. He sat down again seeing the next teacher was already in the classroom.

'*Oooo*, sir, sir.' The boy behind him sprang from his seat. 'Tarun has done urine on the chair. I don't want to sit near him.' He pulled his desk back. In no time the whole class was shifting chairs and desks, creating a deafening racket.

'Be quiet,' the teacher yelled, 'or I am going to expel all of you.'

The boys stopped. But the silent command is still very noisy. Tarun shut his eyes as if he were in a nightmare and would wake up to perfect normalcy. When he opened his eyes, he found a heavy jaw and stench of tobacco looming over him.

'Filthy little Hindu. Look at the mess you have made. Go and stand outside for the rest of the class.'

The desks started screeching again.

'Quiet.'

As soon as the final bell sounded Tarun was always the first pupil out of the main gate, running like a fleeing convict. He would walk back home leisurely, sometimes with Hardip who lived two streets away. The boys often bought *jamun* from roadside sellers. They would eat and spit out the stones forcefully, competing who could project it the furthest. One time the projectile, accompanied with a fair amount of spittle, landed on the face of a man passing by. The boys took off running. Tarun was unfortunate. He tripped on a rock and fell. 'You son of an owl, have they not taught you any manners,' the man yelled and whacked him across the face, 'do you know who I am? I am Chief Engineer at the waterworks department. I can have the water supply cut off to your house.'

Tarun refused to say how he got an imprint of fingers on his cheek. If the water supply indeed ceased, he feared getting the blame. He would have to lug buckets from communal wells or beg the neighbours.

He began feigning stomach aches, headaches, mastering the art of holding his breath for extended periods to appear pale and sickly. 'Oh, poor boy,' Pabiji would feel his temperature by placing a hand on the forehead, 'all right, don't go to school today, but you must do some studying to catch up.'

The day of reckoning was delayed for a brief period. Even so the ever-tightening knot of fear would not leave him, for he knew one day they would ask him to recite the times table. The teacher will stand back with a mocking smile shaking his head from side to side, I know you can't do it. Tarun would stay silent to prove him right.

●

'Take that rubbish out of here,' Pabiji said, kicking the battered tin box out of the way.

Tarun rushed to save his collection, dropping on his already bruised knees. The box contained pens and ink pots, mangled watches, watch straps, discarded metal objects, small rocks, and pebbles. Only he could see the colours and hues of the rocks: pink, green, copper, and blue. His brothers mocked him, calling him a dirty scavenger.

'What's that?' Hardip said, pointing at Tarun's crotch. They had wandered into the woodland and were now sitting side by side on a fallen log.

'What?' Tarun looked down at the fly buttons of his faded blue short pants.

'No, no, what's inside?' Hardip said as he slipped closer.

'You know what's inside you fool,' Tarun replied.

'Show it to me, you can have my guava.' Hardip took out a half ripe guava from his pocket.

Eager to please his friend, Tarun stood up and lowered his pants to the knees.

Hardip bent down and started stroking Tarun's limp penis. This went on for about thirty seconds until they heard leaves rustling nearby. Tarun swiftly pulled his short back up.

That was Tarun's first ever sexual encounter, though not

with the opposite sex. It meant nothing to him, but he was confused by Hardip's curiosity. If a girl really did make such a request, he would never be able to do it. The embarrassment would kill him.

At a *satsang*, where his mother often insisted on taking him, a clutch of ladies was singing praises of Lord Guru Nanak. Chanting and clapping with dedicated enthusiasm. They urged him to join in. He shied away, sinking into himself. Later he spotted three girls, his own age, sitting huddled across the room. He shifted position to get a clear view. In the midst of the religious fervour Tarun's penis hardened. He crossed his legs to hide the embarrassment, convinced people were looking at him and could read his thoughts.

He loved exploring the school grounds, the outer peripheries, feel the gratification of pebbles crunching under his feet. He had studied the shape of the land, knew where the ground curved like a cradle and the spider legs of tree roots rippled above the soil. He knew the crevices that could hide his body among the snakes and thorny bushes. The bearded groundsman often gave him fruit plucked from trees.

❦

On the day exam results came out Tarun did not go home from school.

'Where is Tarun?' Pabiji asked Krishan, anxiously peering out the window, 'he should have been home four hours ago.'

No one had noticed his absence until it was dinner time. Krishan went to Hardip's house.

'I didn't see him leave school, uncle. Don't know where he is,' Hardip replied. His father offered to help in the search. They took Hardip to retrace the route to and from school. The old caretaker, well past his retirement age said, 'I don't know who Tarun is, but you can search the school if you like.' He fetched a heavy bunch of keys.

Neighbours started pouring in, offering to help. 'Check the canal…' someone suggested, leaving the sentence unfinished. The words hung heavy in the air with the ominous meaning.

Pabiji began weeping in her sari. Father raged at Pabiji for not keeping an eye on the boys. He ordered Krishan and Suraj to accompany him to the canal, to the bend with the steep bank and swift flow of water, which he knew was a favourite spot for people who had had enough of life.

They found Tarun sitting on a rock staring into the shimmering water. He had already torn up the result sheet into twenty pieces and dropped them in the water one at a time, watching them float erratically in the ebb and flow. The attached letter from the head teacher, which said he wanted to see the parents to discuss 'young Tarun's future' suffered the same fate.

'What are you doing here?' father bellowed.

Tarun refused to budge from the rock.

'You are to tell me what this is about,' father said, threatening him with the cane.

Tarun's stare stayed locked on the opposite bank. Father followed Tarun's line of vision across the water, the moon light reflecting in the ripples. He nearly slipped on a wet rock as he yelled for Suraj. 'Look over there.' He pointed at a half-submerged boulder, the water flowing around it. Trapped between the rock and a fallen log was a human body, floating face down, naked from waist up.

Krishan put his foot in the water, to walk to the rock.

'Don't be a fool son,' father said pulling Krishan back by his shirt, 'the water is deep here, and the man is dead anyway. Better inform someone in the colony.'

Krishan was about to set off to the small labourers' settlement when they heard voices. Five or six men were running towards them. They waded in with long poles and lanterns. Following behind were a clutch of women, wailing into the night air.

'Quick, let's get out of here,' Suraj said, 'in case they try to implicate us.'

Brothers Suraj and Krishan threaded an arm under each of Tarun's armpits and hauled him up off the ground. Tarun stiffened his body, shut his eyes, and maintained the sitting posture while they carried him all the way home. Even when they dropped him on the floor, he refused to relax his muscles. While the family screamed and cajoled and begged him to explain the strange behaviour, he doggedly kept his mouth shut.

Doctor said it was selective mutism, a severe anxiety disorder where a person is unable to speak in certain situations. It is not that the person is refusing or choosing not to speak, he or she is unable to do so.

'What causes this?' father asked, attempting to regain his composure, while Pabiji stood behind him, a corner of the sari in her hands, worrying it into twists and knots.

'The cause is not always clear, but it's known to be associated with anxiety. The child will have difficulty with taking everyday tasks in his stride.'

Father raised his eyebrows. 'Is this permanent? So, what to do.'

'Usually, they recover in familiar surroundings. Your child is an extreme case, but he will come round. Be patient. It is a misconception that a child with selective mutism is controlling or manipulative.'

'Yes, doctor, is there any medicine to give?' father asked.

'The only medication is a good dose of love,' he said and laughed, 'I wish I could get some of it.'

'*Oho*, doctor sahib, what are you saying?' father said, 'you have a very loving family.'

'You haven't met my wife then,' Doctor said, 'I am in danger of catching selective mutism myself… with a bit of luck.'

The two men exchanged knowing glances and laughed.

'What did he say?' Pabiji pounced on father as soon as the doctor left. She hated it when people spoke in English in her presence, convinced they were doing it to exclude her from the conversation.

'You need to go easy on the boy.'

Father sent for a duplicate school report. When they learned Tarun had failed in every subject Pabiji vanished. The space in the room of existence gradually shrank as days passed. She stopped talking. She went about her tasks with exaggerated motions, like a mime actor in silent movies. Words pooled in her brain, but little leaked out. When father, fretting over the strange behaviour, pestered her to speak, she broke the regime of silence and complained bitterly that he should not have sent her son to that school. Tarun caught phrases from intense arguments conducted in whispers and behind closed doors

Years later, those vivid flashes of memory seemed like pieces of a bad dream, as if none of it had happened. The only narrative Tarun could impose upon this jumble of images was the narrative of ritual, changeless since he was a boy. The sound of a free-flowing river, moonlight on rippling waves like mini flares, the smell, all these often reignited those memories in bitesize flashes. Yet at family gatherings they did not discuss the canal episode, as if it never happened. Even Pabiji did not talk about it, though he had not expected it from father who was a man of few words.

8

Malviya Nagar 1954

The clock on the wall demanded Tarun's attention. The hour hand was on one. The minute hand rested between five and six. It was a fading remnant of another time, broken down, never replaced. The most diabolical part was the second hand, which was the only part of the clock that moved. The tick-tock-tick was silent. This one only did tick, tick, tick.

He had an urge to bring it down and check its mechanisms. Not that he knew how to fix clocks. Salim could though. 'I will ask Dr Mallick if he wants to throw it away,' he whispered in Dev's ear.

'What?'

'The clock.'

Dev made a face. 'Don't embarrass me by asking for that broken down contraption. What will he think? That we cannot afford to buy a clock.'

Tarun huffed and crossed his legs.

When the call came for him to go in Tarun hesitated, made a face as if he already knew it would be a distasteful experience.

'Go in,' Dev said, fingering Tarun's back, 'if you did not want to see him, why have you come all this way. Waste my time too.'

A large wooden desk occupied the centre of the consulting room without windows, but with an odour of tincture iodine. A stethoscope, a Chelpak ink pot, dip pen with steel nib and a piece of blotting paper, sat by the doctor's elbow.

'Mallick is on leave. I am standing in,' the occupant of the chair explained as he opened Tarun's file, 'my name is Suraj Dutt,' he said and scanned a page hurriedly. 'Have there been any more episodes?'

'Yes,' Dev said quickly, 'my uncle had a seizure last month.'

'Last month,' the doctor repeated and made a note on the file with a pencil, 'why didn't you come earlier?'

'My uncle was reluctant to come. He was insisting it will not happen again. We have had to force him.'

'How long did it last?'

'Two or three minutes. Is that right uncle?'

'But doctor I was all right afterwards, ask anybody,' Tarun said as he puffed up his chest, 'I am perfectly fine now.'

'Epilepsy is a chronic disorder. You can't wish it away. The only solution is medicine.'

'I am taking the medicine doctor sahib,' Tarun said, but omitted to mention he was irregular, there were days he forgot altogether.

'Yes, I see that here. You are clearly prone to Colonic or Atonic seizures rather than Focal type,' doctor said and scribbled some more.

Tarun eyed the long-handled dip pen lying flat on a glass plinth. Dev pinched his thigh under the table.

'I have seen your file. Nothing else to do. Keep taking the same medicine. Come back when you run out.' He whistled as he spoke, a speech impediment. 'Good night's sleep, avoid stressful situations, no skipping meals or overeating and no alcohol,' he said and then peered deep into Tarun's eyes, 'you drink?'

'I don't drink, doctor. What are you saying?' Tarun said.

'Calm down,' Dev said.

'You calm down if you want to, I am going.'

Doctor wrote something hurriedly on a chit and handed it to Tarun. 'Pay Gopalji on the way out and come back if there is no improvement. We may change the medication.'

Tarun studied the chit. It said Rs 25 consultation fee. 'Oh, what's this,' he cried, 'so much for just fifteen minutes of your time.'

Dr Dutt raised his head in surprise, and then leaned back on the chair, 'you are right. Ten rupees would be more than sufficient for fifteen minutes.'

'Then why are you charging so much more? What is the meaning of this?'

'Well, my friend, the rest is for the six years I spent studying medicine at Patna Medical college. Then five years practical experience at Safdarjung Hospital followed by two years in general practice... Am I still overcharging?'

'Didn't I say there was no need to see him. Didn't I?' Tarun ranted as they walked home, 'twenty-five rupees just to hear I should continue with the same medicine. As if I did not know that already.'

9

Lyallpur 1920

Holding up at arm's length, the gilt-framed picture of a near naked Jesus Christ she had found in Tarun's satchel, Pabiji railed against it, as if it were a poison potion, or an evil charm that had cast a spell on his son. 'See this,' she said, waving the picture in father's face, 'I told you not to send him to that *Isai* school... now see what has happened.'

'Woman, have you forgotten your brother, Diwan Kochhar sent his sons to the same school, has it done them any harm?' father retorted, rustling an Urdu weekly he was reading at his desk.

'Why don't you have a word with them. Ask them not to expose my son to this nonsense.' She held the frame at arm's length. 'Our son should be learning Hinduism.'

'I can't do that. How can I dictate to them what religion they should or should not be teaching? It is a Christian Missionary school. Or have you forgotten. Besides, the Commissioner will not be happy if I try to interfere.'

'But they have appointed you inspector of schools now.

Why can't you?'

Father rustled the paper again, shifted on the chair. 'I am an inspector, not a dictator.'

The District Commissioner, an Englishman, as tall as he was broad, had come to the house six months earlier, unannounced, taking father by surprise. Pabiji had panicked, running around in disarray in the kitchen, how to entertain an Englishman, what food to offer.

'Very good Sukhdayal, I like your honesty and no-nonsense attitude, just like us English,' the commissioner had said and boomed with laughter, 'I am recommending you for the position. Take this letter to the District Office.' Father hated the comparison to an Englishman but kept his cool with a fake smile. The commissioner put his hand out for his assistant to hand him a pen. The assistant dutifully uncapped the fountain pen, checked the nib was in order, and handed it to the boss. The commissioner signed the document with a flourish that nearly ripped the paper. Again, father smiled, shaking his head agreeably, hiding the dislike he felt for the British. He saw them as ruthless oppressors. Sooner they leave India the better. He admired Gandhi and others in the freedom movement. But he would not allow his sons anywhere near them. Career is more important than a stint in *azadi* jail, he had told the boys.

Pabiji's sister Kamala, suggested a school for Tarun, a boarding establishment run by a Baba in his ashram. 'Listen to me Rajwanti. I have heard from dependable sources that it is a good school. It will be exactly right for our Tarun. They teach everything from history, geography, mathematics, including our Hindu *sanskara.*'

'Hindu *samskara.*' Pabiji cried as if she had finally hit on the solution. She stopped kneading the dough on the brass tray and punched the wet ball with both fists. '*Baas,* I am sending him to Baba's ashram school.'

'Ashram? what is he going to learn there except sing bhajans.' Father was horrified. Everyone knew he did not tolerate talk of ashrams and gurus, seeing them as a preserve of women and the weak. He wanted his sons to grow up with discipline and education suitable for civil service, international commerce, or engineering.

❋

A padlocked zinc metal trunk already hauled on the horse-drawn tonga, father sat on the front seat, erect like a maharaja, a hand resting on the walking cane. Tarun and Pabiji clambered onto the back seat. She had not told the boy where they were going. But Tarun guessed it had to be somewhere important with an overnight stay. He did not ask again, fretting silently for the break in the routine. At home he compulsively went around correcting the order of things. In his mind everything had a place and a hierarchy. He found comfort in meeting the same people, seeing the same cracks in walls or chipped footsteps, the same leaking drain pipes collecting moss, the familiar sound of life in the neighbourhood.

From the rear seat Tarun watched the tonga driver with a dusty turban, grunting lazily but cracking the whip on the poor horse with vigour. The horse speeded up when whipped, but not for long. It slowed down gradually, as though hoping his tormentor would not notice. The animal raised its tail and defecated while still on a trot. Tarun marvelled at the animal's ability to shit while on the move. Pabiji pressed a fold of her sari on the nose. They were in the countryside, parched open land on both sides with clusters of wild bushes. Tarun saw a convoy of four bullock carts lumbering achingly slow on a dirt track and wondered where they might be going. A boy on the crest of a hill appeared to be throwing stones at flying vultures.

'Not long now,' father said. Tarun nodded, but still did not ask where they were going. He trusted father, felt secure in his company. Though he never rushed to greet or hug when father arrived home from work. His presence in the house was enough for him. Father's grunts as he released his feet from the uncomfortable footwear, calls to Pabiji to fetch him a glass of water, fortified a dependable aura. Tarun's duty was to put father's shoes away while still warm and smelling of sweat and shed skin. Mohan's task was to polish them once a week, get them ready for Lyallpur's toxic red dust that clung to surfaces like leeches to the skin. Mohan hated the menial task and often subcontracted it to Tarun, offering him one paisa and a slab of *ampapar*. Tarun felt delighted, considering the brass coin a regal sum. When father found out he sent for Mohan to put a stop to the illicit commercial activity. 'Show me your hand.' Mohan exposed his palm and received a whack with the walking cane.

The tonga driver made a series of clucking sounds with his mouth. The horse started slowing down, and finally stopped with an up and down roll of the head and a loud snort. On the right was a heavy metal gate, beyond which stood an old colonial style building.

'We are here,' Pabiji said and placed a hand on Tarun's knee.

Tarun looked around him mystified. 'What is here?'

'Your new school. You did not like the old one *na*,' Pabiji said, injecting enthusiasm in her voice, 'we are taking you to a brand-new school. You will like it so much, make hundreds of friends.'

Still reeling from the bone rattling tonga ride, the unfamiliar surroundings, mother's words taking time to sink in. 'New school,' he said, looking around in confusion.

'Yes, a brand-new school for you. You will love it here.' Mother's excessive enthusiasm confused him even more.

'But it's so far,' he said, imagining he would have to take a tonga ride every day.

'No son,' father said, 'this is a residential school. You will be staying here. We will bring you home when the holidays start.'

The reality struck him with a bang. He felt his hands go cold imagining walking into a classroom full of mocking sniggering faces.

A young man in a crisp white shirt came to greet them at the gate. He had that pious upright expression of a resolute disciple. 'Please this way,' he said and with minimum of fanfare walked them to the main building, to a small room with a desk and chair. Books, boxes of chalks, black board dusters, pencils and twelve-inch rulers lay scattered in a glass cabinet secured with a padlock.

'Please sit down,' he said pointing out a bench and two easy chairs set against the wall, 'I will order some cold drinks, you must be thirsty after the journey.'

A woman in white sari entered with a jug of water and glasses. Tarun managed just a sip, he could not swallow, as if his throat were lined with cotton.

'I will show you the school now,' the young man said after they had finished with water. They came out of the room from a door at the rear, along a path bordering flowering bushes. Up front the path split into two, one leading to an open-air assembly area set in green lawn. The other path led to three identical barracks.

'As you know,' the young man said pointing proudly to a signboard erected high on two poles, 'we are Baba Ramdas Pyarelal Jhandewal Ashram. The local people commonly refer to it as Baba da Ashram.'

Tarun, following close behind his mother, tried to stay invisible. He heard a loud hectoring voice of a teacher coming from a hall on the right and his stomach lurched as if injected with acid. Past a boundary fence, woodland on the other side, a stream running through it, they entered an L-shaped room with high walls and corrugated slanting roof. Tarun clutched mother's hand. He had never seen so many beds in one place. There had to be at least thirty, all arranged in a straight line against the walls, barely two feet apart. The air reeked of sweat and soiled clothes.

'This is sleeping quarter A,' the man said, 'B is across the path.' They walked the entire length of the hall and exited at the other end. The young man stopped to explain the daily routine. 'The boys wake up at six,' he said, eyeing

Tarun to include him in the conversation, 'they have a bath and breakfast, and then sit with the Baba for two hours. They learn about our religion and study Bhagwat Geeta and Mahabharata.'

'What did you say?' father stopped suddenly beside a thorny bush, 'you are teaching Geeta to nine, ten years old.'

'Yes sir, that's correct,' he said brightly as if father was impressed that the children were learning the holy book.

'What good will it do? Will it make them scientists, doctors, or barristers?' father asked.

The young man shook his head puzzled. 'But this is our policy,' he said, 'you must have known before applying for admission.'

'No, I did not,' father said, his eyes wide with rage. 'Did you?' he said to Pabiji, glaring at her, as if accusing her of deception.

Pabiji kept a resolutely straight face. Tarun realised the squabble was about him. He wished all this would go away, and that they were back to the familiar aura of home, to the routine he was comfortable with.

'I believe teaching Geeta, and Mahabharata for two hours every day is unnecessary. Absolutely no need for it,' father said after a pause, a little calmer, expecting an offer of compromise, an alternative subject for those who didn't want to learn the Gita.

'If you don't like our curricula sir, you are welcome to take your son back with you,' the young man replied bluntly.

Stunned outrage on father's face. Pabiji stepped in

quickly, 'no, no, we like it here very much. We have no objection about religious studies. Our boy will stay.'

Two hours later Tarun saw the back of the tonga, kicking dust as it picked up speed, taking his mother and father away from him. He stood his ground, refusing to let the tonga out of sight, imagining Pabiji will stop the vehicle, wave at him frantically, urging him to come running, quick, quick, quick. When he rubbed his eyes and looked for her, she was gone.

A woman in white sari and enormous bosoms came out of an office. Tarun recognised her as the one who had brought the water. 'You must be Tarun,' she said. A bald man by her side kept nodding to every question she put to Tarun, as if his name was Tarun.

'I am Rampyari Shakuntla Devi,' she said. The emphasis on the word Rampyari suggested it was a hard-earned title and she intended to flaunt it.

They walked Tarun through the school, the classrooms, sleeping quarter and then the common hall where twenty boys were sitting with open books. He did not know the books were Bhagwat Gita, which they will ask him to commit to memory, a feat never accomplished by anyone, not even an adult. The boys saw him coming and their eyes lit up as though he was carrying toys which were up for distribution.

The orderlies carried the trunk in and placed it beside a bed. Big bosom said, 'empty your suitcase and settle down. You will be happy here.'

Tarun shook his head. He did not like people telling him when and where he would be happy. She eyed him severely.

'You WILL be happy here.'

Two weeks later, one lunchtime he noticed an overexcited crowd in the play yard. They had formed a close-knit circle like an ugly patchwork tent. Tarun knew they were bullying or beating someone. He had already learned there were no private humiliations in the school, they were all mercilessly public. A boy he recognised from dormitory B was lying on the ground with blood dribbling from his mouth. The boy had neither the guts nor physical attributes to put up a fight. Someone said explaining, 'see he bumped into the fist of another boy and hurt himself.' The boys were laughing because their leader was laughing. The leader, a big boy with round face and short cropped hair, looked Tarun's way. Their eyes met. Instantly a taste of terror fumed and smothered Tarun's mouth, and again he felt acid in his stomach.

10

Malviya Nagar 1954

'No need to repair it,' Tarun said cheerily, pointing out the crack in the wall running in a zig zag pattern like a lightning strike, 'we can cut a door for the annexe... just over here.' With an expansive gesture, he traced an imaginary door on the wall, the hand going up and over and back down again to the floor. 'Isn't it a stroke of luck the foundation has heaved at this very spot.'

Pabiji scanned the wall from ceiling to floor, turned and left the room mumbling, 'what cheap house they have given us, made of paper.'

Pali gave it a casual up and down. 'This is nothing,' he said with a dismissive wave of the hand, 'get me some cement, I will fix it.'

Pammi came over, the heels of the hands out in front, as if she were pushing a car, or acting out the mortuary ghost (elaborate tales of the ghosts' antics were kicking around the college). The room rapidly filled with a metallic odour of her wet nail polish. 'What do you know about building work, nothing,' she said to Pali, 'you better stick to your social work, go spread peace and love by screaming at people.'

Padma said, 'I agree with Pammi. You are not a doer; you are just a talker.' She did a hand gesture of a barking dog, 'you never air your ideas in a forum where they might be challenged, you just say them to yourself and congratulate yourself when you agree with what you say.'

Pali batted the air with his hand. 'Not true,' he said, 'I speak to people all the time, debate the issues, and usually win. Do you know what your problem is? You are choosing books over life. Books don't solve problems of life and society. You must go out there and get your hands dirty.' It was true, Padma was in the books reading phase. Tarun had noticed too, and he was in owe, how she could slouch on a chair with her hard brown face, and go through books borrowed from friends, for hours at a time as if she were in a competition.

'We are going to knock this section out and build a room on the other side,' Tarun said, slapping the wall lovingly.

'Really? For what?' Pammi said.

'It's for me. I am going to live there,' Tarun replied, a winning smile on his face.

'What about planning permission? Isn't that required before breaking walls?'

'*Hanh, hanh*, it is. Suraj *bharaji* is coming soon. He is going to talk to a builder friend. Everyone agrees it is a clever move.'

'I know someone who can do the work,' Pammi said, blowing on her nails, 'my friend's uncle is a builder who knows the owner of Regal cinema, and, and, and that's not all, he says he can get free matinee tickets. I am going next month. Want to come uncle?'

Tarun snorted. 'You know I don't go to cinemas....'

Pammi cut him short and said sneering, 'yes, yes... only people of low moral values spend three hours indulging in tasteless fantasies in stuffy theatres and then come out behaving like vulgar screen actors.'

Before he could respond she left the room and moments later a scream penetrated the dividing wall.

Tarun and Pali rushed to the front room and found Pammi sitting crouched under a table. 'Lizard, lizard,' she croaked, a finger stabbing the air. 'Kill it.'

About eight inches long from head to tail, translucent and pale like a skinned chicken, it was a common house lizard, appearing stuck to the wall like someone had plastered it there.

'It is only a *chipkali*,' Tarun said, 'harmless.'

'But it could fall on my head.'

'They don't fall, they have suction pads on their feet. Now if you spend less time watching movies and more studying animals you will know these house geckos are common all over India, and they live on insects, not humans,' Pali said.

At that instant Salim appeared at the door. He stopped abruptly seeing Pammi crouched under the table. 'Am I interrupting something.'

'It's the lizard,' Pali said. He pointed at the little creature with splayed legs and head raised. stalking a prey, 'she is terrified.'

'That,' Salim cried surveying the room, 'you are afraid of that.' He strode over to the wall light, jumped, caught the unsuspecting creature in a full swoop. 'There you are,' he said and took the struggling reptile out and released it on the boundary wall.

Pammi emerged slowly from under the table. 'Why couldn't you have done it?' she said to Pali with admonishing eyes and left the room.

11

Lyallpur 1920

Exactly six months and twenty days after Tarun's admission to the ashram school father received a letter. Headed: Baba Ramdass Pyarelal Jhandewal Ashram, School Division.

> *… your son, Tarun, has committed an act of gross indecency. He was running naked in the grounds of the ashram where Baba was giving a lecture to an assembly of his devotees, majority were females from good, respectable families… the ladies felt terrorised… their honour violated… in view of this wanton misbehaviour by your son the school has decided to expel him from Baba Ramdass Pyarelal Jhandewal Ashram, School Division… please take notice… arrange to have him collected…*

The signature at the bottom was strangely amateurish, like a child attempting joined-up writing: Lalla Ramlakha Chandok.

Father, as usual maintained a studied silence as he reread

the letter. His eyebrows in a tight knot, tapping the cane to the floor repeatedly as if swotting insects. 'Not possible my son would do such a thing. This is not in his character,' he said finally.

Pabiji listened with a hand on her mouth, as he read the letter aloud, translating it into Punjabi for her benefit. 'What are we going to do now?' she said, 'first your Christian school rejects him and now this.'

'Woman, you wanted to send him to this school, not me,' father said and slammed the letter on the table. A glass of water toppled over, crashing to the floor. 'Now look what you have made me do.'

❀

When father arrived at the school, enduring a two-hour pounding in an overcrowded bus on the hottest day of the year, he was in a foul mood. The principal welcomed him in the office with a namaste. A middle-aged man of rounded stature, a thick moustache which dropped at each end of the mouth. A large turban with a pointed *tura* sat on his head like a crown, letting it be known he was senior in hierarchy, an elder chief. 'Please sit down,' he said.

Father studied him. The face was not one he recognised, nor the name attached to the door, Lalla Ramlakha Chandok – Headmaster. He had not come across that name in the teaching fraternity. 'Are you from outside Punjab?' he asked.

'No, no, I was born right here, in Gujranwala district. May I offer you water?'

'No need, I have come to collect my son,' father said and impatiently tapped his cane to the floor.

'Yes, I will send for him,' the principal said and hit a brass bell on his desk.

A fresh-faced young boy arrived within seconds and stood erect with arms straight by his side. 'Yes, sir.'

'Call Tarun, hurry.'

While they waited, father tried to make small talk. 'How long have you been teaching?' he asked.

'I am the principal here. I don't teach,' he said with a scowl.

'Yes, I can see that, but you must have taught in the past.'

'Teach? No, no I have never done such a thing.'

'Then how did you become headmaster?' father said, rolling his forefinger briskly in the air as if ticking off an upstart pupil in his class.

'You see, I have dedicated my whole life to Baba. I have been his *bhakt* from day one,' he said and raised a forefinger, 'then last year he called me in and said, Ramlakha you have been so loyal to me for ten years, it is time I reward you. I am making you principal of the school. So, who was I to disobey? I said, yes Babaji, whatever you say I will do.'

Father tapped the cane to the floor forcefully and sat upright, grim faced as if he wanted to lash out at this fool. He was about to say something when Tarun walked into the room and stood staring at father with fearful eyes, as if expecting father to give him a stern talking to.

The boy presented a pathetic sight. He was half his

normal weight, pale, and frightened. The strangest sight was his head. He was half bald, the hair sheared right down to the roots in haphazard patches.

Father took Tarun in his arms. It was a rare show of raw emotion. 'What have they done to you?'

Tarun began weeping.

'How do you explain this,' father demanded, 'he looks half dead. This is not how we brought him to you.'

'Your son had stomach trouble. We gave him the best treatment available; our ashram doctors are the best in the country. Also, your son is difficult. He refuses to eat.'

'Refuses to eat?' father said, 'he has an extremely healthy appetite. And why have you cut off his hair?'

'It's our school's policy. Punishment for gross misconduct. Discipline, discipline, discipline. That's the school's motto.'

'I will give you discipline,' father roared and raised the cane threateningly in the air.

The principal cowered with hands above the head. 'There is no need for this, sir.'

'I want a full report. I want to know why you forced my son to run around naked. I do not believe he would have done it voluntarily. You understand. Or I will report you to the authorities.'

The principal nodded, nervously readjusting the turban.

'Do you know who I am?'

'No sir.'

'Just as well or you will be running to your Baba for protection.'

12

Malviya Nagar 1954

Before they stepped inside Moti Mahal, which was quieter than the last time, Salim warned Tarun, 'I do not want a repeat of the grand drama from you. You understand.'

'Is it my fault that it comes without warning. Anyway, I am taking the medicine now.'

'And I am hungry. I am going to eat like a horse.'

'Whatever you fancy, order it,' Tarun said as if money was not an issue.

With exaggerated hand gestures Salim began ordering the food, 'I will have this… this… this… and this,' stabbing the menu wildly with a finger.

'Yes, yes, you can have that, no problem,' Tarun said while trying to appear equally flamboyant but failing miserably.

'Do not worry my friend,' Salim said, picking up the signal, 'we will share the bill.'

'It's just that I have had to give money to my mother this month,' Tarun said, relieved and guilty at the same time.

'Didn't I say don't worry about the bill,' Salim cut him short, 'but tell me what happened to you the other day. You said you wanted to meet the girls and when I took you there you clammed up like a monk.'

'It's not like that… I… I…'

'What are you; a man or… or something else.'

'It's just that I couldn't… anyway I want to meet that girl again, the one with red bangles.'

'Bangles?' What bangles?'

'The last girl on the right, the shorter one. Oh, what beauty she was, and the jingling glass bangles.' Tarun raised his forearm.

'I know where girls wear bangles, you fool.' Salim studied his friend again with narrowed eyes. 'Ho, ho, ho, what is this I see? Are you in love with the girl with red bangles?' He slapped his thigh and gave a high-pitched hoot.

'Love? Nothing like that, I just like her.'

'You just like her?'

'Yes.'

'You like *tarka* dhal with boiled rice too.'

'Yes.'

'What would you do if *tarka* dhal was not available? Kill yourself?'

'No, I will kill you,' Tarun snapped.

'Listen to me my friend,' Salim said, 'listen to me. Don't fall in love with these kinds of girls. They are only good for an hour's fun and fuck. Then you forget about them and go home. Or you will get into trouble.'

'What trouble will I get into? I only want to meet her.

You can arrange that for me, can't you?'

'Do you know her name?'

'Err, no.'

'So, you will go there, pay the money and demand to see the girl with red bangles. Do you know what will happen? No… *Abbe saale*, let me tell you what will happen. You will find six girls standing there. All wearing red bangles, making eyes at you. Pick me, pick me.' Here Salim did a crude hand gesture and laughed just as the waiter began setting the table with the bowls of *matar paneer, tarka dhal, mutton bhuna.*

'I want to meet her outside the house.'

'What?' Salim slapped his forehead. 'You want me to go and ask Abida Bai to send the girl out because Tarun wants to have the fun but not pay for it. Do you know how stupid that sounds?'

Realising he was making impossible demands Tarun shut up. This will never work, he thought, even if he met the girl what were the chances she would reciprocate positively? Pammi had said the other day, pointing out an article in Filmfare, 'uncle did you know only about twenty percent of the female population will find an average male attractive by looks only, so long as nothing else was known about the person.'

A dismal figure, he thought. He had placed himself in the eighty percent category, seeing himself as an abominable ogre who would never find love.

He looked around him and was amazed how quickly the restaurant had filled up. The general hubbub, the blaring radio, noise of the kitchen. It reminded him of the previous visit. He glanced at the table they had sat the last time. A family of four were occupying it now, mother, father and two children, girl, and a boy. A tick on the back of the neck made him look up. The ceiling lights felt far too bright. He shielded his eyes with a cupped hand and looked at the family again. This time he felt annoyed as if they had trespassed on his territory, his domain. The little girl looked at him and smiled. He felt a force urging him to go and claim the table and recreate that scene in every detail, including the overturned chairs and frothing in the mouth. He heard Mita's high pitched voice. *Have you seen what kind of people go there? Chi, chi. I hope you don't.'*

'There is one way you could meet her… *oi, saale*, are you listening, or have you gone deaf.?… Abida Bai opens her house to visitors at twelve in the afternoon. The girls start arriving half an hour earlier. You could wait outside and catch your girl before she goes in.'

'Oh,' Tarun muttered and crawled deeper into himself.

Salim waited for his friend to recover. Getting no response from him he slid into a ditty in English:

my beloved darling with red, red bangles
for you I am in such a tangle
say two words to sooth, sooth my heart
or I will break an angry fart

'No, no,' Salim giggled like a schoolboy, 'the last line should be – or I will go home on a rickshaw cart – or even better – I will throw myself under a rickshaw cart.'

'Shut up Salim, sometimes you talk a lot of nonsense, stop it.'

13

Lyallpur 1920

Pabiji was crying on the day Tarun was due back home. She heard the front door open and looked up from the fog. Her son came in and stood with head bowed, as if summoned to the headmaster's office for a talk down. Shoddily cropped hair, he was wearing dirty canvas shoes, laces undone, shirt hanging half out. She burst into a loud howl again.

'It's all your fault,' she said later to father.

'How is it my fault, woman. It was you. You were so keen to send him to that school or have you forgotten.'

'If you had let them know you were inspector of schools, they would not have dared mistreat your son,' Pabiji screamed while father cleared his throat repeatedly.

'You know it is against my principle to flaunt authority.'

'Principle, principle, where has your principle got you? And that smooth talking Englishman, did he give you a raise? No, just promises, promises.'

Their neighbour Gupta's boy, on hearing Tarun was back home, knocked on the door and came right in. 'Is Tarun here?'

She grabbed the boy's shoulder and turned him around, 'now run along home to your mother. It is supper time.'

The boy shrugged free. 'Does he want to come out to play?'

She had taken a dislike of the whole Gupta family ever since this boy had pushed Tarun in the canal and nearly drowned him. Had it not been for a quick-thinking passing farmer, her son could indeed have died. To make matters worse none of the Gupta family had ever apologised. Now in her moment of grief the boy had come to taunt her. 'This isn't playtime,' she snapped, 'I will send him when he is ready.'

She called Suraj and Mohan over. 'Keep an eye on your little brother today,' she said, 'he is so upset.'

❋

When Tarun went outside to sit on a rock, he found Suraj and Mohan following him. They sat with him, casually chucking pebbles, targeting a bird, or passing goats.

'I was always hungry there,' Tarun said, running the back of his hand across the dripping nose, 'they gave too little to eat and half of it got stolen.'

'Stolen. How.'

'The bigger boys. They would just pick up a roti or *puri* from the plate. We were supposed to have a banana every day. That too they snatched before it reached us.'

'Didn't you complain?' Mohan said and pitched a pebble at a passing dog. The animal scurried off squealing.

Tarun shrugged his shoulders. He did not tell them

hunger had forced him to the kitchen in the night. To his surprise, he had found two boys from another dormitory, stealing biscuits and slices of bread, and eating by the handful, delirious and hurried, fear in the eyes. Emboldened, he started doing the same. The taste remained illicit for him, something swallowed too quickly giving him a stomach-ache, something in danger of coming back up, something that went immediately to the brain, which was always foggy, stuffed perpetually with fear and loneliness. One day walking through the kitchen he saw three watermelons (his favourite fruit) sitting alone on the counter. He waited until it was pitch dark before sneaking back. The watermelons were still there, undisturbed. He began breaking them open with the side of his hand, gorging on them. Only after he had a stomach full, he noticed the foul taste of decay. He got runs the next day, soiling his clothes and stinking the classroom.

Even when he was older, he never told Pabiji that a portion of his childhood was always hungry and had been searching for fullness ever since. Talking, or listening, had never been easy for him. Voices echoed in his brain, confusing him more. There had been a breakdown somewhere about what he was to his family and what the family was to him. The problem was that he and family were standing side by side facing in the same direction, looking into emptiness.

Whenever he met a person, the face became embedded in the brain cells like the negative of a photograph and so with places he visited. He could recall a building, layout of a street, the shops and what they sold, after the first visit.

But he could not place the face or the building in any context. He forgot names promptly.

Suraj said and swung his fist in the air as if punching someone in the chin, 'I will take my friends from the hockey team and give them a beating they will never forget.'

'Yes, I will come too,' Mohan said and swung an imaginary hockey stick, left and right, like a warrior smashing skulls.

Tarun told them about Laxman. Whenever he shouted at the boy, to keep his hands to himself, the dormitory would come alive with laughter. Laxman too would laugh as if he were playing the fool. But it was no innocent prank, for Laxman's probing hands always went for his private parts. One day an older boy beat up Laxman, warning him not to harass Tarun. Unfortunately for Tarun, the older boy left the school soon after. One afternoon, while the boys were in the ashram tent, Laxman sneaked back to the dormitory, picked up Tarun's belongings, and shoved them in a suitcase. He refused to return the case until Tarun apologised for grassing him to the older boy and to submit to a compromising position. It took exceptional courage for Tarun to scream loud enough for the dormitory head to take notice. This time the boys did not laugh. They cheered when Laxman was slapped and kicked.

Hardip whistled with delight, 'ha, you are back,' he cried when Tarun knocked on the door. But Tarun felt neither delight nor remorse. The months away had seemed like years, felt as if his whole life was upside down. He did not know how to upright it.

He told Hardip about a boy with a baffling rash on his body, and whenever the boy was late in the class the teacher made a face as if he were defecating; another teacher turned purple with rage if the boys did not stand up when spoken to?

Hardip laughed. But Tarun did not want to laugh.

Pabiji eased herself onto a chair that creaked as though it was giving voice to all her own aches. 'Tell me about the ashram,' she said, 'I am curious. Is it true women fall to the ground as soon as Baba makes an appearance?'

'Up to two hundred people visit the place every day, mostly women,' he replied, 'on Saturdays and Sundays, the number is more. Baba lives with his most devoted followers who kiss his feet each morning, wash his toes and sprinkle flowers.'

'Tell me more.'

'First thing in the morning we had to sweep and wash the prayer hall, including the toilets. It was compulsory.'

'What! They used you like *bhangies*, toilet cleaners,' she cried a little too loud, and looked around quickly, guilt suffused with fear on her face. Tarun guessed she did want father to hear this, for it would give him another stick to beat her with.

'Visitors had to wear white. The tents were white, the floor sheets were white too. Baba's bodyguards wore white with a tilak on the forehead. When off duty they smoked, drank alcohol, and made a racket which we could hear,' he said, and noticed Pabiji's face getting tighter as he spoke, as if the mechanism inside her, connected to the skin of the face, was shrinking slowly and surely.

Tarun had begun to abhor this colour, associating it with the white of widows, of mourners, the living dead who wept and touched Baba's leathery feet. The white of gurus and followers. He started shielding his eyes from white. Hating it felt good, gave direction and relief. Even at age twenty-eight, this kind of contempt came to the fore the moment he felt uncomfortable. He would disown before it disowned him.

'We will never send you to a place like that again,' she said, drawing him closer, 'father has decided to educate you at home. We will hire good teachers for you, and Krishan, Savitri and Balraj are going to help you with English and maths.'

The relief he felt on hearing this was like hollowing out of his insides, such lightness. For the first time after arriving home, he cried. The tears that welled out were simple tears, uncomplicated, pure in origin. With a sweaty palm he wiped the snot and drool.

One day Mita asked him why he was dancing without clothes in front of ladies who had come to celebrate *Janmashtami*. Was it a dare or a bet with a friend?

'I wasn't dancing,' Tarun said, narrowing his already thin chest in indignation, 'in any case I don't want to talk about it.' He was finding small talk laborious, and the way people were looking at him with pity irritated him, as if he had a limb or something missing.

'Go on, you can tell me. I will keep it a secret. Was it a bet with your friend – what is his name – Laxman is it?' she said and handed him a generous sized slab of *ampapar*,

'I was saving this for you only. We are friends are we not?'

He knew she was manipulating him by offering the *ampapar* and sweet talk, but he told her what she wanted to hear.

'After the beating by the head prefect Laxman became obsessed with taking revenge,' he said, and then haltingly told her how Laxman had started stealing his belongings. Every other day something went missing, book, a notepad, or a pencil. Sometimes they reappeared, mangled, and stamped on by dirty shoes. But there was no way of pinning it on Laxman. Going to bathrooms, which were open topped cubicles with little privacy, became a terrifying experience. Boys had to fill buckets from communal taps to take to the bathroom. Sometimes when he slipped out to the latrine for a minute or two, he would return to find the soap missing or the bucket tipped over. His dry clothes would mysteriously slip off the hook. Tarun was sick with worry and was beginning to lose appetite.

'One day I was in the bath, pouring water over me when I felt something slippery fall on my head. It was a snake,' Tarun said gravely and stretched his arms out to indicate the length, 'what could I do? I ran from there. I did not know where I was going. I just wanted to be as far away as possible from the snake.'

'And then…?'

'As I said I was running from the snake and somehow it felt as if it was following me. Baba's bodyguards caught me near the main tent. They took me to the principal. Principal took me to Baba who was combing his beard at the time. Give him a good beating, he said to the bodyguards.

That will not be wise sir, the principal said to Baba. Then Baba stopped combing the beard, tilted his bottom and farted. It was so loud the bodyguards became alarmed,' Tarun said, at first with a straight face, then burst out giggling, 'no I made that up.'

'Tell me the truth,' Mita said.

'Baba ordered them to expel me from the school. Throw him out, he said. That was it.'

'Didn't you protest that it was not your fault?'

'I tried but they wouldn't listen. Baba said I was a vandal, an evil person.'

'Did anyone ever beat you?' Suraj asked, looking up from a book on radio technology, his subject at college.

Tarun rolled his eyes as if it was a dumb question. He pulled up his trouser leg and showed Suraj a healed scar just below the knee. 'I was playing *gulli danda* with the boys. One of the boys was so desperate to win he started cheating. When I asked him to stop it, he said I had insulted him, called him a liar, and he wanted to fight.'

'Did you. Did you,' Suraj said, springing up off the chair with excitement.

'I refused to fight. I told him I am not playing anymore. That made him even more angry. He came after me and pushed me to the floor.'

Tarun had told his family everything they wanted to hear. He did not think they would be interested in small matters like his personal hygiene. He used to wear the same underpants for days at a time, for he was afraid to send them for a wash in case they never returned. He had already lost all but two and was too embarrassed to ask the authorities for replacements, and too embarrassed too to admit he had stolen one or two from the clothesline. Then there was the toilet at the rear of the dormitory, a dreary dark place with hole in the ground on which one had to squat with a certain amount of precision. Rats were all over the place. One could hear them scuttling and squealing, as if with glee, as the turd fell in the dark hollow with the echoing sound of *plop, plop, plop*. He had managed to keep the phobia of rodents a secret by not going to the toilet. He had become adept at keeping the food tightly squeezed in the stomach for two or three days at a time. When he could not hold it any longer, he would rush to the hole, defecate half standing, and come out running with the pants still down by the knees. He was too shy to admit his weakness and endured the pain hidden from view of others, getting weak and sickly as days went by.

So, there was nothing more to say, nothing of importance, except one. He was too guilt ridden, ashamed, to tell anyone what he did to young Samanth. One afternoon he heard laughter and catcalling in the playfield. That meant someone was suffering. He felt sorry for whoever was at the receiving end. Near the boundary fence a small crowd had gathered in a tight circle. Little Samanth, who had been at the school only a month, was looking up into a mango tree. They had ripped the shirt off his back and thrown it high into the branches and were urging him to get it. Whether Samanth knew the authorities had forbidden the students to go near the mango tree, which was just beginning to bear fruit, was not clear. He had started climbing. His tormentors cheered. When he was a foot away the boys pulled the shirt a little further out with a long pole, teasing him to go further. This went on for a good fifteen minutes.

'Oi,' Tarun shouted.

Everyone looked over at him. This was his first stand against the school bullies, against the ruthlessness of the human pack animal. He was determined not to disappoint himself. But then three things happened in quick succession.

The first was that he noticed the person with the pole was none other than Laxman.

Second, the shirt had slipped off the tree and had fallen by his feet.

The third, the boys had interpreted his shouting of 'Oi!' as heroic 'Oi, well done' not as 'Oi, stop it.'

Laxman shouted, 'pick it up Tarun, throw it over the fence.'

Not daring to disobey the bully he picked up the blue shirt and threw it towards the fence. Even while doing it, he felt self-hatred. Why are you doing it Tarun, why, why, why? The shirt lodged itself on the top level of the barbed wire fence. It was a six-foot-high military style fence with layers of sharp pins.

Samanth jumped for the shirt, which was within reach, but missed his footing. His arm scraped the fence, drawing blood instantly. He tried to pull away and made things worse by falling further in. He was still putting on a brave smile, as if it were nothing. He tried to extricate himself, but only managed to entangle further into the coil. Like a snared animal he started pulling, tugging wildly, and screaming. Tarun felt something in him sinking, but there was nothing he could do. He was certain the headmaster would send for him. He would have to take the blame entirely upon himself, for he did not have the courage to implicate Laxman.

The boy was hospitalised. For reasons he still does not know, the authorities never questioned him about the incident. What he did that day, the sheer cowardice and butchery had seared in his brain permanently. His heart ached with shame and guilt. Only time had dulled it.

Mother left Tarun with a melodramatic sigh that trailed after her like a smell. Tarun did not know how long he stood in the sun trying to see past the veil covering his future.

In the absence of a closure Tarun's appetite remained subdued. Pabiji spent a great deal of time trying to convince him to eat. When he said he was not hungry she threatened to call someone to take him away. A policeman, sepoy, a ghost, bogeyman. The ultimate threat was the 'big man.' She would open her eyes wide as if this 'big man' were the fiercest of all.

Tarun felt awkward about her warnings. He was old enough to understand she was unlikely to hand him over to a bogeyman when she had taken so much trouble rescuing him from one in white garb. More than that, he was curious what kind of punishment he should expect, the specifics of it, will it be beating or mental torture. He sensed she did not know he had already visited the place she was alluding to in her barren threats.

14

Malviya Nagar 1954

The heat of sun's rays on the skin can feel as if there is a lit fire near you. Half of Tarun's face was in the sun when he woke up feeling the burn and the sound of a fruit seller's cart squeaking painfully loud as if it was inside the house. The hawker hollering, 'mangoes, mangoes, mangoes.' Tarun sat up and held his head in both hands. In no time, Salim's words about Abida Bai's girls came prowling, loud as the fruit seller's call. 'Abida Bai opens her house to visitors at twelve in the afternoon. The girls start arriving half an hour before.' A perfect set up, he thought, I could wait for her outside. Talk to her before she goes in. Where is the harm in that?

'You don't look well,' Dev said, peering into his face, 'not taking the medicine, are we?'

'You shut up, I am all right,' Tarun replied and turned away, as if Dev was somehow able to read his thoughts.

After a quick wash he took a stale roti from the steel container, scooped two spoonfuls of leftover *aloo gobi*, rolled it into a wrap and walked out the door. Past Budhia Singh's flour mill, he walked to the bus stop in long sturdy strides and ate the roti-wrap in three enormous bites, as if it were a mere snack.

On the bus a man asked him for time. Tarun raised his wrist casually to show him the watch, a brand-new HMT with black leather strap.

'How fast the time goes,' the man observed with a yawn as if he had just woken up, 'half an hour ago it was nine o'clock, now it is nine thirty.'

Someone sitting behind them laughed. '*Arre bhai*, if the time was going fast, it will not be nine thirty now, it will probably be nine forty or nine forty-five, even ten o'clock, depending on what speed the time is running.'

'I was just saying – I didn't mean in the literal sense that time is running fast. How can it?' the man replied.

A wiry old man with long grey hair butted in. 'No, no, time can run fast or slow. I have experienced it myself.'

'O grandfather, then could you do me a favour. Slow the time for me; I am late for my appointment,' a young man said. He looked at his watch, contemplated for a moment. 'About twenty minutes will do fine.'

The boy's friends tittered.

'This is no laughing matter,' the old man said, 'I have spent a long time exploring the mountains. Once I met a sanyasi in a cave high up on Nanga Parbat. He said he had meditated for twenty years straight and had developed supernatural powers. I can make time stop completely or make it run faster at will, he said. At first, I did not believe him of course, like you all. So, I asked him to prove it. He said, ok, look at your watch and tell me the time. Three thirty exact, I said. Then he asked me to shut my eyes while he meditated. We sat like that for a while in complete silence. Open your eyes he said finally. I opened my eyes. Now look at your watch.' Here the old man paused for suspense. 'You will not believe it, but it is *bilkul* the truth. My watch still said three thirty.'

Silence in the bus.

It broke with a solo laughter. 'No *jadoo, phadoo* here. I know how your sanyasi pulled the trick,' someone said.

'Oh, then tell us.'

'He asked you to close your eyes and you as an obedient *chela* did as he asked, both eyes tightly shut. And who can blame you. The sanyasi took out a powerful magnet from under his buttocks and placed it quietly against your watch. So, what happens? The hands of the watch become stationery. He keeps still, meditates to create an effect, hides the magnet, and then asks you to open your eyes. *Phatak* magic done.'

The bus erupted into laughter. The man who had asked the time nudged Tarun. 'Does your watch run on time?'

'My watch runs on time, always. Made by Hindustan Machine Tools, latest model. A gift from my boss,' Tarun said.

'*Arre, wah,* they are making watches in India too.' The big man's eyes lit up. 'Absolutely marvellous,' he said in English with a colloquial Punjabi accent which only an Indian would understand.

Tarun felt a kick in the stomach as Abida Bai's green door came into view. Ordinary exterior, regular door, but inside he knew it was vastly different. The street was strangely quiet. As if by magic of a sanyasi's magnet, time had stood still there, like it was seven in the morning. He consulted the HMT. It said two minutes past eleven o'clock. He positioned himself at a vantage point under a peepal tree with low overhanging branches. It offered an unobstructed view of the house and of people turning into the lane.

He was feeling acutely self-conscious, fearing he might come across as someone with criminal intent. He waited, and in time drifted into his usual obsessive thoughts: wishing she would fall into a danger so he might rescue her like a hero, a longing to take a personal memento from her as a holy relic, and then he was indulging in sexual fantasies of extreme kind and plotting a systematic exploration of her body. A fly buzzed in his ear. He was about to take a swipe when the door opened. A tall man in white shirt, an embroidered waist jacket and black trousers came out. He started crossing the road with an assertive swagger. Why is he coming this way? Tarun looked around him. There was no one else nearby.

'You have been standing here for twenty minutes. What business do you have here?' His manner was courteous, and the Urdu had a pleasant Benares lilt to it. The scar above the left eyebrow danced as he spoke.

'I am waiting for a friend.'

'Who is your friend?'

Tarun did not reply.

'If you must wait, then do it someplace else. Over there.' He gestured vaguely into the distance.

'I will go when I am ready,' Tarun said.

The man stepped closer. 'You will go now,' he said in Tarun's face.

Tarun folded his arms across the chest.

'You will go now,' the man repeated.

This time Tarun detected a hint of threat in the voice. The green door opened again. Out stepped another man. This one was in a black fez on the head, curls of tassel covering his ear. He had a soft feminine skin and smiley face, but when Tarun looked into his eyes, they were round and cold as steel.

Tarun offered a compromise. 'I will go and stand there,' he said, and without waiting for a response, walked to the turning and assumed position.

They gesticulated, asking him to go further.

He retreated ten more yards. Still, they wanted him further back, out of their sight.

Tarun decided to stand his ground this time. 'I will go when I am ready. This street doesn't belong to you,' he yelled.

Taking it as a challenge the men came over and stood facing him.

Tarun started backing away, hastily, tripping as he did.

'Yes, yes, keep going. That's a good boy.'

The smiley face lifted the fez off his skull. 'You can have this as a gift,' he said and placed it on Tarun's head, adjusting it for a snug fit.

Tarun swiped it off his scalp as if it were a filthy rag. Dirty sons of swine. He started walking away, picking up speed as he went.

'Faster... one, two... one, two.'

Tarun heard them laughing, like street dogs who had driven an alien out of their neighbourhood.

At the bus stop, he stood in line, humiliation oozing from his stooping shoulders.

The bus was late. He coughed, and the coughing turned persistent, the chest wheezing. An old memory from school days came gushing back. He was walking to school when a dog had started barking, an Alsatian, the biggest he had seen. He stopped and barked back at the dog, playfully, safe in the knowledge the animal, incarcerated behind the gate of a rich merchant's house, could not harm him. Maddened by Tarun's taunts, the dog's barks had turned ferocious, and it had somehow managed to nudge the gate open by its snout. Tarun ran as fast as he could, but his short skinny legs were no match for the animal's powerful hind. Screaming, convinced death was near, he tripped and went tumbling down an embankment on the edge of a brook. It felt as if he was in a free fall down a mountain. Passers-by had shooed the dog away by then, and when he stood up the coughing started.

❁

'You look so strange here,' Pammi said. She held up an old sepia photograph of Tarun for everyone to see. The boy is sitting on a bench, staring intensely into the lens, statue like with a puffed-up chest.

It was Sunday morning. Still in his pyjamas, Tarun had spread out his collection of photographic paraphernalia on the floor, including the latest acquisition, a Kodak Brownie

127 camera, picked up from a street vendor.

There were photographs of father, and grandfather, of Pabiji sitting on a charpoy with baby Pammi in arms, standing erect were Dev and Pali in ill-fitting short pants. There were black and white photographs, faded with pinked edges, pulled from an album.

'I look hideous here,' Dev cried. He wanted to tear up the photograph.

Pali and Savitri were leafing through another album in which Tarun had attempted clumsily to mount the smaller photos begged from brothers Krishan and Mohan, both keen photographers themselves.

Mita yelled, 'oh my God, look at this one, looks like I have just woken up.' She too wanted the photograph banished from the album.

'Be careful, don't spill tea on my collection,' Tarun yelled at Pali.

'I am not spilling anything, am I. See the cup is empty,' Pali protested and picked up a brown envelope. 'What's in here?'

He spilled the contents on the floor and gasped with delight at photographs of his mother and father's wedding. Father is a young groom mounted on a bedecked horse, dressed in a safa wrapped around his head and stiff collars edged in gold thread. There are men in a circle around the musicians, cheering and dancing, to the beat of the dholak. There are women dancing, managing their saris, and waving one arm in the air.

Savitri picked one of Tarun's photos to examine it up close. 'Poor boy,' she said absently, as she drifted into the past, recalling her brother as a toddler, 'he was so lovable and sweet. He used to shake his head so violently or make a face when he didn't want to eat.'

Unlike children of his age Tarun's guttural clamour was a mystery, she recalled. To interpret it as mama, baba was fanciful. At first, they ignored this limitation. One day when Krishan hit him on the head, frustrated at his refusal to play with him, father explained to Krishan that there are children who develop at a slower pace, and it can be both physical and to do with the brain. Krishan did not understand any of it. 'Then why don't you send him away?' he said. That shook father into silence. Things had changed swiftly after that. Pabiji sought Savitri's help in taking care of Tarun.

'But *ayah* is capable of looking after Tarun,' Savitri protested.

'You know we can't leave him to servants. He needs proper attention – proper,' Pabiji said vociferously and then repeated, 'proper attention.'

Although she or father did not say anything specific, but from their sometimes grave, unspoken exchange of glances, it seemed to Savitri things were not as they should be. Pabiji and father looked upon Tarun with identical expressions, nervous, questioning, and sometimes doubtful.

So, Savitri had to tend to her small brother's needs, from feeding to bathing. Milk was Tarun's pet hate. Even with added *shakar* or disguised as runny porridge one could not fool him. Pabiji watched over him like a dragon, determined that a fixed quantity went down his throat, whether he wanted it or not. Then, when father returned from office, he would demand to know the exact quantity Tarun had consumed, if not enough then why not?

The exercise of feeding Tarun and father's interrogation regarding its success or failure always left Pabiji spent and in a raging mood. While father would say, 'and have you seen Lalla's son? He is already playing hockey.'

A neighbour suggested feeding him boiled egg and cod liver oil twice a day. Pabiji baulked at the idea, 'I am not allowing no meat or eggs in the house. That is final.' But she relented at cod liver oil if she did not have to administer it herself. Savitri took the task. But Tarun thrashed his matchstick legs and arms, refusing the foul-smelling liquid. He snapped his mouth shut on Savitri's finger. She pulled her hand away as blood oozed from a cut.

Years later when her wedding preparations were in full swing Savitri reminded Tarun playfully, 'you remember biting my finger? Do you?'

'Yes, it tasted good,' he had said giggling cheekily. Aged nine then, he had already run through illnesses like measles, mumps, bronchitis, nosebleed and more, keeping the family doctor and *Jariwala* baba with herbal medicines terribly busy.

In time Tarun had grown into a thin, gangly young boy, still learning the way around his new body. A dusting of dark powder seemed to coat his upper lip and his eyebrows scampered about before meeting in the middle. Savitri could never forget his odd body movements, as though the limbs' hinges were of incorrect size, the torso closing in on itself. Father had to give him an occasional knock to straighten him up.

15

Trains, buses, cars, trucks, motorcycle rickshaws, horse drawn carriages, all offloading passengers at the station. The riverbank was a good half a mile away. Tarun stood at a high point, looking down. All he could see was a river of bobbing heads heading in the same direction. Tarun and Mita allowed themselves to go with the flow, bumping into people carrying rolls of bedding and other possessions, including pots and pans, pails and buckets, sticks, flags, pennants. There were families who had brought along servants and maids. An entire population on the move guided by blaring loudspeakers and yelling police officers. Heat rising from parched soil like wisps of steam. Air reeking of old leather and incense. The sun beat down at an angle. No shelter. Not even the shade of a tree. They had covered a quarter of a mile, and already they could smell the river, warm moist air wafting in their faces. 'Ganga mata ki,' someone yelled a slogan. The crowd responded with, 'jai, jai, jai.'

Not a tall woman, but Mita assumed space as she

walked, bumping, elbowing, and blocking the path with her wide stance.

'Why is he called Handiwalla baba?' Tarun asked.

'Because he carries all his possessions in an earthenware jar.'

'How is that possible? A shirt or two and a dhoti will fill up a standard sized *handi*.'

'Yes, that's all he possesses. He wears one shirt and washes the other. He has devotees who take turns in cooking for him. He eats only one meal a day.'

'What does he do all day long?' Tarun said, 'I suppose he keeps busy killing flies. Haridwar is full of them.'

'Don't make fun Tarun. He is a very learned man. You should see his face; light radiates from it day and night.'

'Ah, then we will not need a light bulb.'

Mita ignored his joke. 'This is what I was saying Tarun. Follow him, renounce everything. See how content you will feel. Then you will not want to get married. Avoid the headaches that go with it.'

Tarun's thoughts travelled back to the ashram school, the torture and humiliation he had endured there under the tutelage of the hideous baba in all white. What a nightmare that was. Even years later he was struggling to exorcize those bad memories. He had lost so much weight then. When he started eating again, he was gobbling everything to compensate for the missed lunches and dinners. As if there was someone else living in his body, taking up temporary residence and trying to push him aside. He had begun to suspect there was something wrong with him. He was opening from the inside and strange pimples were sprouting on his face like overnight mushrooms. Father said there was nothing to worry about, they will go away. The confusion he felt was nothing compared to the changes he was witnessing in the outside world. He noticed men were beginning to treat him as an adult and women of the family looked at him as a young innocent boy one moment and a lecherous grown man the next. It did not help when mother started giving him Krishan and Balraj's shirts and trousers to wear. 'Look how smart you look in this shirt,' she would say, standing back and admiring. Tarun was convinced she was lying. He wanted to rip the shirt to pieces.

Now Mita was asking him to become a slave to another baba.

'How do you know I will be happy and content if I give myself up to your Handiwalal baba?'

'He will teach you how to be at peace with yourself.'

'Are you saying happiness and peace will only come if I am a bachelor?'

Mita narrowed her eyes into slits.

'Have any of our sisters and brothers complained that marriage has given them misery?'

This time Mita opened her eyes wide, shocked, and scandalised as if he had doubted her integrity. She elbowed a man who was walking too close and eyed him fiercely. The man backed away, startled by that look. And then she turned to Tarun as before, 'if you hear baba's story, you will understand what I am saying.'

'What – that he was married – they quarrelled like cats and dogs – he ran away with a *handi* and became a sadhu.'

'Don't be so disgusting.'

Another half an hour of trudging like a farm donkey Tarun threatened to drop the bag in the dust. 'Where is your Handiwala baba?' he demanded.

'We will find him soon. Shall I carry the bag?' Mita said but not meaning it, as she walked on ahead with sturdy steps, her slippers filling with sand and dust.

'At last,' cried Mita on seeing familiar faces and stopped fanning herself with the little reed fan.

A hand-painted sign attached to poles said simply Handiwala Baba, like public information signs ENTRANCE or EXIT. Or was it deliberate? To induce curiosity, encourage people to walk in and explore, Tarun wondered. In the centre of the camp was a large shamiana enclosed with windbreakers, the epicentre of the activity. Scattered around the main shamiana were tents and sun shelters made with sheets stretched over wooden posts.

A young man rushed to meet Mita with hands joined in namaste. 'Mita *bhahan* welcome, welcome.' People were greeting her enthusiastically, astonishing Tarun. What is so likeable about her?

To the left was an open-air kitchen. Cooks stirring vegetables in blackened pots like witch's cauldron. Stoves release greasy steam while flames licked the black bottoms. A drop of sweat from the cook's brow fell into the oil; it spat viciously.

He spotted a man sitting on a raised platform under the shamiana glowing orange by the sunlight. Facing him was a gathering of about twenty men and women, all with heads bowed deferentially. Tarun assumed he was Mita's

Handiwala baba. He had imagined a potbellied oily man with a handi by his side. But this man was thin and bearded, with overgrown rowdy hair as if he had just emerged from a wind tunnel. Tarun took an instant dislike to the man, as if he had declared marriages immoral just to annoy him.

He saw Mita hurrying from one tent to another. She had left without telling him what to do with the bags.

He sat down at the rear of the congregation and took on a persona of a monk locked in prayer. At one point Baba's gaze settled on him. Tarun's heart dropped an inch, believing the holy man was about to ask him to the podium. But nothing happened. A man sitting beside him cleared his throat and said, 'namaste, how are you?'

Tarun nodded, 'I am well.'

'Where have you come from?'

'Malvyanagar, Delhi.'

'I am from Delhi too, Greater Kailash. I am a vet,' he said.

'Ah, you are a doctor for animals,'

'Yes, yes, just that. Do you like animals?'

'I do.'

'Wild animals?'

'Wilder, the better. Tigers are my favourite,' Tarun replied eagerly.

'Very good, very good,' the vet said and settled back facing Baba again.

Later, at lunch Tarun grabbed a platter of food and offered it to the vet. 'Here this one's for you doctor sahib.'

'Oh, it's too much,' the vet said in mock horror.

'Eat, doctor sahib, this is an auspicious occasion, not every day you come to a mela like this. There is halwa to follow.'

The vet laughed. 'Are you trying to fatten me? You want to feed me to the tigers?'

'They won't eat you, doctor sahib, not at all. They know you are a friend, even if you sometimes scare them with your sharp needles.' Tarun was delighted how easily he had befriended this man.

'So, you like tigers,' the vet said nodding, 'good, but did you know we may not have any left in the wild in the not-too-distant future.'

'Why is that?'

'Because of our greed and utter selfishness.'

A man standing nearby raised a dhal stained finger. 'How do you surmise we will have no tigers left sir?' he said.

'We are in the year 1954 now. At the beginning of the century, we had an estimated forty thousand tigers in the wild. Today the population stands at half that, and that is a generous estimate. So, you can see where we are heading.'

'You are saying the tiger population is decreasing, but only two months ago a woman from my village disappeared, picked up by the animal. The poor woman had only stepped out to relieve herself.'

'Yes, that's exactly my point. The human population is increasing, with it our demand for food. So, what do we do? We destroy forests to plant crops. When we destroy forests, we also destroy the natural food source for animals. So, in desperation they come into human populated areas and take whatever they can catch. Normally tigers are shy of us humans. They will only attack if they are desperately hungry.'

'*Hah,* tigers are coming into our villages because they are hungry. But we humans, are we not hungry too *bhai sahib*? Everywhere you look in India there are people begging for food.' To make his point he lifted his shirt exposing a flat stomach and patted it, *slap, slap, slap*, with an open palm. 'What are we to do? You tell me.'

'Yes, it's a dilemma of modern times,' the vet said, 'classic case of conflict of interest. But we are also killing animals just for the pleasure of it. Are we not?'

Another man standing close by joined in. 'What you say is hundred percent true. Did you know many thousand tigers were killed while George V was the king? According to records, which I have seen sir, he personally killed thirty-nine of the best and took the skins back to England to decorate his palaces.'

Detecting the Bengali accent, Tarun asked if he was from Calcutta.

'Yes, Calcutta only,' he said, 'my mother wanted to come to the mela, so I thought why not I come too and cleanse my soul. Not that it needed cleansing.' He winked and laughed. 'How about you? You here for cleansing as well?'

Tarun chuckled. 'No, my sister dragged me here.'

Calcuttan continued in his strong Bengali accent, 'the British invaders, for three hundred years they have been killing, killing, killing.' He narrowed his eyes and gestured with raised arms as if shooting with a rifle. 'Now that the numbers are down, suddenly they are remorseful. Like the cat, after swallowing a mouse it feels sorry for it and tries to save its tail.'

'That is correct,' the vet said, 'but it is also true our rajas and maharajas have been hunting tigers too. In fact, the tradition of *shikar* began long ago by the Mughal emperor Jalaludin Mohammad Akbar. Fortunately, they were not mass killers. It was the hunt that gave them the thrill. In more recent times Hollywood has become interested.'

'Oh, Hollywood,' the young man said, as if he was a connoisseur of English language films, 'I have seen Between Savages and Tiger produced by George Kleine? What remarkable hunting scenes?'

'Do you know how they shoot the scenes?' the vet said, 'they mount big cameras and guns on elephant backs and film real hunts, killing the tigers in the process. They make far too many hunt movies with actual killings. All for the American audiences, for mere titillation. Tiger's Claw was another one by Joseph Hannebery.'

'Yes, I have seen it,' the young man said as if not to be outdone.

'Well, they employed my father as an advisor for that film. All this only stopped when the war started. Thankfully.'

'I am impressed by your knowledge. What is your line of business?' the Bengali from Calcutta asked.

'Have you heard of Jaiprakash Puri?'

'I have heard of Jaiprakash Puri. Is he not that well known wildlife expert at Delhi Zoo?'

'I am that Jaiprakash Puri, one of the two directors at the zoo.'

'*Orre baba*,' the Bengali screamed and grabbed the vet's

hands. 'I am honoured to meet you sir.'

Tarun looked astonished, feeling privileged to have met such an eminent animal doctor. A small crowd gathered around the vet wanting to know more about Indian wildlife, why wasn't the government doing anything to preserve it.

'I too have shot tigers, barasingha, sambar, all from elephant backs,' Jaiprakash Puri said with a straight face, and then chuckled at his own joke, 'with a camera.'

Next day Jaiprakash Puri said to Tarun, 'Come, we are going for a walk.'

'Are we going hunting?' Tarun said.

'Yes, but on foot this time, there are no elephants.'

'And no tigers either.'

They left the encampment as though setting off on a hunting expedition. Soon they were jostling with excited Hindu pilgrims from all over India. Groups of women singing bhajans. Others were getting ready for a dip in the Ganga to shouts of *ganga mata ki jai*. Rough terrain, soft ground trodden over by thousands of eager feet. Wide ramps laid over ditches, handrails constructed from bamboo poles, painted arrows and one-way signs, loudspeakers blaring instructions, police officers with sticks funnelling the crowd, screaming children and lost footwear, hustlers, and potion sellers. Commonplace people hoping to meet God and make a deal for afterlife salvation, for a one way ticket to heaven, but first tell us what is there to see and the facilities on offer.

They arrived at an elevated spot overlooking the route of procession. They could now see a fair distance back. 'Stay close,' Puri said to Tarun.

In the procession trail long haired sadhus in orange garbs were ambling along in their hundreds, a disorganised rag tag army, swinging maces and relishing the attention. Others had solemn expressions as if meditating on the go. One or two were slowing down to fill their chillums with tobacco and marijuana.

Following the sadhus was a line of marching bands, representing various towns and villages. Attired in tunics and epaulettes of gold braid, playing clarinets, drums, trumpets, and janglers. Each band was jamming a different tune. Cacophony, disharmony, and white noise. No one was caring.

Tarun and Jaiprakash went further up the ramp for a closer view. People were still arriving, straight from the station, pressing into the crowd. Every now and then someone would holler a slogan: *har har Mahadev ki*. The crowd would respond with, *jai, jai, jai*.

Another half hour, the sadhus gave way to a troupe of painted elephants decked with flowers, bells, and trinkets. Long haired swamis sitting atop, white chadar slung over the shoulders.

Tarun nudged Puri. 'See your elephants.'

'Hunting elephants are better trained than this lot,' Puri said.

Following the giants of the jungle were sadhus in full nudity, the emancipated limbs smeared in ash and the unwashed hair matted like ropes, garlands of flowers hung around the necks, the flaccid penises swinging merrily, dust of ash on pubic hair, tridents held high in their right hands. Inebriated on marijuana they were marching in disorganised arrogance. Women in the crowd gasped, covered their mouths with saris and looked to their left or right, while others strained for a better view. Some of the older women broke rank and rushed forward. They threw themselves on the ground to collect dust and ash where the nagas had trod. The nagas hissed and threatened the women with their tridents. 'Don't come near.' The crowd jeered, not at the nagas, but the women, for antagonising the holy men.

Another troupe of elephants arrived; this lot was suitably adorned with religious symbols painted on the body. Sandwiched between the elephants were sanyasis sitting cross-legged on palanquins. The devotees carried the palanquins on their shoulders.

Two hours and thirty minutes, the procession seemed never ending. Jaiprakash Puri, exhausted, said to Tarun, 'let us go now.'

But it was impossible to go anywhere. They had managed to reach the front row, hugging the barricades, within touching distance of the imposing elephants.

'We shouldn't have come,' Jaiprakash Puri said, shaking his head, sweat dripping from his face. 'I am not well, get me out of here.'

Worried for his friend, Tarun looked around him. The crowd on the opposite bank appeared less dense. He said to Jayaprakash, 'be ready, we will dash across to the other side as soon as there is a break.'

Tarun stood on an upper rung of the barricade, leaning forward, looking for a suitable opening between the animals.

'Tarun the procession is slowing down,' Puri cried, alarmed.

The elephants had slowed to fits and starts, their massive behinds shambling lazily, like pregnant animals. The music bands ahead were keeping up the cacophony, like valiant soldiers on a battlefield.

People began craning their necks. 'Why has the procession stopped,' someone asked a policeman.

'I am standing here only six feet from you. Did you see me run up to the front to find out why they have stopped?' the policeman said irritably, mopping sweat on the forehead with a dirty handkerchief.

'No.'

'Then how do I know why they are not moving?' the policeman replied and spat on the ground.

A woman fainted. They passed the body from shoulder to shoulder to the rear. People began yelling for water from the police officers. 'Do something. Don't just stand there.'

One of the policemen threw his hands up in exasperation. 'Do you think we are not thirsty too. I have been here since six in the morning.'

An older woman slumped over the barricade. The bands ahead had run out of steam, barring sporadic blows of trumpets. Loudspeakers were still blaring instructions which made no sense. The elephants began shifting their weight from foot to foot.

'We need to get out,' Puri said again, shaking his head in despair. He mopped his face with a handkerchief and attempted to sit down on the ground. 'Oh, oh, don't do that. You will suffocate down there,' the man behind him said, urging him to stay upright. The loudspeaker above their head cackled hideously over an urgent announcement. It said something about an accident, 'do not panic… we will get everyone out of here safely… stay calm.' It had the opposite effect. People began looking around for a way out. And then it started. A stunning chaos as the crowd started dispersing. The sky appeared to darken in the entanglement felt arms and elbows. Puri grabbed Tarun's shirt front, the buttons popping in quick succession. The heat streamed over them in sharp waves of foul air. Sweat glistening over the arms and neck Tarun started guiding Puri away, though he didn't know where he was going. Someone yelled, 'that way' and the crowd surged in that direction. Tarun stumbled on something soft by his feet. His stomach wrenched seeing a woman on her back. She was trying to protect her face with dirt caked hands. A man pulled her upright. They had hardly made any progress when he heard someone screaming in his ear. He turned around to see Puri's terrified face.

'Did you feel that?' Puri yelled again.

'What,' Tarun said, 'I don't feel….'

He had not finished the sentence when they heard a crack, the sound of wood splitting.

Bodies were tumbling forward. Tarun felt a bump on his head, as if struck by a hammer. Suddenly it was dark. Tarun opened his eyes. He was staring at huge teats. It took a while to realise he was staring at the underside of an elephant's body. A woman fell on him. The sari covered his face. He lashed out with both hands. The elephants were snorting, lowing like cows, shifting from foot to foot, as if marching on a spot. A child was screaming behind him. He started crawling. An elephant foot inches from his face. Terrified it could land on his face, he rolled sideways. Overpowering animal odour in the air. The elephant lowered its haunches and released a torrent of urine. He felt the warm splatter on his face. Someone was pulling him by the arm. He looked up. Saw a familiar face. He recognised the man from Calcutta.

'I saw you on the other side. Where is Mr Puri?' he yelled.

Tarun shook his head and pointed at his throat.

'Water? OK but first let us get out of here.' He pulled Tarun up.

Tarun caught a glimpse of a child in the mud. A moment later it's skull split open, like a trampled guava fruit. Tarun howled as if he were a child too. A fence gave way. An avalanche of bodies went tumbling down a bank. Tarun felt a blow to the head. Two men were fighting to stay upright, each pulling the other down.

Hazy. Deathly screams. People calling names, desperation in their voices. Children howling.

Handiwala baba's encampment was silent. No lectures or bhajans. Baba was in his tent refusing to come out. Mita came running. 'Thank God you are safe.' She poured water on his face and arms and scrubbed them with a towel. 'Sit down in the shade,' she said. There were others in the tent, sprawled out like wounded soldiers.

An hour later Jaiprakash Puri arrived limping and angry, supported by two police officers. They lowered him into a chair. 'You can go now,' he said to the officers as soon as the weight was off his legs.

❋

Savitri was sitting on the divan bed in the front room, knitting a yellow sweater. Pali hated the colour. 'I don't like it. I will not wear it.' She had dismissed his gripes as childish. 'You can wear it for Vaisakhi, so appropriate for the occasion.' In a momentary lapse of concentration, she had put in a wrong stitch and was unravelling it to the previous row when she heard footsteps and the door flung open, flooding the room with sunlight and a blast of warm air.

She gasped seeing Tarun and Mita silhouetted against the sun. 'My God you two look a mess.' She dropped the knitting on the floor. 'Why are you back early?'

Neither said a word. Tarun walked straight through the room dragging a sack behind him, face red as beetroot.

Mita dropped heavily on a chair spreading her legs wide, turning her clammy face to the ceiling fan.

'So, what happened?' Savitri asked again.

Mita could barely open her mouth. Too tired, I will tell you later, she gestured.

'Tell me now,' Savitri said.

Mita turned around and peered into Savitri's eyes. 'Why are you so agitated? Has something happened while we were away?' she asked.

❋

'Did you know Mohindra Pal has a grown-up daughter?' Savitri asked Tarun. Her head silhouetted against the hanging light at the rear, giving her a ghostly appearance. The worried face, jumpy eyeballs, excessive clearing of throat, reminded Tarun of Pabiji during the days of the partition.

Savitri had called him to her room. Made him sit down on a chair while she stood over him. He wondered why the theatre, why she had shut the door and made the room darker.

'Yes, I know,' he replied, massaging his bruised shoulder, 'but you knew that already.'

'Last week, I was talking to Mrs Sharma. By chance we discovered she knows the Pal family well. They are both of the same *gotra*.'

Ah, Mrs Sharma, he thought, the snooping cat, claims to know half the population of Delhi.

'What does she want?' he said, 'I am in no mood for games.'

The night under the tent had been his worst ever. He had dreamt naked sadhus in saffron colours were chasing him to the edge of the river. When they caught up with him, they had miraculously transformed into tigers. He thought he could subdue them by patting the mane, until one of the beasts roared in his face.

'Did you know they are trying to get Sangeeta married?' she said.

'No. But what has that to do with me?'

'They have been searching for a boy for quite some time.'

'So, you want to help them find a suitable boy. Is that it?'

'We thought of you.'

Tarun slumped on the chair as wind sucked out of his lungs. 'You thought – of – me.'

'Yes, I discussed it with Pabiji and Mrs. Sharma.'

'It won't work,' he said decisively

'It's too late for that,' she said and took Tarun's hand. Her fingers were damp. They felt like a pond-pulled frog.

'Too late...' His throat dried up. When he spoke again it felt like sandpaper had scraped his gullet. 'What did they say?'

'They were not keen. They didn't think it was a good match.' She wrenched her shoulders as if she were not to blame. 'That woman, Sharma, overstepped the mark. She opened her big mouth too soon. We had sent her just to probe, to gauge the reaction. You know what I mean.'

Tarun shot up from the chair and exploded. 'No, I don't know what you mean. How will I face Mohindra Pal after this? How?'

❁

She had not told Tarun everything, held back bits which had displeased her in more than one way. She had made Pabiji promise not to tell anyone.

After visiting the Pals, Mrs Sharma had barged into the front room where Savitri was sitting with her knitting.

'You have a word from the Pals?' Savitri cried, and then realising she was being over eager, she had invited Mrs Sharma to sit down and offered her warm *suji* halwa with the tea.

'No, no tea, no halwa for me, I have just eaten.' Mrs Sharma had sunk into a chair and mopped her face with the end of the sari. She had looked up at Savitri in horror and slowly mouthed the words, 'how can I tell you this.'

'Say it, say it,' Savitri yelled encouragement.

'You know what Mrs Pal said?'

'What? What?' Savitri cried, sliding forward to the edge of the seat, 'did they say yes?'

Mrs Sharma touched her ears to show what she had heard had scandalised her, 'they said yes all right, but – not Tarun. They want Dev.'

'Dev, Dev,' Savitri screamed with such incredulity, as though she did not know who Dev was.

'They want our Dev for Sangeeta because he is going to England.'

'How did they know he was going to England?' Savitri said and beat her thigh with a hand.

'I may have told them he is applying for jobs in London. But did I know this will happen?' Mrs Sharma said, sinking uncomfortably into the chair.

'Don't they know their daughter might be as old as Dev. We show them Tarun and they want his nephew. What kind of family do they think we are?'

'Shh, shh,' Mrs Sharma begged, 'I will tell them…'

But Savitri would not shut up. 'Such people. Do they think we will marry our boys into that family?'

'No, not all. But I am only the messenger…'

'How dare they? Shameless people,' Savitri screamed in Mrs Sharma's face and then snatched the knitting off the table and started clicking the needles with immense ferocity, as though she had a deadline to meet, and failure was a punishable offence.

◆

Tarun did not want to go to work and face Mohindra Pal. But he knew staying away was not an option. He entered the office trying to appear casual, unaware of the damp patches on his check shirt under the armpits. He picked up the odour of copper flex and detergent, a faint uplifting smell that usually reminded him of the first day at work.

'Boss has gone to meet a client,' the peon informed him at the door. Tarun relaxed his shoulders. A moment of relief.

He went over to the filing cabinet and placed his tiffin box at the usual place, filled a glass with water from the tumbler and walked over to the inner office to fetch the job sheets from the in-tray. To his surprise the metal tray was empty, barring two or three paper clips and dust. He searched the desk and then the cabinet. Did not find anything. When he looked up, Harilal Yadav, the part time office administrator was waving a brown envelope at him, beckoning him over to his ridiculously bulky wooden desk stained with spilled blue ink. A retired Indian Railways employee he appeared more like a debt collector who was perpetually having a dreadful day.

'Boss has left this for you,' he said.

Tarun went and snatched the envelope from Yadav's bloated fingers. A big man with rolls of fat rippling under the belt, Tarun imagined his penis getting mashed between the thighs.

'What's this?' he exclaimed, seeing a wad of rupee notes and a letter in the envelope. He pulled out the sheet of paper and began reading it, and his eyes came to rest on the sentence... *employment terminated forthwith...,* like a mirror falling to the floor, his world shattered.

He had lost the only paid job he has ever had, a job he loved. He looked at Harilal Yadav. The rascal was leaning back on the chair with a smirk. It was no secret the man had been waiting for just such an opportunity, so he could pull in his nephew.

'Do visit to say hello if you are passing this way,' Harilal said, making out he was sorry to see Tarun go.

Tarun gave him a scathing look. 'You typed the letter.'

'I only did what my boss asked me. What could I do? You must have done something to deserve this,' he addressed Tarun's back.

A pigeon flew in through the open window. Seeing the strange surrounding it panicked and soared higher to the ceiling in a bid to escape. Tarun could feel the displacement of air as its wings flapped. Going round and round in a circle it dropped a great white blob on Harilal Yadav's desk. Yadav pushed his chair back and threw a ruler at the bird. '*Saale chutia*, get out,' he yelled. The twelve-inch metal ruler hit the spinning blades of the fan, creating a clanging racket, and panicking the bird even more.

Tarun walked out the door with his unopened tiffin box.

16

A dreamlike winter began. Even awake he was sleeping. Home was like the base planet around which the world must revolve. Each day a series of sequential vistas. It ruled every aspect of his life, the daily trudge to the market to buy fresh groceries. On Thursdays collect rations from banya's shop. Fridays: have the wheat milled for chapati flour. Hang winter quilts on the line, beat dust and leave to air. The *whap* of the rug beater, the hiss of the steam iron, the distant hoot of the factory siren, the call of the knife and scissor sharpener who came round every month carrying a giant grinding wheel on his shoulders. Emergencies like blocked drains, leaking pipes, electrical faults were for Tarun to deal with, but he ignored the cracks on the wall.

He had spoken to people in the trade. 'I will do anything, work free, try me out, just see what I am capable of.' He went to places where they hired trades people on a day rate basis. Joined queues of fifteen, twenty men, all more experienced than him. He had taken the rejections to heart, letting their poison seep in till the urge to look for a job was gasping its last breath.

He took to banging his body against the wall or going down on hands and knees, hitting his forehead to the floor and screaming silently. He fretted if food was not ready when he wanted it. Stormed out of the house at minutest criticism. Doors opened, doors shut, shadows rose and sank. He stayed put, staring at objects fixedly. There she was, Savitri embroidering a tablecloth, fabric stretched on a ring, scissors and reels of thread spread out on the floor. Dev standing over her, teasing, 'mama you have missed a stitch… there.' Why won't they do it somewhere else? Why in my face?

He saw the anguish and disappointment on Pabiji's face, all day, and every day, but felt powerless to alter it.

Rainy season was upon them. Usha arrived with eight-year-old Uday, but not her husband Prakash, who was too busy designing cars at Hind Motors. Dressed up in high colour, ready to party, she said to Tarun, 'I am meeting old friends, why don't you come along. We will go to the cinema later.' Tarun made half-hearted attempts to clear the cobwebs from the brain, extricating himself from the sticky molasses of hopelessness.

One day he saw Uday on the floor thumping through a book. 'Udi,' he called softly, 'show me what you are reading.'

The boy pretended not to hear. He was uncomfortable with this strange uncle who gripes so profusely but said little else.

'Udi, come to uncle,' Tarun said again, tapping his

thighs. Uday eyed his mother from under his unruly thatch of hair.

'Go on, show Tarun uncle your book,' Usha said while ironing a pink sari.

Uday rose from the floor reluctantly and went to the uncle who was sitting on a sagging string bed. Tarun took the book from Uday's little fingers. It was not a comic book as he had expected. 'Ah, good,' he said, turning the pages. It was a book of animals, with titles printed on top: languor monkey, giraffe, deer, crocodile. He stopped at the tigers. '*Hoh*, tigers, do you like tigers?'

The boy hesitated.

'Do you want to see real tigers, big ones in the zoo?'

The boy's eyes lit up. 'Yes, yes.'

'We will go soon,' Tarun said, turning over more pages and for long moments remembering his own childhood, recalling little flat books with bold writing and sketched animals.

'Let us go for a walk, come,' he said and rose to his feet. He stood still for a moment as if breathing life into his legs, reminding them of their purpose, which was to carry the weight of the body. He put out his hand. The boy cautiously inserted a finger into his fist. Walking side by side, through the gate, onto the road, he looked lovingly at Uday, surprised the boy had agreed to come out with him. Usha followed their movement leaning over at the window until they were out of sight.

They walked in silence at first. Feeling awkward, how to entertain an eight-years old. He pointed at a climbing red bougainvillaea outside a house. 'Do you like flowers?' he said and offered to pluck a handful.

The boy did not reply.

Radio was blaring in the house. They progressed slowly down the lane, past familiar edifices, children playing cricket, the crack of ball-on-bat. A puppy yelped at them, secure in the company of the children while above them a flock of black crows balanced on a power line, as if performing a circus act.

It was the time of evening when everybody switched on their radios, set to high volume. Tarun could hear the same programme in uninterrupted instalments

They entered another neighbourhood past the elementary school, freshly painted exterior, shocking orange, and pink. He adored the colours. 'Do you like it here?'

'Yes, it's different. Can we go to the zoo now?'

'We will go, but first get your mother's permission.'

'Oh, she will let me go, she will, she will.'

A man was roasting peanuts by the roadside, spreading an enticing aroma.

'Would you like peanuts?' Tarun asked.

'No.'

'Don't you like them?'

'Mother will scold me. She said I must not be greedy.'

'How will she find out?' Tarun said making eyes and a conspiratorial gesture with a finger on the lips: we will keep it a secret.

They munched the nuts out of paper cones. Clouds appeared suddenly, obliterating the sun. Uday jumped up with delight at the sound of distant thunder and gust of wind. He ran into a flock of crows feeding on the grass, roaring like a tiger, 'haaar – haar.' The birds took off in fright. The boy laughed. Tarun joined in. 'This is a Bengal tiger,' he said with childish enthusiasm and made a loud roar. Soon they were competing and rolling in laughter.

Next day they went to the maidan where a stage stood overlooking tall effigies of demon Ravana. Buntings, light bulbs on cables stretched over trees and lampposts, music blaring from loudspeakers. Tarun said pointing, 'see that podium over there? The actors will arrive soon to perform. It's called Ram Leela. There will be a battle between Lord Rama and Ravana, and then everything will explode. There will be jubilation, fireworks, bonfire, flames in the sky.'

'Fireworks, where?' the boy said, eyes round as ping pong balls, shaking in anticipation.

'It will happen soon, but first Ravana has to be defeated.'

The loudspeakers crackled an announcement. The actors were on the stage, followed by Lord Rama, tall and grandiose in colourful costume, a crown on the head. Tarun stood on tiptoe, craning his neck for an unobstructed view of the high point, the ultimate battle. Lord Rama issued the final blow. Demon slayed. The crowd erupted in jubilation. This was the moment Tarun had been waiting for.

'Look, fire,' Uday screamed, 'let's go there.' The effigies were burning now, flames lighting up the faces in the crowd. They could feel the heat. Fireworks set off in the sky in a series of explosions, sparklets raining down in wide arcs. The crowd roared, and the loudspeakers burst into religious songs.

That was the climax of the brief halcyon passage, as if the moon had appeared from behind the clouds casting a small pale illumination upon his flattened grey world.

⬥

Back from the ration shop Tarun dropped the hessian bag of wheat on the floor to catch a breath. He dabbed a handkerchief on his sweaty eyebrows. The book he had purchased at a second-hand bookshop in Darya Ganj was still in his left hand. Flicking through it earlier he had learned something new: Bengal tiger is the biggest cat living in the wild, no two of its black stripes are identical, differing in shape and length and even hue.

'Tarun uncle.' He heard a child's voice.

Tarun turned around sharply and saw a boy standing on a rock, behind a bush. About thirteen years old. His hands outstretched. On the palms sat a white envelope, as if the boy were proffering a gift. '*Didi* has asked me to give you this.'

Tarun studied the boy, trying to assess if he was from the neighbourhood, if he had seen him before.

'Who is your *didi*?' Tarun asked, expecting one of Savitri's friends in need of an electrician.

'Sangeeta *didi*.'

'Sangeeta,' Tarun mouthed. The only Sangeeta he knew was the boss's daughter.

'Sangeeta Pal from Pahari Gully?' he asked.

The boy nodded.

'Come closer.'

The boy obliged.

Tarun picked the envelope from the boy's palms while

making eyes at him, as if warning him he better not be playing tricks. The boy pulled his hands away as soon as they were free, as if relieved he had completed his task.

Tarun ripped the flap open. Felt a sudden kick in the heart. Is this a trap set by an angry Mohindra Pal. Does he want to humiliate me even more for having the temerity of asking for his daughter's hand in marriage?

Tarun pulled out the piece of paper, cautiously as if working with exposed live wires. He unfolded the paper. The words began jumping out at him like jack-in-a-box, in haphazard fashion.

It was a brief note:

Tarun, you will be surprised to receive this letter I am sending with my brother, Sachiv. I have asked him to hand deliver for obvious reasons. I feel really bad the way Daddy has treated you. It was most unfair. I want to apologise and explain everything personally. Will you meet me tomorrow in Khanna Bookshop at 5 o'clock? I usually go there on Mondays to buy books. I hope you will come.

Sangeeta

He reread the letter wondering what kind of relationship she had with her father. Was it acrimonious? Would he get into more trouble by meeting her? His voice shook as he said to the boy, 'tell your *didi* I will be at the bookshop.'

The boy appeared relieved as he turned and sprinted down the lane at great speed.

❦

Outside the bookshop Tarun lingered, mustering courage to enter. A man squatting on his haunches by the entrance saw him hesitating. 'Go in, go in,' he said gesturing with his hand, 'many books inside, new and just like new.'

Tarun took a deep breath and stepped inside, into a tranquil world, like a temple for books. The shop was deceptively large, stretching deep on the side and back. Mr Khanna and his son were behind a desk working on ledgers.

He surveyed the interior of the shop and spotted a girl scanning a row of books on a tall shelf. He recognised Sangeeta, even though he had met her only once before at her home. Now she was wearing a light blue *salwar kameez*, casual like a college student, but not the type one saw hanging out in coffee shops around the campus, the loud and argumentative types, smoking cigarettes, thumping tables, claiming to know how to solve India's problems. This girl appeared studious, the type that attends lectures, goes home to do homework, and returns next morning fresh faced for more learning. There was so much beauty. Her startling face was concentrating on a book, the long fingers stroking the spine. He strained to see her feet. But they were not visible from the angle he was standing. He concentrated on her head. Her thick black hair tied at the back, casually, with a ribbon, as if she had left home in a hurry.

His head reeled. It was true he was desperate for female company, and wanted a wife and family. Yet, now watching her standing there surrounded by books, he felt an unexpected sensation, one of relief. Thank God she will not be my wife. He would have felt inferior, out of his depth with someone so educated, so sure of herself.

She looked up. 'Oh, you have come,' she said. Her voice was soft but firm. She did not make eye contact with him, choosing instead to address the book.

Tarun couldn't find his voice at first. 'I told your brother I will come,' he said hesitantly.

'Yes, you did.'

They were silent, each waiting for the other to take the lead, and just as he was about to ask why she wanted to see him, she closed the book with a thump and showed him the cover. 'Have you read Untouchables?'

He shook his head. How could he tell her he could hardly read?

'I love Mulk Raj Anand. I have read his other book also, Coolie, one of his earlier works,' she said.

He had assumed the bookshop was merely a convenient meeting point. He hadn't expected her to talk about literature. She replaced the book on the shelf, carefully standing it up. 'It was Coolie that had brought him into prominence, particularly as the British had tried to ban the book.'

Her voice sounded far away from the roar of his thoughts. 'Do you read a lot?' he asked. The words came out before he could stop them, the worry in his voice obvious, but the question mark was absent.

'I do,' she replied, 'I enjoy books which are genuinely heart-warming or hard-hitting political polemic.'

Tarun did not reply. He looked uncomfortably at the exit door.

'Sachiv told me you were so surprised when he gave you the letter,' she said after a short pause.

'Should I not have been? A boy I don't know produces a letter and says it is from my *didi*.'

'Yes, you are right I suppose,' she said, 'have you found a job yet?'

'Not yet, but I am looking.'

'When I heard daddy was going to ask you to leave, I begged him not to do it. But he would not listen. What a stubborn man he is. I asked to see you because I wanted to apologise personally.'

'It's all right, you don't have to apologise.'

'I pleaded with daddy. Even afterwards I asked him to think again. Call him back. But he would not listen.' She shook her shoulder as if she were helpless.

Call me back? Tarun wondered if he indeed received such a request, would he respond aggressively, ask Mohindra Pal to get lost, or accept it, however demeaning it might be.

'I wouldn't have gone back anyway,' Tarun said.

She began toying with a clump of hair on the forehead, twirling it on her forefinger. Her mouth opened and shut. Tarun could see she was struggling with inner thoughts.

'Mother has told me everything,' she said, and her face went red.

'Told you what?'

'That your family were interested in me.'

'Yes, that's true, but my family didn't consult me first,'

Tarun said.

'I want you to know it was not my decision. They didn't consult me either.'

If they had asked you, would you have said yes, or no, he wanted to ask, but did not dare. If the answer were no, how could she say it to his face? It would be embarrassing for her.

'What I think doesn't matter to them,' she continued, 'they never listen to me anyway. I am not important. Anyway, I remember you when you last came to the house.'

Tarun detected a hint of approbation in the voice.

'I wanted you to stay... longer,' she said.

He read it as: I love you. His heart soared for an incredulous, gorgeously cruel moment. There was an awkward silence. It began to swell, and the shop assumed the shape of a balloon. The balloon burst with a raving laughter from two boys from another aisle. It went about the interior of the shop like a book slung with force by a joyous customer. Tarun turned his back on the boys, suspecting they had been eavesdropping and were laughing at him.

'You can speak your mind,' she said, 'I will not go running to him. Why would I?'

He felt the throat drying up. 'I am a bit shy,' he said, 'I wanted to stay a little longer too, but how could I? You were the boss's daughter.'

'Ah, the boss's daughter. It wouldn't have mattered,' she said, 'anyway that's past. I asked to see you today to apologise for my father's behaviour.'

Tarun realised there was discord between father and

daughter, but he did not know the extent of it until she said, 'they do not let me go anywhere. They will not let me do anything I want to. If they find out I have been talking to you, they will beat me.'

'What if someone has seen us together already?' he said.

Her face darkened and she went silent.

'Why is your father angry with me?' he asked. The question jabbed the still air like a thrown punch.

'He is angry with your family. The only way he could take revenge was by picking on you. He just does not think,' she said and then gathered two books off the shelf and walked over to the cashier.

He noticed her left leg was visibly shorter and slightly bow shaped, making her right hip protrude as she walked.

'I have to go now before they send the servants to look for me,' she said to Tarun behind her.

'Madam will you pay for them now or shall I send the bill?' the cashier asked.

'Send it home, and send two notepads, same as before,' she said and then seeing Tarun was waiting for her to finish the transaction, said softly, 'you go. I don't want anyone seeing us leave together.'

'When will you come here again?'

'I don't know… I'll let you know before *Diwali*.'

17

In the backyard Tarun picked up an old Caltex motor oil can, packed with dark mud, in which three chickpea seeds had sprouted. New life, new beginning, fathered by an erstwhile pessimist. He carried it to the tap and soaked the mud with water while regarding the tender shoots paternally. A crow cawed above his head. He returned the tin to the corner where a mature *tulsi* plant already stood in a clay pot.

Mita arrived home later that morning. Gaunt and dishevelled. She insisted on building her own hearth in the backyard, using clay, straw, and bricks picked up from the building site. 'I will be doing my own cooking again,' she announced. She would set off to the temple early in the morning with an air of determined privacy, as if defying others to accompany her.

No one dared ask her what the matter was, except they speculated something must have happened in Rishikesh for her to turn so choleric. One day Meenu Dass from number thirty, whispered in Pammi's ears, 'my police officer brother was at the mela. He knows about Mita.'

'He knows. Tell me, tell me.'

This is what Pammi learned of her wayward godly aunt: Five days after the stampede at the mela, where two hundred people had died in the stampede, Mita was at Handiwala baba's deserted encampment. They found her quarrelling with idlers sheltering in the few tents which still stood upright. She wanted to know where the Baba was, when did he leave and who was with him? She harassed a police officer who had merely stopped for a short rest. He asked her why she wanted to know so much.

'He is my baba,' she said indignantly. He read her words as 'he is my husband.' Convinced she was a widow of an unstable mind; it was his duty to help those who had lost their way, he advised her to go to Benaras without delay. 'Sister there are places in the holy city you can stay for the rest of your life. They are specially designated for women. Why, I too have an elderly relative who lives there.'

In response she grabbed the staff he had placed on the bench. 'Oh, oh, oh, that's a police property. You must not touch it sister.' He demanded she put it down.

Instead of returning the stick she raised it above her head, threatening to hit him. 'How dare you tell me all this rubbish about homes for abandoned widows. Who do you think you are? You are only a boy.'

The policeman, taken aback, begged her to calm down, not to do anything she might regret. But Mita would not calm down. She created such an unearthly row that people stopped to enjoy the spectacle. 'You think I don't have a home. Well, I have news for you, my home is bigger, and better than the *chhaupadi* you live in.'

'I accept sister, you have a big comfortable home. I am only a poor constable. Now can I have the staff back,' the young constable said wheedling, worried the inspector would discipline him for being careless with government supplied weaponry.

Inspector Dass arrived in his jeep. 'What is the problem here?'

'I will tell you what the problem is,' Mita screeched, 'your man here has insulted me; calls me a homeless widow and nonsense about going to Benaras. I would like to make it clear I am neither a widow nor homeless.'

'Very well madam, you have a home,' Dass said, 'you better go back to it. This place is not safe for lone women.'

'Then give me a lift to the station.' She clambered on to the back seat of the police jeep and refused to budge.

Back home she began quarrelling with Tarun again. 'Didn't I tell you, didn't I? Marriage is not for you. Not everybody has to get married. Now look at what they have done. Even that lame, one legged girl has rejected you. What a shame. What an insult. You should drown yourself in a spit of water.'

Tarun was shocked. How could she say such a thing?

'You still haven't learned a lesson, even after this.' Spittle flew from her lips. 'Look at me. How contented I am not married.' She dug a finger into her chest as if assessing the strength of her ribs.

'You don't look happy to me Mita,' he said finally, shaking his head in pity.

'What. You have the temerity of speaking to me in this

fashion, your older sister.' She raised a hand as if to slap him. 'I will give you one across the face.'

'It is my life. I will do what I like,' he said, 'you be content and happy if you want to, I am happy being miserable. So, leave me alone.' He stormed out of the house and walked to the edge of the woods half a mile away to be alone. He stopped at the well, which still existed in this part of the town, and used sparingly by the villagers. He looked down through the rusting grill into the water. A bird was just visible at the water's skin. It was an egret, still alive, but only just, for he could see slight thrashing movements. The bird was too large to pass through the slatted metal grill. He puzzled how it got there. Someone must have raised the grill and released it inside. His heart wept for the hapless creature. It must have flown for hours in the confined space looking for a way out, finally falling in the water exhausted. He looked around for the bucket on a rope normally used to fetch water. But nothing was available that day. He turned away, unable to watch the creature in the final throes of life.

❁

Later that night he overheard Savitri telling Mita, 'all those astrologers we consulted about him, what liars they proved to be.'

'Not astrologers but my Baba you should have conferred with, ask for his blessings.'

'And you think your Baba will have blessed him when he considers marriage a sin.'

The thought that haunted him and ate into his heart was that he may spend the rest of his life a single man, and that Mita would forever snigger and point fingers at him.

❋

Padma came in carrying a tray laid with fried pakora and samosas and the air took on an oily aroma. Once again, she had taken to cooking with passion, and everyone knew it was a passing phase, like her on and off love affair with yoga. She had started yoga classes as if her life depended on it. Only to give up after two months when someone said jokingly, 'this *hathi* (elephant) *yoga* suits you to the ground.'

Tarun snatched a samosa from the tray on the way out.

In Khanna bookstore two boys were sitting on the bench, their heads side by side, sneaking a peek in an adult magazine. He had met Sangeeta previously at this very spot with a Mulk Raj Anand book. The only female now was a grey-haired middle-aged lady inspecting the spine of a book with gold embossed lettering. The room was so quiet, you could hear the rustle of pages turning. The gurgle of the watercooler by the counter, sounded like a dyspeptic gut. It reminded him he had forgotten to take the medicine that morning, which he usually swallowed with a glass of water. Mr Khanna was standing beside a smartly dressed man. His voice broke the silence, echoing through the room like the flapping wings of a startled pigeon. 'No money in this business brother, no one buys books these days, they want to read free or ask stupid questions… Now look at that man over there. He thinks this is a library,' he said in a lamenting tone, 'people come here to read everything for free.'

Tarun shuffled quickly to a darker corner under a fused light bulb to wait for Sangeeta. She had said she would be in touch well before Diwali. But there had been nothing from her till after the festival. The remnants of the fireworks were still lying scattered on the grass; burnt out shells of *chakri, annar*, scorched sticks of rockets, unexploded crackers, when young Sachiv had appeared walking through the debris, as before with an envelope in hand. The message read:... *meet me on Tuesday at 4 pm in the bookshop...*

The manner of the writing was unlike the previous one. This was a one-liner, hurriedly written in pencil on a piece of paper torn from a notebook. It conveyed desperation.

Another half an hour, still no sign of the girl. He was getting worried Mr Khanna would ask him to leave for treating his bookshop as a waiting shelter. He left the shop fifteen minutes later to go back home, angry, and disappointed. What a fool I am to have fallen for this stunt. He had hoped Sangeeta would be different, a friend like Salim. The previous meeting, though brief, had carried a great weight. He had sensed she too was lonely. So, what has changed?

Suddenly dark clouds appeared, blocking the sun. He continued walking as if unaware of the cool breeze hitting his face or the thunderclaps in the distance.

The downpour began with a sudden burst, drenching his hair within minutes. He made no attempt to take shelter.

A black dog by a crumbling wall stood up and shook water from its pelt. He was certain this dog was one of a dozen fed by the bearded old man from the dilapidated house. Every afternoon at one o'clock, he would stand on the steps of his small dwelling, give a loud call, and click his tongue, like a farmer calling his sheep. The dogs would come running, poor hungry creatures, and snap the pieces of chapati the old man lovingly tossed at them. He would chuckle with delight at the spectacle, calling each dog by the name he had given them.

The neighbours objected. 'These animals are disease ridden; they should not be encouraged to come here.' The old man was like a goaded tiger. Tarun had heard him thunder out an ancient Urdu poem, the gist of which was: yes, there are diseased animals living in this neighbourhood, but they are of two legs variety, not four.

He passed the house with long flag poles where entangled paper kites were disintegrating in the rain, and then he saw from the corner of his eyes a girl sheltering under the canopy of a tree, arms crossed tight over the chest.

He stopped and wiped the raindrops from his face with his shirtsleeve. 'Sangeeta… you,' he cried.

She placed a finger over her lips: keep the voice low. She made herself even smaller against the tree and looked up at the sky.

'I was waiting for you in the bookshop,' he said.

'I know,' she said, 'I could not leave home on time.'

He thumped his shoes on the grass to rid them of mud.

'I sneaked out like a thief. They think I am in my room.'

'Why did you want to see me?'

'I don't know,' she said.

'You don't know.'

She hesitated and then said demurely as if as an afterthought, 'no... I don't.'

'Me too. I don't know,' he said and smiled.

She smiled back.

'What if your father finds out you are here?' he said.

She shrugged her shoulders.

'Do you want to go to the shop to buy books?'

'It's too late now.'

'Do you read every day?'

'What is there to do but read. I look out for books by little known authors. They tend to be more honest in their writing. Like Shivaji Pandit,' she said, 'I also write. Filmfare published one of my stories in the December edition.'

'That's wonderful,' he said.

'I write my diary too, a kind of autobiography. But no one knows about it. It is a secret.'

'If no one is going to read it, then why write?'

'When I have children, I will let them read,' she said.

He detected a trace of steely resolve in that voice. She knows where she wants to be, he thought, and will get there eventually.

'Have you more brothers and sisters?'

'You have met Sachiv already. I have a younger sister. It's all in the diary.'

Above their head birds had started rustling the leaves, releasing water droplets. He took her arm and guided her to a more sheltered spot on the other side of the trunk. An aeroplane in the sky reflected in a pool of stagnant water where a centipede slithered.

'Sachiv is not my real brother,' she said.

'Oh... adopted?' he said, turning to her sharply and noticed a little mole on her upper lip, slightly to the right, but the lips were perfectly shaped.

'No, I was adopted,' she said and stopped twirling her hair.

Surprised, Tarun considered her closely. Is she telling the truth?

'I want you to imagine this,' she said and then shut up. Tarun could see the slow resurgence of pain in her eyes.

'What am I to imagine?' he asked.

'This...' She was quiet again.

'Yes, go on.'

'Someone is dangling a small child held upside down by its leg out of the window of a building. The window is three storeys up. You cannot see the face of the person, but the arm is clearly visible. It is a female arm. She is swinging the child back and forth. A small crowd has gathered on the path below. They are pleading with her to stop. Don't do it, don't do it. Someone has fetched a bedsheet. Men rush in and stretch it out like a hammock. They are positioning themselves under the window.

'She is teasing the crowd, sometimes pulling her arm in as if she has changed her mind and then pushing it out again. This goes on for a long time. A woman screams suddenly. The men with the sheet spring into action, scuttling this way and the other. One of them stumbles but they manage to stay upright.

'This is what a twelve-year-old boy saw that day. He knew instinctively the arm belonged to his sister. The vivid scene had seared into the wall of his consciousness. Everything else, before or after, was hazy, as if time had stopped flowing.'

'You... did it?' Tarun asked.

'No, you fool, I was the baby,' she said with raised eyebrows and then sat down on a fallen trunk.

'How do you know all this? You were only little.'

'My uncle, mother's little brother told me everything when I was older.'

'Why did your mother want to hurt you?'

'Not me. She was trying to hurt someone else.'

'But it was you who fell three storeys,' he said, unaware his mouth was agape, until she said, 'close your mouth, I can explain.'

'I suppose this is also in your diary.'

'But of course, everything exactly as it happened. I don't leave anything out,' she said and then swallowed air as if stifling a sob.

Tarun kept quiet. It would not be right to interrupt someone in that state.

She sighed and slapped a hand to the chest. 'I have been out too long. Its already dark. I must go now.'

'But you were going to explain...?'

'I will when we meet again.' She got up off the log and dusted the back of her dress.

He watched her go around the trees, picking her way through the muddy patch and on to the pavement. Her walk slightly lopsided as if she were suffering from an injured foot.

Suddenly saddened he turned away. The naked intimacy of the past hour pulsed through him inflaming the desire to meet again. Yet he knew they could never marry. The knot of hostility between the two families was too tight to unravel. He could smell the fragrance of her hair long after she was gone.

The nightfall had created a dark cavern under the trees. He thought he would spend the rest of the night sitting there.

18

'Namaskar Pabiji.' Salim greeted Tarun's mother as he bent down to touch her feet. Pabiji blessed him, stroking the head, distressing his meticulously styled long black hair.

'*Munde di nokari lag gai hah*, your boy has landed a job,' he said brightly, exposing a set of symmetrical white teeth. A healthy glow on the face, well mannered, restrained – enough to melt any woman's heart. What mother would not want a son such as him. Bloody rascal Tarun was thinking, making me look gross and inadequate.

Forced into unemployment, encounters with Sangeeta, his life was spinning out of control as if he were on a boat adrift in the middle of a storm. He had to talk to someone. He had gone to Salim's place of work and waited for him to come out. '*Oi, bahandi... saale*, what are you doing here?' Salim cursed in his trademark foul language, his way of expressing pleasant surprise.

Sitting on opposite stools in a crowded chai shop, Tarun had gabbled out everything, to the minutest detail, relieved himself of the troublesome load sitting on his chest.

'*Saale*, Punjabi *jat*, you have been sitting at home for six months, troubling your poor mother, why didn't you come to Salim, your friend?' He raised the glass, sucked the hot tea. 'Never mind, you are here now. You leave it to me; I will speak to my boss and have you gainfully employed in no time.'

Two weeks later Tarun received an invitation for an interview with a senior project manager at Dalal & Co, a man of forty who, Tarun learned later, was a nephew of Mr Dalal.

Sameer Dalal was sitting behind a massive table, folders and tools sat at one end, his booted feet, one on top of the other, sat at the other end. He was reading a ledger book with eyebrows knotted in concentration. Tarun sitting opposite wondered if he should clear his throat.

'You are hired,' Sameer Dalal said after a while without raising his head from the ledger.

Tarun stared at Sameer's thatch of hair, wondering if he was talking to him or reading something from the ledger.

'We work hard here and play hard as well,' Sameer Dalal said, this time looking up and pointing at a half empty bottle of Johnny Walker sitting on a flat board over a coil of electric flex. 'If you are going to sit around nursing your bottom you will be out of here in two days.'

'Don't worry sir, I am a diligent worker,' Tarun assured him, rocking his head fervently, 'just like Salim.'

'I will be the judge of that,' Sameer Dalal said harshly, showing him the white of his eyes, 'you can start tomorrow. Be here at eight in the morning. Your first assignment is at the Ritz.'

'Ritz cinema hall sir,' Tarun blubbered, 'in Kashmere Gate.'

'Yes, yes that one. And keep this in mind you are going there to work only, not to sit on your fat bottom and watch Dilip Kumar and Nargis.'

'Oh, no. I don't watch movies sir. Strictly against my principle,' Tarun said. He had sounded so very sincere it made Sameer Dalal look up and study Tarun's face, suspecting he had a short fuse in the brain.

'Look around, familiarise yourself with the place,' Sameer said and yelled at a peon styling his hair with a metal comb, '*oi* you, son of a hero, show Tarun sahib to the warehouse.'

Ecstatic at landing a job, Tarun had hurried home to break the news, running to the bus stop, whistling jauntily but badly, and boarding number nine. A week later he had gone to Salim's house and left a message with his wife, 'please ask him to see me at home on Sunday.' He wanted to thank Salim by taking him out for a slap-up meal. But of course, money was a problem. He did not have any. He was going to borrow it from Salim with a promise to pay back from the first salary cheque.

So, Salim had arrived at Tarun's house with plans to go for a posh dinner.

Salim said to Pabiji, 'I am taking your son with me, but don't worry I will bring him back in one piece.'

From somewhere in the shadows, they heard a badly stifled giggle.

Pabiji laughed. 'Both of you are my sons. I have nothing

to worry about.'

Pammi came over casually pleating her long hair and expressed a poorly faked surprise. 'Oh, I didn't know you had a guest,' she said.

'Guest? No, no, I am no guest. This is my second home,' Salim said.

'Then why haven't I seen you before?' she said.

'But you have. I was here only the other day, remember. I rescued you from that dangerous man-eating lizard,' Salim said.

Pammi laughed. 'Do it again.'

'We have to go now,' Tarun said and pulled Salim away by the arm.

'She must be a terror,' Salim said once they were out of the house.

'Yes, she is.'

'It reminds me of my sister before she got married,' Salim said and after a pause made a face, 'take my advice don't even think about it.'

'About what?'

'Marriage.'

'Why did you get married then?'

'Her family trapped me. I was young and didn't know better. Anyway, you do as I say, not as I do. It is a huge responsibility, catering to her demands and her family's, educating the children, school fees and uniforms, and a hundred other things. Do you think you can manage all that? And... and... you will have to cut out running after girls on the side.'

'*Hah,* but you do it all the time,' Tarun said, reminding

him of Abida Bai.

'*Saale* didn't I tell you, you do as I say, not as I do.' Salim said, admonishing him, 'anyway, where are you taking me tonight?'

'I thought we would go to Kaka di Hatti near Connaught Place, their Kulcha are delicious, so I have heard.'

At Kaka di Hatti they were astonished to find a crowd at the entrance waiting for their turn to go in. 'Follow me,' Salim said confidently and barged into the waiting crowd asking people to move aside.

Someone blocked his path. 'Brother, we have been here for over an hour. Why must you go in before us? Are you a minister's son-in-law or something?'

'Don't you know who I am,' Salim said, putting on an air of a VIP, 'I have come from far.'

'We all have come from far, brother. Very, very far… haven't we?'

A chorus of 'yes, yes, yes, very much far' rang out. The doorman in white livery stood with folded arms. 'Unless you can prove you have a table booked, you must wait sir, like these people.'

'But I have a table booked,' Salim said, raising his voice, 'let me through, I want to speak to the manager.'

'No manager available today sir,' the doorman said firmly, 'he will be back tomorrow.'

'All right,' Salim said, backing down, 'you make sure we get our turn in the right order.'

They sat down on a bench, sharing it with two others. Through the half open door, they could hear the chatter and laughter, and aroma of hot sizzlers filtering out to the street, adding to their woe. 'I am dying of starvation,' Salim muttered.

'O babu,' a beggar shoved his grimy hand at Salim, 'have mercy on a hungry, homeless man.' Sprawled on a dirty mat under the lamppost, a leg missing, he was haranguing passers-bye with his pathetic cry, frequently changing the pitch. 'Sahib, for every coin you give a poor man, God will compensate you with ten.'

Tarun's neighbour on the bench, puffed on a cigarette, leaned forward. 'Oi, where is your other leg?' he demanded, as if the beggar had hidden the limb under his clothes.

The beggar lowered his head and exposed the stump which ended in a ball just below the knee. 'I have lost it,' he said.

'That I can see. How did you lose it?'

'What to tell you. It's a long story,' the beggar said despondently, splaying his arms wide.

'Come on, tell me.'

'If you like,' he said. He shut his eyes, opened them, cleared his throat as if he were psyching himself for a stage performance. 'Landmine sahib, *BADHAAM*,' he said aloud mimicking the sound of an explosion.

'What landmine, what are you talking about?'

'I was in the army *bada sahib*.'

'You were in the army. You trying to make a fool of me. How can a man with one leg join the army? *Hunh*?'

'Sahib, you misunderstand. I was in the army fighting the Japani in Burma. Incredibly good fighter *sahib*. My Captain even gave me a badge of honour. I was in the logistics... driver.' He did a salute with his grimy deformed fingers.

'What did you drive?'

'Everything, jeeps, trucks…'

'Bicycles,' someone pipped at the back, producing a chuckle from the crowd.

'Why are you talking nonsense? Making up stories. You think you will get more money this way,' someone yelled from the rear, a gruffy scornful voice.

The crowd turned to look. A young man was standing by the paan shop, the lips-stained red. He spat at the lamp-post, a thin red stream, and glared at the beggar's head, contemptuously.

The beggar continued, 'once they let me drive a tank, just from here to there. *Oof,* difficult that thing. But my speciality was jeeps.' He did mock steering of a vehicle, dramatising by leaning left and right. 'Up mountain, down mountain, reverse, sharp left and right, top speed, without making my passengers fall out.'

'You hit a landmine with your jeep?'

'No sahib, one day those cunning Japani surrounded us from all sides. What to do. They took us to their camp and made us prisoner *sahib*…'

'You were a prisoner of war?' Salim cried, springing up off the bench.

'Yes, but I was not worried. I knew my captain – Captain Jameson will come for us. So, we waited, waited, all the time spitting at the Japani, at their back. *Thooo.*' He did mock spitting. 'Ten months we waited. Then one day our helicopters came early in the morning, hundreds, firing at the camp, *thak, thak, thak*. The Japani were jumping like frightened monkeys. We fight them with our hands, break the fence. We knew where our trucks would be hiding, in the jungle up north about a mile away. We were running, running, and laughing, Captain Jameson has saved us, God save Captain Jameson, God save the Queen. Then suddenly *badhaam*, a big explosion.'

'Shut up you *natakbaj*. I am warning you or I will have you picked up by the police. We don't want to listen to your nonsense,' the *paan* spitting fellow interrupted, scoffing, and stamping his foot.

'*Arre bhai*, leave the poor man alone. How is he hurting you?' the cigarette man said to the young fellow.

The beggar said quickly, buoyed by the support, 'this boy is here every day, harassing my customers. You only see him today. I see him every day.'

'So where is the captain now?' someone asked.

'That I don't know *sahib*, maybe go back to England.'

'How did you get back from Burma without the leg?'

'Captain brought me here by train after the hospital discharged me. What treatment the army doctors gave me, absolute first class. Six days on the train, in the medical buggy. When we arrived at Delhi Junction, the Captain shook my hand and said, Ramdass you are home now, it is time for me to go home too. But I knew he had no home to go to and no family. He had already told us bombs had fallen on his house. His wife and children were sleeping inside. *Baas* I did not see him again.'

The crowd went silent again. Tarun scrutinised the beggar's face. The wide nostrils, skin like old leather, deep hint of exhaustion, but there was something about his eyes. They appeared alert, and this theatre he had set up was deliberate, of his choosing.

The sound of a slow hand clap at the rear broke the silence. '*Wah, wah, wah,* what stories the monkey spins,' said the *paan* spitting fellow, projecting his voice like a stage actor, 'yes, there is no harm in listening to his yarns for cheap entertainment, a bit of street theatre. But believe me he has never been in the army. There was no Captain Jameson. The only captain he knows is his penis. He hobbles to the brothel every night after he has collected enough money, to make his captain happy.'

The beggar beat a palm to the floor in exasperation and started rolling up the mat to leave.

'See, what I told you, see – he has been caught out and is ashamed to speak,' the *paan* fellow said.

The beggar tugged forcefully at his half shorts and slammed the rolled-up straw mat to the floor. 'You want to hear the truth sahib, then I will tell you.'

'Yes, go on.'

'This man standing behind me, all the time eating *paan*, masticating like lazy cows. This man is my nephew, my older brother's son. The rascal has nothing better to do, so he comes here every night to torment me, laugh at me. And you want to know why…'

'I am warning you…' The *paan* fellow stared viciously at the beggar's head as if he would like to split it open.

'My brother and I were both in the army, in the same unit. When we found out our unit was going to Burma, I was excited but not my brother. He did not want to go. He did not want to leave his wife and young children. He said there is no one to look after them. I told him not to be a fool, there are enough people in the village to care for them. Think of the money you will earn on active service. You could come back after two or three years and start your own catering business, as you have always wanted. So, we went. Everything was working all right. We were safe from Japani because our job was in the camp only. One day after we escaped the Japani prisoner of war camp Captain Jameson called me. Ramdass, I want you to be careful how you drive. We are running short of drivers. I knew that was true. The poor fellows were driving the jeeps over landmines the Japani's were planting like potatoes.'

'Hah, have you ever seen a monkey drive,' the *paan* fellow jeered and hooted like a baboon, '*hooh, hooh, hooh.*'

This time the crowd ignored the *paan* fellow's taunts. 'Did your brother come back to start a restaurant business?' Salim asked.

'Yes, yes, he is most definitely back. His name is Kaka,' someone said pointing at the Kaka di Hatti signboard.

A raucous laughter erupted.

'Is this a laughing matter?' someone yelled.

The laughter died instantly.

The beggar resumed speaking. 'Babu what to tell you… one day there was an attack on our camp. The enemy was raining artillery shells. I was outside the store's compound with a group of machine gunners. A shell exploded on the water tank trapping my brother. When I saw what had happened, I left my gun position and ran to help him. I pulled him out from under the mountain of metal, carried him to the jeep and while bullets were flying everywhere I was taking him to the medical unit. A shell exploded on us.

But it was God's wish babu, what could I have done...' He paused to wipe tears from his eyes with his knuckles. 'Not a day passes when my nephew does not taunt me. He blames me for encouraging his father to go, for not taking care of him there. He says, *chacha* you have come back but why have you left my father behind?" I say to him, you call this coming back son, look at me, only half of me is back. The other half is still there buried in Burma soil along with my soul.'

Silence again.

'Why are you begging? Don't you get an army pension?' the man with the cigarette asked, dislodging the ash with a flick of the fingers.

The beggar looked bewildered. 'Pension? What do I know about all that? We are poor uneducated people.'

'He was in the British army. In 1947 it ceased to exist in India. How can he get a pension?' someone said.

'That is not correct,' a studious looking young man waved a finger in the air, 'after the British left, the Indian army took over the entire administration. He must apply to the right department.'

'Not true. The Indian Army is not responsible for discharged army personnel prior to 1947. He must apply to the British and Commonwealth Foreign Office.'

'He should not be begging. It gives the army a bad name,' someone said.

'Don't pick on the poor fellow. He is doing public service by begging. Can't you see he is helping the public wash away their sins.'

People were taking sides now, shouting over each other.

The beggar, bemused, like a spectator at a badminton match, his gaze switching from one face to another.

A police jeep sped past behind them.

'You look like a filthy rich businessman. Why don't you give him a job?'

'Filthy rich? Brother I am one step away from becoming a beggar myself.'

'Then ask this beggar. He will give you a job.'

'No, no, you must first make a written application… in triplicate,' another man added chuckling.

'Only those with experience may apply.'

Another police jeep arrived and came to a screeching halt at the crossroad.

'What's going on?' Tarun sat up and looked around him.

'Probably drunk fighting,' Salim said.

They heard a scream. A bearded Muslim cleric appeared, running as if for his life. Behind him a yelling mob, armed with sticks and swords was giving chase.

Tarun ran to the centre of the road for a better view. 'They are going to kill him,' he said.

Salim came over to look. People were pouring into the square from all directions. Someone in the mob pointed at a barber's shop, Ali Hairstylist. The mob hurtled towards it, like bees from a prodded hive, zig zagging around obstacles. They pounded the shutters. Alarmed faces peered out of the windows. People began spilling out of the houses, running in all directions.

Tarun stood glued to the pavement, watching the mayhem spreading like spilled milk. Bricks landing on windows, crash of glass falling on pavements. Suddenly, as if on a command, the mob turned towards Kaka di Hatti.

'They are coming this way,' someone cried and there was a rush to the entrance while the diners from inside were hurtling out. 'Stay with me,' Salim yelled, eyeing a narrow lane across the square which appeared deserted. He hesitated. Another mob from the left was heading their way. This one was shouting competing slogans: *allah hu akbar, allah hu akbar.*

The beggar screamed for his nephew 'Ramesh, Ramesh.' The nephew hurriedly picked up the cripple, cradling him like a child and disappeared into an alleyway between two shops.

'Come on let us follow them,' Salim said, then changed his mind again, 'wait, go towards Regal. We can take a taxi from there.'

The Muslim mob armed with sticks and daggers on the left. Hindus, and Sikhs with swords on the other. Tarun spotted the bloodied body of the cleric lying sprawled in the road, like a dead dog abandoned. Behind them a scuffle broke out between the restaurant staff and customers refusing to pay the bill.

A dozen or so policemen formed a defensive line, beating their wooden sticks to the ground. A police van overtook the Muslim mob and stopped in their path. The mob halted. It started falling back. The leader in green bandana yelled a bloodcurdling slogan. The mob responded with more shouts of *allah hoo akbar,* and then they counter charged in a pincer movement. Overwhelmed, the policemen retreated on foot. The mob cheered. They were picking up debris, hurling it at the van. Someone lit a rag and pushed it into the van's petrol inlet. The driver opened the door and rolled out. The petrol tank exploded in his face. The mob laughed and hurled obscenities, '*saala gandu, bahanchoot, Hindu saala haramkhor.*' Another line of police charged from the right, swinging lathis, dragging blood-clod bodies into police trucks.

Salim spotted an opening. 'Quick, run,' he said. They took off. Past rows of houses which appeared deserted, as if the residents had barricaded themselves in and switched off the lights. They arrived at a crossroad and slowed to catch their breath. A group of local vigilantes standing at the shuttered chai shop stopped them. 'Who are you? Why are you running?'

'Rioting,' Tarun said, gasping for air.

'Are you musalman?' one of them asked.

'No Hindu,' Tarun replied.

'Who started the fighting?'

'Don't know. Didn't see anything,' Tarun said. He knew what was on their mind. They just wanted confirmation Muslims started it. Peaceful Hindus never do such a thing. Aah!

'He is lying, look at his face... look. He is guilty,' someone said.

'Guilty of what?' Tarun asked.

'Guilty of what... guilty of what... guilty of being a *musalman.*' The man pushed his chin in Tarun's face.

Tarun caught a whiff of curdled milk and cardamom. 'I am telling you I am Hindu like you, why do I have to prove anything,' he said.

'Then show us you are not circumcised.'

Tarun laughed, what a ridiculous suggestion.

'There is only one way to settle this, pull his trousers down.'

'Down… down… down.' A chorus rang out. Three men dived at Tarun's legs and began tugging at his khaki trousers.

'No, please, no,' Tarun grovelled. He tried to hold on to the trouser, clutching the belt with both hands. The men yanked. The trousers came down. The buttocks were in full view, the shirt tail flailing. Tarun began whimpering. 'Please leave me alone.'

'Let him go you brainless animals,' Salim screamed, 'I will give you such thrashing, you will cry for your babysitters?'

They released Tarun.

'Anyone dares touch him will have to deal with me. I can take you all at once. Make you shit in your pants.'

'What can you do to us?' said a short bespectacled man.

'You want to see?' Salim lunged at him.

'*Arre, arre, arre,* no fight please.' He shuffled backwards.

Salim did not see it coming. A bamboo pole crashed on his head. Someone had sneaked behind him with a scaffolding pole. Salim swung around and snatched the pole in one swoop. He took the end of the pole in both hands and began whacking the little fellow across the legs, making him dance as though he was barefoot on a bed of burning charcoal. Others fell back fearing a similar onslaught.

'Run,' Salim yelled, 'to the taxi rank.' He threw the pole by the wayside.

Tarun fell into a heap seeing the deserted taxi rank, like a hurriedly cleared warehouse. 'Where are the taxis?' he moaned.

'They have all run away,' said the solitary peanut vendor standing on the pavement which normally heaved with street food sellers, their shouts, and suffocating odours.

'Why?'

'They don't want to end up in the *danga*. Makes sense. No? Even buses are not coming this way.'

'What can we do?'

'You might find a scooter rickshaw if you are lucky or you walk,' he said and made a grave face pitying them, 'where do you have to go?'

'Malvyanagar,' Tarun said, 'seventeen miles.'

'Seventeen miles,' the vendor said with an amused smile, 'it's nothing, you could do it in three or four hours if you walk fast.'

Tarun looked around him, at people waiting, anxiously scanning the horizon, intense eyes scrutinising every passing car. Is that a taxi?

Those with sharper hearing heard it first: the phut-phut-phut of a scooter rickshaw. Salim sprang to his feet and ran towards the source of the noise. A beeline of people running, waving frantically. Salim elbowed his way to the front and hopped onto the back seat, spreading himself wide to stake a claim.

The driver, a big man with a blue turban, turned around and wearily flicked his head. 'Where to?' he said in a tired drawl.

'Malvyanager,' Salim replied.

'All right, I will take you there,' he said grudgingly, as if he was doing Salim a favour, 'you pay me only double.'

'Double?' Salim cried.

'You don't understand, it's a coincidence that I live in Malviya Nagar, I am going home too, otherwise on a day like this the rate is to get as much as you can.' He spat on the sidewalk. 'If it doesn't suit you, get out of my scooter.'

'We will pay,' Tarun cut in sharply, 'now take us home quickly.'

With a grudging shake of the head the driver revved the engine and took off raising a cloud of dust.

Tarun sat back on a resin plastic seat, every road bump travelling up his spine as if reminding him of the stupidity of venturing so far out from the comfort of hometown. He was still feeling the hands of the thugs stripping him naked and their disgusting breath, glimpse of the communal animosity inches from his face.

Ten minutes into the journey, the driver said shouting over the grumbling engine, 'life is tough, sahib. We must make money when the opportunity arises. This thing can break down any minute.' He smacked the handlebar of the scooter. 'More expense and the police harass us day and night.'

'Why do the police harass you?'

'What else,' he said, spitting again, 'they want a cut.'

'But you are also cutting our pocket by charging us more than what's on the meter.'

The driver chuckled, adjusted the turban with one hand and swept the night air with the other. 'Life is like a circus babu, what to do. There is no escape from it, whether you like it or not.'

'Are there any eating places open?' Salim asked.

'No *babu*, all shut for the night. You are hungry?'

'Yes.'

'You eat in my house.'

'Very kind, but you just drop us home.'

'*Babu,* you must eat. My wife runs a tandoor kitchen. She supplies to all the neighbours, best tandoor roti and naan in the whole of Malvyanagar. *Wah*, what tasty.'

'All right, we will have one or two nans.'

'My name is Harjeet,' he said in a loud sing-song voice, 'don't judge me by outward appearance. You can't see my heart, but I can assure you it is extremely sweet. Sweet like ladoo.' He laughed – a series of lazy chuckles.

An hour later he was swinging the scooter rickshaw into a very dark narrow lane, past a hill of rotting fruit and vegetables, the night air thick with sulphuric stench. There were animals rooting in the pile. Dogs. But in the dark one could not be certain. Jackals were known to inhabit the nearby forests. As they passed, paper from the heap flew like scattering pigeons. Finally, the driver silenced the engine in front of a tiny house with a spacious front yard. Tarun caught a whiff of cow dung and became aware of two buffalos resting in the dark under a tin roof. Their bulk and grey coat appear sinister against the background of a brick wall. Nearby stood two full size tandoors. But they appeared cold and unused.

'Don't worry, she has tandoor indoors too,' Harjeet said as he ran to fetch two old chairs from the shed. 'Sit, sit please.'

The wife appeared on the steps; a large lady dressed casually in loose fitting salwar kameez. 'You are late again,' she bawled at the husband, ignoring Tarun and Salim.

'O, *bibi*, bring hot nans, quick, quick, the *babus* are very hungry. What *sabzi* have you got?'

'Sabzi,' she sneered, 'saag only.'

'Then bring, what are you gawking at?' he waved her inside. Turning to his guests, 'food will be here in minutes, relax,' he said and then gestured with his forefinger and thumb as if estimating the size of an egg. 'A small whiskey?'

'No whiskey, we have to be home soon.'

He made a face as if disappointed for not having drinking partners and settled down on a chair, pulling his trouser legs to the knees. 'I want to ask you what you were doing out so late in Delhi. Don't you know how unsafe it is these days?'

'We had gone for dinner at Kaka di Hatti,' Salim explained, 'and then the rioting started. No taxis, no buses, until you showed up.'

'Delhi is a dangerous place even during the day. But at night – *hai* – there are dacoits everywhere looking for innocent people like you. We see it all the time,' he said, and opened his eyes wide, as though it was something grave and sinister, 'and there are other things. Even the police are afraid.'

'What things?' Salim said with a dismissive wave of the hand.

Harjeet looked over his shoulder into darkness beyond the shed, in the depth of a black barrage. Tarun followed his line of vision, seeing nothing but still feeling a dash of fear.

'Where do you live babu?' Harjeet asked.

'Near the post office, only a quarter of a mile away.'

'Exactly, only a quarter mile,' he said, 'but will you dare walk home at this time of the night?'

'What rubbish are you on about,' Salim said.

'Once you hear what I have seen on these very roads, you will be afraid to walk even to the end of the lane outside.'

Salim laughed. 'Nonsense. But you can tell us what you have seen.'

'Then I will.' He gestured at them to come closer. A bird beat its wings somewhere in a tree and then there was silence again. Harjeet cleared his throat, looked over his shoulder. 'Six months earlier my cousin Jinder came to my house. He wanted to see a film and was looking for someone to accompany him. I said all right I will come with you. So, we went to a late-night show. The film finished about ten o'clock at night, and by the time we came out of the theatre hall and walked to the bus stop we discovered the last bus had come and gone already. There were no rickshaws or tongas, not even taxis anywhere. We had no choice but to walk home. It was a dark moonless night. Deserted streets. Shops shut. But it did not bother us, we were enjoying the walk, Jinder fooling around, acting like the hero in the film. We had walked about a mile when we saw a *paanwala* shop with lights on. It was open. My cousin was delighted. He is mad about *paans babu*. Whenever he sees a *paan* shop, he must stop and buy one, always a sweet *paan*. We saw a man sitting behind the counter, rolling a leaf. Jinder stopped suddenly. That man's face is familiar, he said, I am sure I saw him in the cinema. He was sitting in the row ahead of us, and he was turning around, looking at us. Jinder, you are mad, I said, how can this man be in the cinema with us when he is clearly sitting here running a shop. Jinder was convinced, hundred percent. Anyway, we went and ordered a paan each. The man took his time picking this and folding that and finally when he had finished, he offered us the *paan*. Jinder was about to take it when he screamed and jumped backward. Then I saw it too and we ran from there, dropping everything.'

'What did you see?'

'This.' Harjeet made tight fists of his hands and put them out, showing Salim and Tarun the rough knuckles. 'Horse hoofs... the *paanwala* did not have hands like ours. He had horse hoofs.'

Tarun peered into Harjeet's face, expecting him to break out laughing. But he appeared deadly serious, not even a hint of mirth.

Harjeet continued. 'Home was still about a mile and a half. The streets were quiet as a cemetery at midnight. Suddenly we saw a man. He was walking ahead of us. Come on let us join up with him, Jinder said. So, we speeded up and caught up with the man. You do not mind if we walk together, I asked. No harm in that, he replied, company is good, but you two appear as if you have seen a ghost or something. I told him we certainly have seen something; what it is we don't know. Oh yes, tell me about it, he said. I told him about the cinema show and the man in the *paan* shop. He listened patiently, and when I told him the *paanwala* did not have hands but horse hoofs, he did not appear surprised. Casually, he pulled his hands out of the trouser pockets. Like these? he said.'

'What? What?'

'Horse hoofs, *babu*. This man also had horse hoofs, just like the *paanwallas*.'

'What did you do?' Salim asked, clearing the blocked throat.

'What else. We started running again until we were well clear of the man. By now Jinder just wanted to get home as quickly as possible. But home was still a mile away. Ten minutes later we heard something. It was a clip clop clip of a trotting horse. We started running again. But babu, what to tell you, this clip clop clip clop would not go away, like it was following us. It was getting louder. I was running as fast as I could. Then we saw it. It was a *tonga*. The tongawallah sitting on his seat happily singing to himself. I cannot tell you how relieved we were *babu*. I flagged him down and asked if he would take us to Malvyanagar. Jump in, he said, it is only a short detour. We climbed in on the seat behind the driver and asked him to hurry up. Do not worry, he said, I will get you home in ten minutes. He started singing again while whipping the poor beast. When we were well on the way he asked us why we were out so late at night. Don't you know how dangerous it is around here, he said. I told him, brother, we know all about that as we have already experienced it first-hand. He appeared amused, so what have you seen? Jinder found his voice. He told the tongawallah about the man in the *paan* shop and the other one we met later, both with horse hooves instead of regular hands. You believe me, don't you, Jinder said. Oh yes, I believe, I believe, he replied, and then without turning back, he dropped the reins and raised both his arms up in the air. Like these, he said.'

Tarun felt a cold shiver down his spine. 'What... what did you see?' Tarun said.

'Horse's legs *babu*, the *tongawallah* had horse's legs in place of arms, complete with hoofs.'

Tarun sprang to his feet. 'I don't want to hear any more of this. Take us home. This minute.'

❋

Two days later they met again in Chandni Chowk.

'*Hoooo*,' Salim said, showing Tarun his closed fists, mimicking horse's hoofs.

Tarun slapped Salim's hands away.

Salim laughed. 'I say we should go to Kaka di Hatti next time we want some excitement.'

'I don't,' Tarun replied tersely, 'I am never going to Delhi late at night.'

'You can't blame me. I never force you to go anywhere.'

'Yes, you do. You told me you like going out at night to get away from your wife.'

'It was your idea to go to Kaka di Hatti.'

'Anyway, this is not what I have come to talk about.'

'What then?'

'Can I borrow your suit.'

'Borrow my suit. For what?'

'Usha has arranged for me to see a girl in Jaipur. Pabiji

wants me to dress properly, like a man she says.' Tarun rolled his eyes.

'Aha, that's why you are so edgy.'

'You want to lend me your suit or not. It's only for one day. You can have it back after that.'

'*Abbe saale,* when did I say you can't have the suit. Have it. But you will look like a clown wearing a suit when you are only going to see the girl and the family. You are not going to your wedding. I suggest you wear a nice trouser and shirt and leather shoes. Brown shoes are fashionable these days.'

'I will have to spend money on a new trouser and shirt.'

'That's sensible.'

'*Hah*, do you know how much tailors charge these days?'

'You can afford it. You are working now.'

Tarun glared at Salim's face as if there was a fly sitting on the nose.

'Who is the family?'

'What do I know? Usha says they are a good *kshatriya* family. She knows them from her husband's side.'

'And the girl?' Salim said, clowning with his eyebrows. 'Is she sexy?'

'I will find out when I meet her.'

'If she is not sexy, tell her you are not interested.'

'Oh yes, why didn't YOU think of that when you were getting married?'

'Hundred times I have told you, you do as I say, not as I do.'

'Yes, you have. Now can I borrow the suit?'

'*Orff-ho*, you can have the suit if it fits you. Do you want

to know the last time I wore it?'
 'Yeah, when?'
 'I was going to my own wedding.'

19

'After her mother's death mother became a maid in Pal sahib's house. She was only sixteen,' Sangeeta said.

They were standing under the same *kadam* tree where Sangeeta had previously sheltered from the rain, with its heavy foliage and yellow flowers, the odour of wet soil rising like wisps of steam. Now it seemed the most obvious place to convene, in the succour of secrecy, against the coarse bark of the trunk while black ants marched in a straight line by the feet as if offering a military style welcome.

'That is Pal senior, daddy's daddy,' she said by way of explanation, 'at first everything was going well then one day the man turned into an animal. He lured my mother into his room and raped her on the very bed he used to sleep with his wife. This went on for months, he would force my mother on the bed whenever his wife was away… the pig.' Shocked by the slip of foul language she slammed a hand to her mouth.

'Why didn't she leave and complain to the police?'

'Yes, I keep thinking the same, why didn't she go to the wife or someone else for help. But remember she was only a poor village girl and needed the job badly. Moreover, he was a violent, short-tempered man. Even his family feared him. Then, what was inevitable, did take place, she became pregnant. On hearing of her pregnancy, he turned from an animal to a generous, kind human being, reassuring her every day, offering to look after her and the little brother. He moved her into an apartment and started giving a monthly allowance so there was no need for her to go out to work. What could the poor woman do? She accepted it as her fate and did everything according to his wishes. But when the girl was born, he turned into a monster again. This time the old man wanted to take the child away and raise her as his daughter in his household. He was adamant the little girl was his… as though he had purchased her in the market.'

'How could he do that without telling the family?' Tarun asked. A scooter rickshaw rattled past on the street. He instinctively turned to look, wondering if it was Harjeet, even though he knew the possibility was remote. The streets of Delhi were teeming with scooter rickshaws.

'Without telling the family… *baba*, the family knew everything by then. How can you keep something like that a secret for long? They were disgusted with him but powerless to do anything. He was an influential man with contacts. Mother was hysterical with worry. She didn't want to give up her child,' she said and paused briefly, 'here is the answer to your question Tarun – on the day he arrived with two of his men she was like a mad woman, like a cat cornered from all sides. That is when she slung the child out of the window, threatening to drop her if he came closer. By then I don't believe my mother knew what she was doing.'

'Where is your mother now?' Tarun asked, feeling sorry for the woman and Sangeeta. Her story could be his. He often felt remote from his siblings, as if he did not belong to the family, that somehow, he was thrust upon them. One day Pabiji had given him a parcel of dress fabric. 'Drop it at Kamala's house,' she said, 'it is urgent.' He remembered clearly it was an acutely sweltering day and Kamala lived over two miles away. The buses on that route were infrequent, particularly at midday when few people ventured out. He refused to go, complaining of the heat, and because Suraj had already declined, Pabiji had flared, pulling her sari tight over the shoulder. 'Get out of this house and don't come back,' she screamed. When he turned to Krishan and Mohan for support, they walked away. For a long time after that he had carried this feeling, like a load of charcoal sack on his shoulders, that he did not belong to the family, he was an outsider.

'She is dead. They tell me she left the house that day and threw herself in a well.'

'What about the old man?'

'When I was six years old, he died too. After that Mohindra Pal and his wife took me to their house. They said I was to call them daddy and mummy,' she said, and her eyes glazed over, the lips shook. She reached out and plucked a flower from the tree, admiring and sniffing it, and then she said, 'I have told you about my family, tell me about yours.'

He shrugged his shoulders. 'What is there to say about my family. Seven brothers and sisters. I am the youngest but one. I was born in Lyallpur, now in Pakistan. That's all there is.'

'Did you quarrel with your brothers and sisters?'

'All the time,' he said.

While they were chatting, a sparrow, attracted by a half-eaten guava rotting among the twigs, flew down and landed by their feet. Sangeeta watched fascinated as the bird pecked at the fruit and the flies hovered. She cleared her throat and began singing. Her voice flew gently, the notes rising at the appropriate moments. Her eyes drifted towards him and into the distance again. He stood rooted to the ground, his heart beating fast. The song was from an old black and white movie he recognised but did not know the title.

Finally, she drifted into silence. She held it there for a moment, and then she opened her eyes and smiled. The smile was like a ripple passing over a calm lake.

20

Padma and Pammi wanted to go to Jaipur too. 'Five pair of eyes are better than three to suss out the family and the girl, one cannot be over cautious in these matters.'

'I am quite capable of handling it, no need for an entourage descending on the Kapurs. They will think we are desperate,' Pabiji said. The calendar on the wall above her head fluttered briskly, driven by a gust of wind.

'But aren't we desperate?'

'Maybe we are, but I don't want them to know, and I don't want to hear this kind of talk from you about your uncle, just remember your place in this house.' Pabiji's sharp glare sent Padma packing in tears.

'Pabiji we are part of the family, why can't we come?' said an adamant Pammi, threatening to produce her own tears.

'What nonsense is this. It is for Pabiji, and Pabiji alone, to decide who should go,' Pali said walking in from the rain, wet shirt sticking to the skin.

'Why? Why? Why?'

Savitri rushed into the room. 'Quiet, all of you,' she yelled at Pammi, 'let Pabiji and Tarun decide who should go.'

Tarun was quarrelling with Salim's woollen trouser reeking of old naphthalene, trying to press it with a hot iron. Years of fold creases were refusing to flatten.

'I am sick and tired of all this,' he said slamming the iron on the table, 'you all can go – and take all the neighbours with you. I will stay behind.'

After more heated discussion they came to a decision, Pabiji, Savitri and Tarun would take the early morning train to Jaipur to meet the Kapur family for tea, snacks, and matrimonial talk. Savitri sent the neighbour's servant to book Harjeet for the ride to the station, and his wife to deliver five rotis and five nan breads later that evening. Harjeet and his scooter rickshaw had now become their transport of choice.

❁

At Jaipur station they hired a cycle rickshaw. Squeezed in the back seat, Pabiji and Savitri on either side, Tarun gazed around him nervously. The old city, Tarun noticed, was no different from Chandni Chowk of Delhi, only it was smaller and denser, the lanes narrow and overcrowded. The rickshaw driver, red faced with the effort of pedalling, people ignoring his frantic tinkling of the bell, the desperate calls to move out of the way, as if the city were full of deaf or insane people. Half an hour later, in the centre of Johari Bazaar, he stopped pedalling abruptly as if he had reached the edge of a precipice and to go further would be suicidal. The front wheel was inches from a *hakim's* roadside cart packed with jars of herbs and potions. *Instant cure of asthma, impotency, gout, monkey fever* – the placard announced proudly. And there were astrologers, soothsayers, and palmists with tools of their trade – birthstones, gems, and *mynah* birds in cages – all spread out in the lane.

The rickshaw driver spat in the gutter. 'I can't go on. Too much crowd,' he said, shaking his head. Little drops of sweat fell to the ground with each shake.

Tarun readjusted Salim's folded jacket on his lap. 'What's the matter?' he demanded.

'Haven't I said too much crowd?' the driver mumbled irritably, as if they were being unreasonable asking for an explanation.

'But you can't leave us here. You must take us to our destination,' Savitri said forcefully.

'Madam, how to go.'

'How far is our destination?'

'Madam, not far,' he pointed vaguely ahead, 'not even five minutes to walk. I will send somebody to show you the way.' He yelled at a boy outside a jewellery shop, 'oi you, show these people Busti Gulley, house number six and don't fool around or I will get you.'

The boy nodded compliantly as if he had been waiting for just such a mission. He led them into an even narrower lane, the hawkers here were waving their merchandise in peoples' faces. Savitri cleared a path for Pabiji, swotting scarves, belts, cloth bags off her face while Tarun, walked stiffly, like a marching soldier, so as not to break the creases on the strides held up with brown leather braces. 'How far now?' he asked the boy.

'There only,' the boy said, as if the destination was merely yards away. But the boys 'there' seemed forever out of reach. After fifteen minutes Tarun asked again, 'are we there now?' The boy gave Tarun a weak smile, stopped suddenly at a blue door and slammed it with his palm.

'Are you sure this is number six?'

The boy rocked his head. 'Kapur,' he said.

'Yes, you are right, Kapur, Kapur,' Tarun said, impressed. Even street urchins know of the family, he thought. He already knew the family ran a textile business in Johari Bazaar. He conjured up images of lavishly furnished shops with fancy spotlights and air-conditioned interior. Rich, and famous clientele sauntering in, selecting fabric and ordering fashion garments. He swung around to face his mother and sister and gave them a winning smile. Pabiji responded with stern eye gestures, asking him to sober up while Savitri adjusted her sari and relaxed her facial muscles in a futile attempt to erase the worry creases.

The door opened. A maid stood behind it, expressionless, allowing the boy to barge in. Someone yelled from the interior, a female voice, 'Billa why are you walking round the streets like a homeless urchin, go upstairs and change.'

Tarun retreated behind the ladies, embarrassed at his terrible misconception of the boy.

In the courtyard a bicycle was leaning against the wall. A galvanised-metal water tank stood on a concrete plinth, five or six attached pipes protruding at various angles. It reminded Tarun of a Satish Sharma metal sculpture he had seen outside the American Express office. Pigeons were cooing above their heads as if in awe of the artwork. A white sheet hanging on the clothesline, like a homemade theatre screen, parted. A man appeared with raised arms in expansive greeting. 'Welcome, welcome, please come inside.'

White shirt and trouser, pencil thin moustache, fair complexion, handsome face, he resembled Clark Gable. Tarun recalled seeing pictures of the American actor in a magazine or a film poster somewhere. But when Clark Gable opened the mouth, the veneer of Americanism fizzled like spilled milk. His accent was of a Punjabi *jat* peasant.

In the living room Tarun sat with the folded jacket on his lap. Mrs Kapur took a seat with a clear view of the kitchen.

Manmohan Kapur played the opening card. '*Bahanji*,' he said addressing Pabiji, 'I am pleased you have come to our humble abode. We are not obscenely rich as you can see. We lead a frugal existence.' By which he meant do not expect a hefty dowry, Tarun assumed. 'We pray to our God every day and our motto is to treat people with respect and never cheat or double cross anyone.' While Mr Kapur spoke Mrs Kapur nodded dutifully, seconding everything he said. 'While we don't like to deceive anyone, we have to keep up our guard, so we don't become victims ourselves.'

'We too are a simple middle-class family. Our demands are few. We are looking for a good, homely girl,' Pabiji said and turned to Mrs Kapur for her response.

But it was Mr Kapur who replied. 'As you know Preeti is

our only daughter. My wife here has worked hard to teach her how to keep a house spick span, yes, she has. Haven't you?' The wife blushed but kept her mouth shut.

'Yes, we have taught her everything. Preeti is a very homely girl. Your son will have no complaints on that score. She can sew dresses too, mend garments when required. She does not believe in wastage. See the blouse my wife is wearing, can you see? Preeti stitched it,' he said and looked around for approval.

'We are a large family. My husband was an inspector of schools, my sons are all well-settled businessmen, big company directors,' Pabiji said and then added in an exaggerated casual tone, 'foreign returned.'

'Foreign returned...?' Kapur's voice broke, like a trumpet gone wrong.

'Yes, yes, we sent our eldest to *vilayet*, England, to study. He came back with a big degree, and my grandson, Dev, will be going to England very soon.'

Kapur's face darkened as if he was suffering stomach cramps. Tarun chuckled to himself.

'We made sure our daughter received the best of education. She studied all the way to class ten, a top-class student, coming first in every subject. But we stopped her from going to university. It is our belief a girl should be more proficient at running a home. Where is the need for a university degree,' Kapur said.

Pabiji said, as if in an afterthought, 'oh, my granddaughters are at university.'

Manmohan Kapur shifted his weight to the left buttock. 'But we have no objection if her would-be husband wants her to continue studying and take a job. It is up to the husband and wife.'

Tarun again shifted the jacket clumsily from his right arm to the left, releasing a faint mothball odour. He sat back, not making eye contact with Mr Kapur, dreading the moment attention would turn to him. That moment came all too soon, when Kapur asked, 'what line of work are you in son?'

'Electrical contracting,' Tarun replied, stuttering a little, 'our work is mainly with shops and business premises.'

'What is the name of the firm?'

'Dalal and Company, our premises are near Ajmeri Gate.'

'Oh, oh, oh. Dalal and Company.' Kapur nodded vigorously, as if he knew the company well.

How could he know of a firm with only twenty employees and one office in Delhi? It seemed to Tarun, this man was one of those know-alls who never admit to any shortcomings and boast of being on first name terms with anyone and everyone important?

'Companies like these are the future of the country. Yes, technology and modernisation. The British have held our country back for far too long. But our time has come. Magnificent changes are taking place. Credit goes to the Prime Minister.'

Tarun nodded in agreement, but he was more interested in the girl than politics.

Kapur continued. 'Hard working people like you are what we need. Not lazy ignorant millions who refuse to do a proper day's work. My friend Alok, who runs a big international firm, not your two-penny chotta-bazaar outfit, he was telling me the other day that the productivity of his people has fallen so low even a blackface *langur* monkey can outperform them. The only thing these people are good at, *saala*, how to produce children – *thak, thak, thak*, they keep churning them out, a factory production line,' he said, striking a fist to the open palm three times and Mrs Kapur and Pabiji turned away quickly. They began discussing saris, where to buy handwoven fabric in Jaipur and lamenting the sharp price rises since the partition.

'What is your opinion son,' Kapur asked and continued without waiting for a reply. 'So, you see we have a problem here. But every problem has a solution. The scientist Einstain – Ainstan – Anstaan.' He struggled with the pronunciation. 'According to the great scientist – every action has an equal and opposite reaction. I say the solution to the problem is remarkably similar, line up all those who do not want to work, including the workshy beggars on the street with their fake missing limbs and sob stories of destitution – oh God, Ram, what to do I have lost everything in Pakistan. Bullshit I say….'

Savitri sprang upright. 'But Kapur bhai…'

'Let me finish,' Kapur said with a thrust of the hand, 'I say give them a taste of their own medicine, shoot them dead – *baas*, then you will see how quickly the country will progress.'

'But Kapur bhai, you cannot expect these poor people to put in a satisfactory performance, operate heavy machinery when they are starving, half nourished and worried about how to feed the family. Give them good wages and good working conditions like they do in England, your friend Alok will find the productivity shooting up in his factory,' she said, her voice shrill, and then realising she had come across too strident, added in a moderate tone, 'anyway this is my opinion. As for eliminating people by shooting them dead, you cannot do it in a democracy. We are not Hitler's Germany, and even he lost the war.'

Tarun was astonished. He had never heard his sister speak so avidly, with such passion about a subject she rarely showed an interest.

Kapur replied, 'you see if we were a Germany, we would not be in such a mess,' realising this was a poor analogy he corrected himself, 'I am all for democracy. But to make a democratic omelette one must crack democratic eggs. There is nothing wrong with taking strong measures, especially when Pakistan and America are working underhand to destabilise our country.'

'Where are the jobs the government keeps promising? What are these people to do? According to the government's own statistics the unemployment rate is twenty per cent. It means one in every four is sitting idle, not because they want to, but because there are no jobs. You can't deny that Kapur bhai.'

'Here you are wrong. But let us not go into this further – after all we are here to discuss more important matters,' Kapur said, and forced a smile. He made eye contact with his wife and then went back to Savitri. 'Another time I will tell you what my industrialist friend has to say about the job situation. You will be astonished. There are enough jobs to go around for everyone. Even a dead man can find work if he wants it badly enough.'

Savitri interned a laughter and turned her face to the pedestal fan.

Just then the door opened. Tarun turned his attention around, his shining shoes shuffling on the floor. The girl entered. She was carrying a tray in both hands set with plates of barfi coated in edible silver, samosa, and pakoras, releasing a whiff of fried pastry. Tarun froze. The light seemed to slow right down. He looked at her face which had the nervous concentration of someone attempting to ride a bicycle for the first time. He couldn't see the hips because of the tray but her feet were small and manicured with a silver anklet which gave her sexy appeal. She is beautiful, he thought.

'Offer them around, *beti*,' mother said, 'be careful.'

'Yes mother.' Her voice was wobbly but sweet. She walked round the room slowly, from person to person, avoiding eye contacts. Pabiji and Savitri picked up a pakora each. Tarun raised a hand to say he won't have any, but unable to take his eyes off her. She was wearing a fabulous turquoise blue sari with gold thread embroidery. The fabric clung to her slim body, giving the figure a sensual appeal.

She placed the tray on a table and made fleeting eye contact with Tarun. He could not tell if she was pleased. If everything else worked out, if they asked him, he would say yes – yes, yes, yes. Does she feel the same about him? He would like to talk to her in private. Now. Not after the families had done their cynical horse trading. Salim had said if you like her, then tell her, don't fool around.

'Hmm, very tasty,' Savitri said, addressing the girl and nibbling on a cauliflower pakora, 'did you make them?'

'Yes, she did,' mother replied quickly, adjusting her sari, a sober light green but similar fabric as the daughter's, 'didn't you *beti?*'

The daughter did not respond.

'Now bring the teas,' the mother said.

Tarun compared her to Sangeeta. Not a bookworm, this one appeared more outgoing, a coffee house lout, member of girl gang, easy going. Just like Usha, he thought.

She returned with five cups of tea and saucers on a larger tray.

'Be careful,' the mother said anxiously, seeing her hands shaking.

By the time she reached the centre of the circle the crockery was clinking. She tried to steady herself. But it made no difference. A cup rolled over spilling the content on the tray. She appeared exasperated suddenly and dropped the tray on the table smothering the samosas. The crockery fell to the floor, spilling hot tea in a wide circle. Tarun stood up to help, but sat down seeing Savitri's stern glare, telling him not to interfere.

'I can't do this,' the girl cried and instantly burst into tears. She turned and stormed out of the room. Mother ran after her while Kapur stared at the floor, at the smashed crockery, his face a shade of puce.

The maid appeared promptly with a cloth, bucket, and broom, as if she knew the crockery will smash and tea will spill.

'*Bahanji*, I am sorry, an accident has happened,' Kapur said.

'These things happen. No need to apologise,' Pabiji said with a wave of the hand, 'why I have spilled tea so many times.'

Tarun looked at Kapur. Kapur was watching the maid sweeping broken pieces of crockery. Pabiji and Savitri exchanged glances, should we retreat now.

In the absence of conversation, the only noise in the room was the clunk, clunk, clunk of broken crockery falling in a bucket. A fly buzzed in Tarun's ear, as though warning him to get out; there is danger ahead.

In the other room they could hear the girl sobbing. Tarun, still dazed, wanted to barge in to pacify Preeti: it's not your fault, it happens when you are under such intense scrutiny. They should never have asked you to carry the tray. For what is the maid there? He noticed Pabiji was signalling at him. 'We ought to be leaving now,' she said to Kapur, 'we have a long way to go,'

Kapur raised an arm, and then dropped it, disappointed. 'We were hoping you would stay for dinner.'

'No, no, we must be on our way.'

Tarun knew then that Pabiji was not impressed. Once they were alone in the yard Savitri whispered. 'So what do you think?'

Pabiji made a face. 'They are not our type.'

'But I liked her,' Tarun said. They had yet to step out onto the street when they heard a girl's screams. All three turned around. The door was slightly ajar. They could see Kapur's back, the arm in the air. He was assaulting her daughter, slapping her across the face. The muffled screams gave way to, 'papa, papa, papa' as if pleading with him to stop.

Pabiji stared in disbelief, said nothing at first, and then cried out, 'O God's child why are you beating the poor girl, what is her fault in all this?'

The beating continued until Pabiji yelled again, 'leave her alone.'

Kapur swung around realising there were witnesses. He assumed a position shielding the girl from view.

'Leave the girl now. We can talk about it,' Pabiji said in a little conciliatory note.

Kapur made a face, his fiery eyes ordering them to stay out of it.

'Don't hit her, don't,' Tarun yelled, overcome by a desire to protect her.

Kapur raged. 'I want you people to leave. Don't interfere.'

'We won't leave until you stop,' Tarun said, boldly, taking an aggressive stance. Savitri took Tarun's arm to pull him away.

'I told you to leave,' Kapur barked, releasing the girl's hair and then rushed at Tarun.

Shocked by the unexpected threat of violence Tarun stumbled backward with a humiliating cry, as if he had already received a blow. He turned around and rushed towards the exit. Pabiji and Savitri followed. Out of the house Tarun felt his legs giving in and he struggled to breath as if his lungs had stopped functioning. He placed a hand against the wall for support, the eyes glazing over.

Savitri grabbed his arm to lower him to the floor. He went down on the dusty pavement, yards from a goat they had seen earlier with sagging udders. It was now bleating frantically, the tongue darting out and in. Black marbles of faeces lay scattered on the ground. Tarun started flailing his arms and legs. Pabiji slapped his cheeks. 'Tarun, Tarun, Tarun, wake up... he must have forgotten to take the medicine.'

Savitri searched his pockets, looking for the little flat box. She looked around her helplessly, to summon help from passers-by.

'Savitri, try the back pocket,' Pabiji said, battling with his head, trying to keep it elevated to prevent injuries.

The front door opened. The boy came out and stopped abruptly staring at them wide eyed. They did not notice the boy as he rushed back in. Moments later the maid came out with a towel and mug of water. She went down on her knees, dipped her fingers in the enamel mug and sprinkled water on Tarun's face, repeatedly. 'Heat, heat,' she said pointing at the sky.

She soaked the towel and wrapped it around his head, making a small bun at the back for the skull to rest on. Working swiftly, she unbuttoned the shirt and fanned the chest with bare hands.

'It's the heat,' she repeated stepping, 'he will be alright. Give him air.' A small skinny woman, years of worry imprinted on her dark face. She stepped back and covered her head with the cotton sari when Tarun stopped beating his arms and opened his eyes.

'You are a good woman,' Pabiji said.

Savitri asked in a muffled voice, 'what is going on inside?'

The maid shook her head as if she were in deep sorrow.

'Is the poor girl all right?' Savitri asked.

'I don't know... sahib has become like this, a mad man, since his business started going down. He has debt on his head...,' she trailed off as if it were not proper to pass judgement on her employer's financial affair. 'They are forcing her.'

'Forcing her to do what?'

'To get married. They are desperate to wash their hands off her. But she does not want to marry like this. It is not my business to say this...'

Tarun sat up and looked at the door as if he wanted to go back in. He had witnessed beating and degradation of a young girl and done nothing. Confused, shamed, he knew the vertigo of the moment would be with him for a long time. His heart pounded again, and he felt breathless – not breathless of epilepsy but with something close to rage.

❁

Head resting on the windowpane, the rhythmic sway of the train put him into a state of stupor. The tedium of it settled upon him like grey, crumbling mildew. He felt aged and mouldy. He was sure his teeth would loosen in the night; hair would come out in handfuls if tugged. He had learned a lesson, never venture beyond the familiar safe dustbin of his world. Stay clear of the night-time bacchanalia, melodrama, and revelry. This is all he deserved from life.

He looked out the window. Another train was passing by. In one of the compartments a girl was sitting with her back turned to him. Below her short blouse he could see the nuggets of her spine, each demarcated. He thought of the girl indoors and wanted to reach out and touch. Down her back, one bone after the other, reach and touch. The train was gone. He felt a draught of tailwind hit his face.

Pabiji and Savitri were sitting squeezed together. Heat and stench of so many bodies in the confined space made Savitri want to retch. She bunched a corner of her sari and placed it on her nose and mouth. '*Hai rabba*, what time will we arrive in Delhi? I can't take it anymore.' She sighed and asked the man standing over her to move aside a bit, give her air.

'They are desperate to get the daughter married,' the words spilled out of Pabiji's mouth.

'Yes, before it becomes widely known the business is in decline,' Savitri said, 'shift the responsibility and one less mouth to feed.'

'They are not our type of people, best to keep away from them,' Pabiji said, looking ahead ruefully.

'But Pabiji, we don't have to socialise with the family. It is the girl we want. Don't forget we are desperate too.'

'The girl doesn't want to get married in this throwaway manner.'

'If we approach this sensibly, we can turn the girl around. Our need to act fast is just as great. Think of Tarun's age.'

A lady sitting opposite, overhearing the conversation, tendered an opinion. 'Sister it is not easy to get children married these days,' she said with excessive hand gestures, her hips spread wide on the seat, a reed hand fan resting on her lap.

Savitri nodded in agreement. '*Hanh*, what you say is absolutely correct.'

'I have married off three daughters single handed. Only I know how I did it.' She made a face as if she had been to hell and seen terrible things.

'Three only,' Pabiji said, 'I have arranged marriages for six children, and they are all happily settled.'

The woman continued, 'and what did I get in return… nothing but complaints and allegations by the boys' families that I was mean with the dowry.' She paused. 'Sister I was not mean, I gave them nice, homely girls and a good amount of gold, silver, and cash too. What more could I have done? Slice off my head and offer it on a platter? Even that would not have satisfied them.'

Her friend in an orange sari nodded. 'She is telling the truth. The world has gone mad. There is no morality left these days. Boys' sides have become so greedy, they do not want to know unless you talk in lakhs or crores. What is the poor man with daughters to do? Keep them at home all their lives?'

Savitri said, 'what a tragedy, life is not easy these days. I have two daughters myself.'

They fell silent as the train came to a juddering halt at a small-town station. Savitri picked up a discarded newspaper by her feet. In the middle pages was a photograph, a scene of heart jerking profundity. She had to stop and stare and try to make sense. What is it all about? In the photograph were three young women, dressed in petticoats. Each with the end of a sari tied to the neck and the other end hooked to the blades of a single ceiling fan. Chairs scattered under their dangling feet, heads skewed, bodies limp like rag dolls.

She read the accompanying article, her eyes repeatedly straying to the scene that floated like a tableau. The three were sisters, all in their twenties. A handwritten note left by them said they wanted to spare their father and mother the shame of three unmarried daughters, because they could not afford the dowries.

She took the newspaper close to her face to wallow undisturbed in the grief of the family. It seemed to her the sisters looked disappointed, as though they had expected something more out of their daring deeds of hanging, and then discovered death was all there was.

21

The image of Kapur beating his daughter thrummed for days in Tarun's head, like a moth's beating wings. Through force of will he had made it flightless, stupefied it, and removed the wings. He tried to move on and throw himself into the folds of his work, in the comfort of rough and tumble.

'O *chachajan*, what is going on here, you have started arriving before everyone else and you are the last one to leave,' Rakesh said with a mocking laugh, leaning back on the chair and feet on the desk. A wily oldish man who knew how to work the system, how to appear incredibly busy while doing little.

Tarun did not respond. At first, he used to join in on the banter, which was crude and bawdy, talking like mongrels – a mix of Hindustani, Punjabi and Bombay movie speak, swearing thrown in like *chaat* masala. He used to consider it essential to blend in with the crowd. Lately he had figured out staying too close to this lot could be detrimental to promotion. For three months now he had been working hard, keeping himself busy.

'You spend so much time here, might as well bring your bedding and sleep in the warehouse, the boss will be pleased, no. He can get rid of the night watchman, who doesn't do any watching anyway.'

Satpal, Rakesh's assistant, snorted. 'He will be an incredibly good security guard. Meet that face in the dark, even the most hardened criminal will be terrified.'

'Nah, he is looking for a pay rise.'

'Pay rise, pay rise,' Rakesh made monkey noises, '*hooh, hooh, hooh.* You will get peanuts thrown at you occasionally. That is all. I have been here for fifteen years; all I have had is a little bonus and a cheap sari for my daughter when she got married.'

Sameer Dalal burst in and called Tarun over to his office. 'I want you to go to Krishna Ophthalmic Optician in Kalkaji. Show them the drawings and the costing. Get the contract signed and bring it straight back here. Can you manage?'

'Yes, I can,' Tarun said confidently.

'I don't want you to go dressed like this. Go home first and change into smart clothes. Look like a professional.'

'You can rely on me,' Tarun said standing up tall, unable to contain a smile, the smile of a schoolboy declared a winner of a competition he had expected to lose.

Back home he rushed to the trunk and took out a fresh trouser and the shirt reserved only for special occasions. The house was in the sway of usual daytime activities, someone hand washing clothes in the bathroom, pounding them with a heavy stick. In another part of the house, he could hear Pabiji in conversation with someone. 'What exactly is wrong with your mother?' Pabiji said.

'Pain in the back and legs... can't even stand up straight. She asked me to cover for her until she is better.'

This voice he did not recognise but thought nothing of it, as he hurriedly tied the shoelaces. He was about to leave the house when he nearly walked into a girl in the corridor. The girl, bent forward, was sweeping the floor. She appeared younger than Pyari, slim built, long hair pleated. She looked up from the stooping position. Their eyes met momentarily and the girl immediately lowered her gaze. She moved swiftly to another room.

He had seen that face before. That thunderclap of shock and his heart gave a fierce thud. The girl at Abida Bai's house. The same alluring eyes, – light bronze complexion – figure of a dancer. But where are the bangles? He froze. Had his eyes deceived him? Slowly he crept closer. All he could hear was the swish, swoosh of the broom. And then he heard Pabiji giving instructions. 'The floor under the cabinet is dusty... run the broom there... and then go to the back room.'

Why is she working as a sweeper? What is the connection with Pyari? He followed her with his eyes, keeping a physical distance. Trying to see her from every conceivable angle, to get the three-dimensional mental image his fantasies deserved. She moved lightly through the house, seeming to weigh only slightly more than her shadow. He waited for her to move to the front yard. His mind was whirling like a spinning top.

Why is she taking so long? When she finally worked her

way to the open yard he tip-toed to the window. She was running the broom in small semi circles, collecting fallen leaves in tiny heaps, even from the rear there was no denying who she was. Unlike Pyari who worked fast and furious with broad confident strokes, this girl appeared less sure of herself.

He came out of the room, yelled at Pabiji, 'I am off now.' Once outside he stopped at the jamun tree. She continued sweeping without a backward glance.

'What is your name?' he asked. He was torn between putting on a bold front, I have nothing to hide, or slink away in shame. But she too is a brothel girl, he thought, we both have a secret to keep.

'You work for Abida Bai?'

'My name is Manjulata… they call me Manju. Why do you want to know about babu?' she said without stopping.

'I went to look for you.'

She raised her head for a sideways glance.

'I didn't go in. I wanted to catch you outside, but the security men wouldn't let me.'

She did not look at him, but he could tell she was surprised.

'What is your connection with Pyari?'

'She is my mother. She is ill so I am helping her.'

'You knew all along who I was.'

She hesitated.

'Did you?'

'Yes.'

'Why didn't you say so?'

'It was not my business.'

'But you wanted me to leave that place quickly.'

'Oh *babu*, you looked so innocent – I had to get you out of there before they ate you alive.'

He went to the tap, turned it on and off with swift jerks. He wanted to stay, whisk her away somewhere private so they could talk. But his appointment was urgent. How could he let Sameer Dalal down? 'I have to go now,' he said, 'are you coming back here again?'

'Yes *babu*, what to do. I must until she can shake this *jharu* again,' she said and looked at the broom in her hand with a contemptuous glare.

❀

Out of the gate he rushed to the bus stop, breaking into a trot. Changing his mind halfway he hailed a scooter rickshaw. 'Kalkaji, hurry, hurry, to the Krishna bazaar, past the crossing turn right.'

So, this is the daughter. He had heard Pyari talk scornfully of a daughter, a demon of a girl who had run away from home. That wretch, she will see me dead soon. Trouble, trouble, what else to expect from her. The day she was born was a cursed day.

At the client's premises, brimming with confidence, he opened the file and outlined the plan, dealt with queries, explained the procedure, eye to eye like a professional, placed a finger where it said SIGN HERE and watched with bated breath as Mr Sukhdev's fountain pen scratched the paper savagely, and then crossed the t's and dotted the i's with heavy blows as if competing with the builders hammering the wall at the rear of the premises, and finally Mr Sukhdev's bookkeeper pressed a blotting paper over the wet ink. Tarun released his breath with a long audible whistle.

The office fell into deadly silence as he walked in late that afternoon, the folder in his armpit. A dozen pairs of eyes stabbed him. Dubious expressions, cynical smirks, expectation of failure.

Sameer Dalal leaned forward, hands flat on the desk, raised eyebrows. 'Did you… do it?' he said, and then repeated aloud. 'Did you do it?' As though yelling would yield positive results.

Tarun threw his arms up in the air as if he had just hit a six, sending the ball soaring into the pavilion. The office erupted into hoots of jubilation. Sameer Dalal drummed the table. 'Open the bottle,' he yelled, 'fetch the glasses.' He sent the peon for kebabs and tandoori chicken and another bottle of Johnny Walker.

❂

'This will not do. Yesterday you did not clean the kitchen floor properly. Look at this… look.' Pabiji was taking Manju to task, setting down guidelines, and showing who is the boss. 'See ants everywhere. They are after spilled sugar grains.'

'*Hanh*, Pabiji, I will do it properly this time. Yesterday I must have forgotten,' Manju replied compliantly.

Tarun could not see but knew Pabiji was waving a finger. Her trademark finger waving. It amused the grandchildren, who mimicked her finger-waving in each other's faces and then they would cackle with laughter.

Tarun's ears were alert, listening to the swishing broom, screech of the furniture, the shlop of a wet mop. Pammi was sitting under the sun, drying her washed hair. Someone was tapping a foot to the beat of music streaming from a radio. In another room Savitri and Pali were debating the merits of homoeopathic medicines.

Tarun waited. Edgy. Manju was working a different sequence, back to front. Pyari always started with the gate, the yard, before entering the house.

Finally, she moved to the front yard. He was relieved that Pabiji did not follow. Stealthily he came out and stood pressed against the wall to make himself invisible. She continued sweeping, dust rising like mini storms in wake of the swishing broom.

'How is your mother?' he asked.

'Still not good,' she said softly.

'Have you taken her to the doctor.' He cupped a hand over the eyes to shield them from the blinding sun.

'You don't know my mother, she thinks her own herbs will cure her, as if she is a hakim.'

'Ask Pabiji, she usually has cures for everything.'

'No one can cure that stubborn woman.'

A gust of wind unsettled the leaves. She rushed to contain them.

'Have you stopped going to Abida Bai?' The word Abida Bai came out in a mangled tone, as if he were ashamed of uttering that word.

She thumped the broom to the floor. 'Why are you asking all these questions *babu*?'

'Just asking… if you do not want to, don't answer.'

She mopped the brows with the end of the sari, moved to the rear of the yard and began sweeping with vigour. Minutes passed. He could feel sweat inching down his ribs.

'Why are you wasting your time here? You know who I am, don't you?'

'I know all that. I don't care.'

'If you are worried, I will open my mouth, then don't. I never do things like that.'

He did not say anything.

'I am just a sweeper's daughter *babu*. What is it you want from me?'

'Will you meet me somewhere outside; I want to talk to you.'

'Talk. What is there to talk about?'

'I can't say it here. Meet me in the park on Sunday.'

'You can say it in the park but not here?'

'Don't you understand?'

'No *babu*.'

'Why aren't you wearing the red bangles?'

'Bangles?' She looked puzzled.

'You were wearing them when we first met.'

'I don't have them anymore.'

'Will you meet me in the park.'

She shook her little shoulders. 'All right, I will meet you.'

'And don't call me *babu*.'

'Yes, *babu*.' She glanced coyly at him.

The torpor of summer was upon them, and inside the house felt like a pressure cooker. Tarun sat in the open yard, shirtless, fanning himself. The trees and their branches were casting long shadows, each leaf as still as a sleeping cat. He himself was like a pressure vessel, flaring with rage at minor issues. Two hours he had waited for Manju in the park on Sunday, like a bloody fool, he thought, for she had not showed up. 'All right, I will meet you there,' she had said. They had agreed on a time, and she had sounded so sincere. She did not return to clean the house either. No word from Pyari. Pabiji was getting worried. 'Kaka, go and check what is wrong with her.' Tarun refused outright. 'We will find another cleaner if she does not return soon.'

A week later Pyari had appeared at the front door, silhouetted against the bright sunlight, a broom in hand. 'I thought you weren't coming back,' Pabiji said, showing her a very stern face. Tarun knew her anger was fake. Inside she was relieved to see Pyari.

Tarun never found out what explanation she had given for her daughter's absence. He had probed his mother once or twice, asked casually if Pyari's attendance was regular. 'These people can't be trusted, *kaka*,' Pabiji's had replied, 'if she does not work properly, I will replace her.'

Sweating like a tiger, a fly buzzed in his face. Noises, even tiny ones were starting to jerk on his nerves but mostly he felt hammered down by having the same nightmare on and off for over a week. It seemed to hover, waiting for him to drop off. As he lay on the bed, sliding uneasily into sleep, it would pounce and grab him by the hair and tow him down with sickening speed. Terrible as it was, he could not remember the details when he awoke. There were people he had never met, waving goodbye, and crow wings batting frantically, while he felt sucked into a blind, breathless emptiness.

He was beginning to feel faint, the heart palpating at a thumping speed. Somehow it was reminding him of the sunstroke he had years ago. Back in the days, if it was too hot to play outdoors, he used to go to his friend Hardip's house. One day they were playing on the stairs, legs astride the banister, sliding down it and then running up to start all over again. Hardip slipped and landed headfirst on the concrete floor. He howled with such force it terrified Tarun. Fearing the blame would fall on him he slipped away and ran all the way home in the intense heat. On the steps he slipped to the ground, not a fall but gradual, like a sinking boat. Next day they told him he had a sunstroke and was lucky to be alive.

He took sips of water and as he was putting the glass down, he felt a sudden slump in the air. All the lights disappeared into a pit of darkness.

A collective groan rose in the house. 'Lights have gone out,' someone yelled.

At first, they thought it was just their house.

'Fetch the candles, Pali,' Pabiji cried.

'Wait, wait. It may come back any minute,' Pali grumbled, putting down the book he was reading on the French revolution. He had let it be known that he and his friends were hoping to start a similar Indian insurrection. India is ripe for a showdown with the rich and powerful.

'No, no. It is a major breakdown. Even the streetlights are out,' Pabiji yelled, 'Tarun go and inform the substation.'

'Inform them what? Will they not know the lights have gone off?' Tarun yelled back.

'Don't talk to me like that. Go and ask them how long it will take to repair.'

'What difference will it make even if we know how long it will take to repair.'

'Don't argue with me. Just go now.'

'Why don't you send Pali or Dev? Why me only?'

'You know about electricity, they don't.'

Tarun slapped the table.

'What was that?' Savitri said and came out to the yard.

'Mrs Sharma,' Tarun announced, recognising the short plump figure of their next-door neighbour emerging ghost-like from the gap in the boundary fence. Hair streaming over the shoulders.

'Sharma *bhahan*, you gave me such fright,' Savitri said.

'I must tell you this… now…' Mrs Sharma gasped for air as she climbed the steps laboriously with a hand on each thigh in turn. She stopped at the door and gestured, give me a moment to catch the breath.

Pabiji came out, a lit candle in her right hand, left hand cupped over the flame.

'Do you want a drink of water,' Savitri asked and called Pammi, 'fetch a glass of water, quick.'

'No, no water. Have you heard?' she said between the breaths.

'Heard what?'

'About Mohindra Pal's daughter, Sangeeta…' She saw Tarun across the yard and hesitated briefly, switching her gaze between him and Savitri, and then continued, 'Sangeeta is missing.'

'Missing?'

'Yes, missing… no one knows where she is.'

'*Hai rabba*,' Pabiji exclaimed with a hand on her chest, 'what has happened to the girl?'

'She has been gone for two days… but I found out only just now.' She glanced at Tarun again who was doing his best to appear occupied, looking up and down the lane as if checking if any of the houses had electricity. But he had heard every word and suddenly felt cold and listless. They had met only days earlier; she had given no hint she wanted to run away from home. And then it hit him with a thud, they could implicate him.

'Has she run away of her own will?' Pabiji asked.

'No one knows for sure. I have heard father was unhappy with her,' and then with a hand on each ear, as if the words were too scandalous to speak, she mouthed them silently 'I have heard he may have something to do with it, yes.'

Pabiji took a sharp intake of breath. '*Hai, hai, rabba*, what is this world coming to. Why have people become so evil?' The candle accidently slipped from her fingers and at that moment, as if on cue, the lights of the house came on, blindingly with a thump.

'*Bijlee, bijlee*,' Pali yelled from inside the house as if others may not have noticed, 'see it has come back.'

Savitri insisted Mrs Sharma come in for a cold drink.

'No, no, sister Savitri, I have to go now and dismiss the

maid for the night.'

Tarun was still standing in the lane. He had seen the streetlights come on, yet not noticed. Why has Sangeeta left home? Has she quarrelled with the family and gone to stay with a friend? Or is it abduction. These things do happen. I should be looking for her, she needs help, he was thinking, but where and how? He dares not go to Mohindra Pal. It would be fatal even to approach the house. He kicked a pebble. It flew unexpectedly fast and hit a parked car with a loud crack.

❁

'This is what I don't understand about you,' Salim said as he took a swipe at flies hovering over his head, 'you always do exactly what I ask you not to. Why is it you never listen.'

'What did I do?' Tarun protested. 'I didn't ask her to run away. How is it my fault?'

'Were you trying to do it with her, eh, eh, with the boss's daughter.' Salim did a rude hand gesture and flicked his eyebrows.

'Don't do that,' Tarun said, looking around if someone was watching.

'I have told you a hundred times that if you want to do it go to Abida Bai. No complications, no headache – *baas* go home afterwards smiling like a cat with nine mice in the stomach.'

'Can't you take anything seriously.'

'I even took you there because you said you wanted to

do it. Did I not. What happens once we get there – you sit down, all pious like a temple priest doing *aarti– om bhur bhawa sawa*.

'Stop – stop going on and on with this nonsense. It was her idea. I only went because she wanted to meet me in the bookshop.'

'You want to marry her? Then say so,' Salim said confidently, as if he was an authority in arranging marriages.

'No,' Tarun said slowly, 'she is not my type.'

'That is true,' Salim said.

'True what?'

'That you are an uneducated bumpkin. She will keep you in your place,' Salim said, gesturing with his fingers as if ordering a family dog to sit.

'Shut your mouth,' Tarun said.

'All right, all right. Tell me who else knows about this.'

'Nobody, just her little brother.'

'*Oi, yaee, yaee, yaee,* the brother knows,' Salim said, shaking a limp hand, 'then you better start praying – *om bhur bhawa sawa.*'

'But it was her, she sent her brother.'

'That doesn't matter. Mohindra Pal will find out and he will be coming for you. What about your family – do they know?'

'No. Savitri will kill me if she finds out.'

'Then you better get ready for fireworks, *bacchu*,' Salim said, whistling and rocking his head from side to side, as if he would not want to be in Tarun's position. Rooted in his pocket he brought out a walnut in its hard shell, placed it between the heels of his palms and pressed hard. It took an effort to crack the shell. Uncoupling the two halves he took out a broken piece of the nut and offered it to Tarun.

'I don't want it,' Tarun snapped, swiping Salim's hand, sending the nut flying.

'Please yourself,' Salim said, 'I must go now. My lunch break is over.'

Tarun looked down at the pavement. Saw the broken shell of the walnut lying by his feet. Why is it always me, why, why, why? Everybody goes through life laughing and dancing, no worries in the world. He thought of Salim, carefree and happy. Why cannot I be like him? What have I done to deserve this? In a side alley he could hear the beat of drums and laughter. A celebration. It went on and on, like a left-open tap. Tears came to his eyes, tears of rage. He fought to contain them. Then the realisation hit him, no one was going to help him, and that he would have to take control of his own life. Let them all go to hell. If Mohindra Pal comes for him, he will tell the truth. What can he do? What can anybody do? What have I got to lose anyway? By the time he had finished drinking a cup of tea standing at the food stall, the golem that this new discovery had created in him had risen to its feet and shaken off the extra layers of earth.

He hailed a scooter-rickshaw and gave the driver Abida Bai's address. The rickshaw effected a quick U-turn scattering a heap of mango peels in the gutter.

Abida Bai's nondescript house stood aloof, like an abode of silent hermits. How misleading outer layers can be, he was thinking, as he knocked on the door. He knew invisible eyes would scrutinise him before opening the door.

Nothing happened for a good two minutes and Tarun began to fear they had recognised him from the previous visit. Finally, the door opened. He heard a girl's silky voice, 'welcome sir, welcome. Please come this way.'

'I have come for Manju. Can you call her for me?' he said and gave her a flamboyant smile, trying to emulate Salim.

The girl looked puzzled. 'There is no one here by that name.'

'Yes, there is. I met her here a few months ago,' Tarun said and repeated the name, 'Manju, Manjula.'

'But there is no Manju here.'

'Yes, there is. Go and ask inside while I wait.' This time he gave her a hard look, imagining Salim would have done the same.

The girl hesitated and went back in through a concealed entrance.

While he waited, he could hear muffled voices somewhere deep inside the house, casual chat broken by laughter. Minutes passed. Why is she taking so long? He was considering barging in when he heard footsteps, sandals on marble floor and papery chiffon slashing against swift legs. A woman came through the door, dressed in a blue sari.

'Please come inside,' she said with a welcoming smile. The eyelashes flickered as she swept an arm gracefully towards an inner chamber.

'Is Manju coming?'

'Manju is not here sir, but there are others. You will not be disappointed.'

'Why, where is she?'

'We haven't seen her for two months. But we have other girls. Please sit down and I will call them. Will you like a drink while you wait?' Like Abida Bai she had the confidence of an old nobility.

'No drink… I want Manju.'

'I agree with you, Manju is a charming girl, and I am not surprised you want her, but as I explained she is not available today…'

'Are you sure she is not here?' Tarun raised his voice.

'Sir….'

'Call Abida Bai, I want to talk to her.'

'Abida Bai is busy. we cannot disturb her. But I am here for you.' She came closer, flicking her eyelashes and the sari top slipped from her shoulder.

Tarun felt his spirit dissolving into thin air. He knew then they were telling the truth but wasn't ready to accept. 'No, I want Manju. I know she is here.'

'Sashi, can you come here for a moment.' She addressed someone he could not see.

The young girl who had shown him in, entered the room. 'Yes madam.'

'Call them,' she said with a slight flick of the head and began adjusting her sari, now appearing preoccupied with other thoughts.

Tarun assumed she was sending for more girls to make him change his mind. Do they think I am a fool? But he wasn't expecting to see two men in starched khaki shirts, as they rushed in and stood to attention.

'Show him out Bahadur. I have given him enough of my

time,' she said with a nod of the head, and strode away briskly without a backward glance, the chiffon sari swishing against the legs as before.

He stared at the departing figure, wanting to scream obscenities.

'Come with me sir.' One of the men took Tarun's arm.

'Don't touch me?'

'This way.'

'I will tell Abida Bai…'

'Yes, sir.… but first come this way.'

22

'It's a major project,' Sameer Dalal said and gave each face a sharp-eyed scrutiny. On the table was a large sheet of paper with detailed diagrams, figures, and instructions. He had appointed Baldev Singh as project manager, a broad-shouldered turbaned man with a booming voice which overwhelmed the air when he spoke. Tarun was the assistant along with two temporary recruits, Rakesh, and Bhagu.

'Any mishaps and be ready for a kick in the arse,' Sameer said, slapped the table with both hands, 'now let's get cracking.'

They worked silently, drilling, and digging out old wires, making noise, and spreading clouds of dust. At midday Sameer announced, 'all right boys, half hour lunch break.'

The air filled with the smell of hot chicken, dhal, onions, roti, Sameer had ordered from the dhaba next door.

'*Oi, Oi,* Tarun, have some chicken,' Rakesh said, smacking his greasy fingers, '*wah*, what tasty.'

Tarun rolled a roti with lemon pickle. 'You know I am vegetarian,' he said with a mouth full.

'No wonder you are such a weakling, like a puppy,' Baldev said, regarding Tarun with a smile, 'as for me if I don't get meat with my roti at least once a day, I cannot function.'

Sameer Dalal cut in, 'I am thinking of becoming a vegetarian like Tarun.'

Eyebrows rose all around, for no one believed Sameer could give up meat.

'Why do you want to become vegetarian?' Baldev said.

'I saw a tiger kill another tiger.'

'Is that because the second tiger was refusing to become vegetarian?'

A burst of laughter.

'Shut up all of you. Let me explain,' Sameer said, 'last Sunday I took the family to the zoo. Children wanted to see the big cats, lions, tigers, cheetahs. We walked over to the tiger enclosures just as they were about to feed the animals. And then the zookeepers arrived. I expected them to bring meat ready to eat. But no, the jokers had a goat, a live goat. They opened the trap door and pushed it inside. *Bahanchot*, it was shocking to see the unfortunate thing bleating as it ran to cower in a corner of the cage. Horrible. When we complained to the staff, why was the goat not butchered beforehand, they said there was no time for all that, they were too busy….'

'*Arre bap re*,' Baldev said, bringing his hands together as if squashing a watermelon, 'they must have made mince of it.'

'Yes,' Sameer continued, 'do you know what was surprising. The tigers did not pounce on the goat at once. First, they sniffed the frightened animal. *Sniff, sniff, sniff,* like dogs after a bitch and then they pounced. The quickest of the three managed to grab the head in its jaws and tried to run away with it. It's my trophy, and I am not sharing it. The other male was not giving up. He tried to snatch the goat. *Baas* a fierce battle began, *Dhoom, dhaam, dhoom*, dust flying everywhere and blood.'

'Were they Bengal tigers?' Tarun asked.

'Bengal tigers, Punjab tigers, what does it matter,' Sameer said with a sneer, 'the thing is they were fighting as if they were prepared to die for the miserly piece of meat. And then one of the tigers stopped suddenly and dropped to the floor. The chest heaving, thump, thump, thump, the mouth was open wide. And then… and then… after a while it stopped.'

'It died?'

'Yes. We realised it had died when the zookeepers rushed in and started erecting a tarpaulin curtain around the enclosure.'

'What about the goat?'

'Ripped apart. One leg here and another over there.'

Rakesh let out a long burp and said haughtily, '*Hoi, hoi,* that's what tigers do in the wild – they fight. That is no reason to become vegetarian, is it?'

'Not the tiger,' Sameer said, 'it was the goat. Its eyes. I have never seen such terror in an animal. Now whenever I see mutton on a plate, I see those eyes.'

They fell silent, while Baldev ate a chicken leg, sucking

and smacking noisily.

'I know Mr Puri. He knows everything about tigers,' Tarun announced, 'I am sure he would know why the tiger died.'

'Who is Puri?'

'He is a vet, and a director of Delhi Zoo.'

'Yes, yes, you know all the big people,' Rakesh said smirking, 'you also know Dilip Kumar. Don't you Tarun?'

'Yes, yes, he does,' Bhagu added, 'he also knows Raj Kapoor.'

'John Wayne also.'

'Why don't you ask this Puri why their goats are so ferocious that they terrify the tigers to death.'

More laughter.

Humiliated Tarun got up and went to the outer room. He poured himself a glass of water and stamped his foot in the fallen plaster. Dust rose in a thick cloud. He watched it disperse and settle down. He stamped the foot again, harder this time. The dust rose in a cloud, but no higher than the previous time.

After lunch Sameer, Bhagu, and Rakesh went back to the office.

Baldev began whistling as he worked. 'Where are you from?' he asked Tarun.

'Lyallpur.'

'Oh, from Pakistan, refugees, eh. I am from Srinagar.'

'Oh, I see,' Tarun said drily, in no mood for idle chatter.

'Are you *brahmin* or *kshatriya* caste?'

'*Kshatriyas*.'

'We are *Ramgharia* tarkhan.' He did a wood sawing

gesture with the hand.

'If your people were carpenters, what are you doing with this *bijli, shijli*, business,' Tarun said pointing at the consumer unit on the wall, cables trailing haphazardly out of it.

'What kind of logic is that? Because my ancestors were carpenters, I must be one too,' he said.

They worked in silence for a while.

'Have you been to England?' Baldev asked.

'Why are you asking foolish questions?' Tarun said.

'I have… I have been to London,' Baldev said and pointed a screwdriver towards the ceiling as if London was somewhere up there.

Tarun caught a whiff of cigarette smoke.

Bharat Sawhney, the barrister, was scanning the room, from floor to ceiling. 'How much longer?' he asked.

'Two more days, sir. After that you can bring in your desks and cabinets,' Baldev replied and moved sharply to the newly fitted sockets and switches. He flicked a ceiling light on and off and made a face as if it was an object of wonder.

'Are you sure about that?'

'Oh yes sir, maximum four.'

'That means eight,' Bharat Sawhney said nodding knowingly, 'I know you people …. Anyway, I heard someone has been to London. Which of you two?'

'Er, I have been to London,' Baldev said.

Tarun glared at Baldev. The rascal is lying.

'What were you doing there?'

'Wasting my father's money.'

'Meaning what?'

'He had me admitted to London School of Economics. Put me on the ship and said, son when you come back you will be a big man with a bright future. But I came back as a small man without qualifications.'

'Why? You must have done well at school to get admission to London School of Economics.'

'No sir, I cheated in my school exams, made my father believe I was a genius. The only thing I learned in three years in London was the art of chasing girls. As soon as I arrived in London, I cut off my hair, put away the turban, started dressing smart, I even let people believe I was Italian, and changed my name from Baldev to Bill.'

Bill – Bill Singh Dhillon? Tarun chuckled to himself, still not convinced this man was telling the truth.

'I know what you are thinking,' Baldev said, 'but it is true, and I ended up getting married. Even in that I failed, because when my father died unexpectedly, and when the money stopped coming my wife left me. She said she didn't want to live in poverty.'

The barrister lowered himself on a box and lit another cigarette. 'What was your father's occupation? It is expensive to send someone to study abroad.'

'We are from Kashmir sir. My father was an influential man. He worked for Maharaja Hari Singh Dogra, as a *vazeer* and sidekick. He knew people in the right places and got things done. But when he died, everything went with it. No money and no influence. I had to come back home with my son.'

'Oh, you had a son from the girl you married in

London,' the barrister cried, '*wah*, how exciting.'

'No sir, it was not like that. I had not informed my family, nor sought their permission to marry an English girl. They were furious when they saw the little boy who did not look Indian. They said I had disgraced the family. What will Maharaja Hari Singh say when he hears about this. I reminded them of Hari Singh's wives and girlfriends. Why do you think he goes to London every few months? But that is different, they said, he is the Maharaja. A Maharaja can have hundreds of girlfriends, but I cannot have even one, I said. My grandmother slapped me, and mother ordered me to apologise. So, I left the house with my son, determined never to go back.'

The barrister tapped the cigarette with his forefinger to dislodge lengthening ash.

'I left Srinagar and came to Delhi. With nowhere to live we ended up on the street, sleeping here and there, begging for food.' He cupped a hand, acting out a beggar's pathetic gesture, 'we had a terrible time, people spitting, accusing me of abducting a foreigner's child. They said I was training the child to become a beggar. When I said he was my son, they became even more abusive. Police were picking me up, child abduction is a serious crime they said, and they would beat me unless I gave them money. I could see my son was suffering. He had no friends to play with, only a street dog who had more fleas than hair on its body. The worst was when the other beggars tried to steal my son. I fought them off, but it left me devastated. Next day we found the dog dead, its throat slit.'

The barrister made a hard face. 'Throat slit?'

'The beggars did it as revenge. That is when I decided I had to get out of there, or we would not survive more than a day or two. I went to see my father's youngest brother who was living in Delhi itself, near Greater Kailash. He was shocked. He said he had no idea I was homeless. You stay with me until you have sorted yourself out, he said. He had a good business going, working as an electrical contractor for the government. He offered to teach me what he knew.'

'So, you became an electrician.'

'Yes, sir. I try my best to be as good as him.'

'He was a good man, your uncle.'

Baldev nodded. 'Yes, he was an exceptionally good electrician too, one of the best in Delhi. He was in great demand by the English sahibs who wanted to upgrade their bungalows. But his problem was *daru*. He drank too much. That's what killed him.'

'And you took over his business.'

'No sir, I didn't take his business, but I took something else... I married his wife.'

'You did what?... you married your aunt, your *chachi*,' the barrister cried.

'Let me explain, sir. As I told you this uncle was the youngest of all my father's five brothers and sisters. He was only a little older than me, about six years and his wife was three years my senior. They did not have children. I found out the reason for it later, but that is another story. Anyway, he was thirty-one years old when he died.'

'*Phew*, that's an early age to die.'

'You are right there; an early age. He used to pick fights with people when drunk. But to wrestle with someone when you have consumed half a bottle of whiskey is bad for your health. This time unfortunately he did not recover from the injuries. And his poor wife, twenty-eight years old. What future is there for widows in our country? To live the rest of your life alone, with not even a child to look after you when you are old. That's the reason I decided to marry her.'

'*Woh*, this fellow is quite a character. One could author a book about him,' the barrister said turning to his assistant, a young man with a flat face and diminutive figure, who had drifted in from the adjoining office and was listening with amused interest.

The assistant nodded. 'You are right, certainly a book material. Sir, can I ask him why his uncle and aunt didn't have children?'

'Yes, Sunil, you can ask him. Why not.'

Baldev did not wait for them to ask the question. 'The thing is my uncle... he... he... my uncle liked boys only... if you know what I mean. I only found out after we got married. The wife told me she was still a virgin; no man had touched her.'

They fell silent. People have all the luck, Tarun thought. I have been looking for a wife for so long – he has been married twice already, even with his big ugly belly and massive turban.

'Where is your son now?' Sunil asked.

'Son?' Baldev said and looked away with an uncomfortable shake of the head.

He is hiding something, Tarun assumed.

Baldev slapped his neck and rubbed the skin as if bitten

by mosquitoes and his bushy eyebrows met in the centre capping the nose.

Hawk-eyed barrister, picking up the signal, said cocking a finger, 'are you telling us the truth, or a wild story concocted in your head?'

'Absolutely telling the truth sir, everything, except one small falsehood.' He brought the forefinger and thumb together to indicate the falsehood or fib was no bigger than a pea. 'Yes sir. I have already told you my name is Baldev Singh. But what I haven't told you is that my father's name was Balvinder Singh and my grandfather was Balbeer Singh.'

'All that is very well, good man, but what are you getting at?'

'What I want to say is this: Balvinder Singh was sent to London to study economics and Baldev Singh was the name given to his son, half Indian and half English.'

'Fuck me,' the words slipped out of the barrister's mouth, 'are you saying you are not Baldev Singh?'

The sikh shook his turbaned head, first yes and then no.

'Are you or are you not Baldev Singh?' the barrister cried, rocking his shoulder in exasperation, and exchanged glances with his assistant to say this guy is a nutcase.

'I am Baldev Singh sir. But I am not the father that you think I am. I am the little foreign boy who the beggars tried to steal.'

'Fuck me,' the barrister swore again as he stubbed the cigarette butt into an ashtray Sunil was holding up dutifully.

Tarun got up and looked out into the street. Is this

person who he says he is. One thing is certain, this man is an electrician and an employee of Dalal & Co (Electrical Contractors). But what is his name?

'Do you believe him?' the barrister whispered to his assistant.

Sunil rocked his head in a non-committal way, not wishing to contradict the boss and said with a hand covering the mouth, 'sir, there is something about him. If you look carefully, he appears half and half, an Anglo Indian.'

'I am the Anglo-Indian boy,' Baldev said, guessing correctly what they were whispering, 'the only falsehood is that I told you the story from my father's point of view. That's all.'

'All right,' the barrister said, adopting a posture as if they were in a court of law, 'I want you to list the places you have lived in London. But beware I know London well since I have lived there myself.'

'That is easy sir, we used to live in a place called Ealing.'

Barrister Sawhney contemplated for a moment. 'All right, tell me where in Ealing.'

'I was young when we left London. I can only say what I learned from my father. I was born in Perivale hospital, and he used to talk about streets called Grosvenor Road, Sydney Road, and a pub called Grosvenor Arms or Head, something similar, which he said was like a second home for them.'

Barrister's eyes opened wide. 'I used to live in Ealing too. I studied Law in London.'

'*Oi, bale, bale*. If my father were alive, you would talk for hours,' Baldev said, appearing relieved.

'When did he die?'

'Ten years ago.' The sikh shifted the body weight from one leg to the other. 'There is one more thing, sir.'

'What?'

'You mentioned earlier about this being a book writing material. I agree with you there. That is why I am writing a biography of my father right now, from a first-person perspective.'

'Writing a book? An electrician. You're trying to make a fool of us,' Sunil said, narrowing his eyes.

'That is correct. I am an electrician. The fact is I am self-educated. It is not impossible, is it?'

The barrister chuckled, releasing smoke from his mouth in short bursts. 'You are an amazing man. I don't know what to make of you. Do you write in Hindi or Gurumukhi?'

``Actually, I write in English, queen's English,' Baldev replied, this time in English, in an accent suffused with his native tongue Punjabi, but clear enough to understand.

Sunil and the barrister exchanged glances and Tarun said, '*wah*, you can speak English.'

23

Pyari's small house was on the outskirts of the town. Open wasteland dotted with small farms on one side, a busy highway a short distance away. Buses and trucks roaring past, competing with screams of children playing on an open plot. Nearby four or five goats were grazing in the thicket. On the other side of a ditch was the frame of a house under construction, with metal bars sticking out like tall reeds. Even here, amid slum dwellings they are building houses, Tarun observed. Trudging cautiously, head down, he approached the small house, no bigger than a village hut. The yard door was slightly ajar. He peeked inside. A path led to an inner courtyard. A young mango tree stood at the centre, its branches throwing heart shaped shadows on compacted mud flooring. Two black goats were resting in the shade of a string cot. A hand pump at one end, a set of heavy grinding stones covered in powdery flour stood embedded to the ground. A typical village scene, one he was familiar with in his younger days, but not since they had arrived in Malviya Nagar. He flinched seeing an old woman crouched before a brazier trying to light a fire with a bundle of twigs. She was tiny and emaciated, a brown leathery creature, so decrepit she could be hundred years old. Pyari had said her mother had died young. Who is this woman?

'You are looking for her?' the woman said. Though her voice was high-pitched and rusty there was purpose and life in it, and she did not raise her head or turn it his way. Tarun sensed she was younger than she appeared.

Who else will I be looking for? The only thing that was giving him a sense of purpose was the idea of Manju, her sudden disappearance. And his desire to find her. The thought was itching at him – has something bad happened to her – again, and again – perversely, as if bearing down on a rotten tooth. He had tried not to think of her, wipe the face from the memory board. But it was a failure. Around and around turned his mind in the same well-trodden groove.

'What do you mean… looking for who,' Tarun said.

She raised the veil over her head revealing henna dyed flat hair. 'How often I must tell you she has gone back to her man?'

'Who has gone back?' Tarun said, and instantly felt his lips drying up.

'The girl – aren't you looking for her?'

'What's her name?'

She looked at him scornfully, as if he had hurled a cheap insult at her. A mole on her forehead caught his attention. It had a small tuft of black hair growing on it, like a tiny shrub in the vast expanse of a desert.

He guessed she was referring to Manju and the people looking for her were Abida Bai's men, desperate for her to return to work, to earn them money, which he assumed was substantial.

A long silence followed. Tarun did not know what to say, how to explain he was looking for Manju.

'O babu, what do you want then?' she said and blew at the fire, making it come alive with a thrum. Smoke rose in thick bursts as she blew repeatedly until satisfied the fire had caught. She picked up an aluminium pot and set it on the stove. Once done she sat back on her heels with a sigh, to wait for it to boil.

'Where is she. I want to help her,' Tarun said.

'She is not here,' she said. A note of acquiescence crept in her voice.

'Where will I find her?'

She raised the lid off the pot, clanked it back down again and finally turned to face him, appraising him up and down. 'Who are you?'

How could he tell her who he was? He dares not reveal his name in case it reaches Pyari's ears. That would be a major scandal, for she was bound to tell Pabiji. 'Have you heard? Your son has been chasing my daughter,' she would say with a cruel mocking smile. He could hear the laughter, the teasing and taunting from nephews and nieces, and what of the brothers. Have you no shame, they would say, having an affair with the sweeper's daughter, bringing the family's reputation down into the gutters. What face will I present to society? Pabiji will wail, beating her chest. What if they find out the sweeper's daughter is also a dancing girl in a brothel? Tarun thought.

'I want to help her,' he said.

'You want to help her then get her away from that man,' the old woman said.

'Who is the man?'

'Babu two years he had been away, no house and abode, suddenly comes back from God knows where, and demands she live with him. Yes, that one. He beats her.' She did a slapping gesture with her bony fingers.

'Where will I find her?'

She did not reply but broke some more twigs and pushed them in the fire. Smoke rose again, bending to the wind.

'How can I help if you don't tell me where to find her.'

'You can find her here. She comes early in the morning.'

'What time in the morning?'

'At six. She only stays an hour.'

'That early, no way,' he cried. He knew everyone would be in at that time of the morning, including Pyari.

'You do not have to come inside. I will ask her to meet you at the top of the road.'

'I will come. You make sure she will be there to meet me.'

'All right, but you will have to be careful,' she said.

'What do you mean?'

'Don't let him see you,' she said in a tone of voice, which implied great danger.

Before leaving he handed her a set of six red glass bangles tied together with strings and wrapped in green crepe paper. 'Give her this, she will know who I am.'

24

At the ration shop Tarun joined the long queue, rolled up cloth bags in his hand. He watched as two bare-chested coolies, dripping with sweat, were unloading wheat and sugar from a truck. Stabbing huge metal hooks into the gunny sacks and carrying the load on their backs to the rear and laying them down in neat rows, like dead bodies in a morgue.

The banya, his body coated in grain dust as if he had taken a dive in a grain silo, was sitting by massive scales attached to the ceiling with chains and pulleys. He was weighing the grain and unceremoniously dropping the produce in cloth bags held open by customers.

He saw Tarun, and without a word began weighing the wheat. He looked up at the pointer at the top of the scale, added more grains to the bowl and flicked his head, asking Tarun to open his cloth bag. Tarun said, 'I want one extra seer today.'

'Why didn't you say that before?' Banya barked and grudgingly drove the scoop into the sack by his side, 'you are not the only customer here. Can you not see, there are so many people waiting behind you?'

'I have only asked for a seer, not your whole shop,' Tarun said.

Someone in the queue spoke up, 'don't be so rude. Give the man what he wants.'

'Who said that?' Banya yelled angrily, looking over Tarun's shoulders, 'go away, you won't get any ration today.'

'What do you mean? I have a ration card here' The man waved a tattered brown card in the air. 'Issued by the government. Not your grandfather.'

'Saala, gandu,' banya swore under his breath and began weighing sugar for Tarun.

Outside the shop the grain truck was rolling away. A sprinkle of wheat marked the spot where it had stood. A man was collecting the spilled grain into a Dalda tin. The truck took off and he ran after the truck, presumably to its next destination. Tarun looked on feeling sorry for the man. He would have offered him a handful of his own grain. But the poor fellow was already halfway up the road, running on his bendy legs. It reminded him of a scene he had witnessed before. It was the middle of the day. So hot even the tarmac on the road was melting. He saw a young boy in short pants following a bullock cart transporting coal. This boy, oblivious to everything, trudging bare feet, was keeping low so the coal merchant could not see him. Every now and then a piece of coke would slip off the cart. The boy would rush to pick it up and stash it in a cloth bag. He was scavenging coal so the family would have a fire to cook the evening meal, Tarun assumed. He had watched helplessly, with a heavy heart, as the bullock cart and the boy turned a corner and were no longer in view.

With the bags of sugar and wheat in each hand, exhausted, he turned into his lane and instantly noticed a police jeep parked in front of the house. In all the years they had lived in Malviya Nagar, not once had he seen a policeman or a police vehicle in their street. Though police often went to the run-down dwellings behind the market where the locals were mostly Muslim and the poor. It was also the place where Ram Lal had his milk depot.

Even before he had opened the gates, walked up to the front door, he had a sense of danger ahead.

He dropped the bags and pushed the door open lightly.

A silent cry leapt out of the throat, and he felt the quality of air thicken. The face he was seeing was Mohindra Pal's. The man was sitting upright on a chair, arms folded against the chest, the oily flat hair sitting on the head like a topee. On his right were two men in police uniform. Pabiji, Savitri and Dev were sitting on the divan bed. Stern and unyielding faces. Everyone started speaking, simultaneuously, except the policemen. Voices began bombarding his brain, jumbled, making no sense.

Pabiji was wailing, 'kaka what have you done, kaka what have you done!' Dev, springing off the divan, waving the hands frantically, 'Tarun don't open your mouth, say nothing, don't open your mouth for God's sake.' Savitri was yelling too, 'Tarun you don't say anything until Kanta's son is here. I have sent Padma to fetch him.' Mohindra Pal springing up and down, screeching, rubbing his hands frantically on the thighs. 'What are you people doing? I have brought Sergeant Rakesh Gupta here to question Tarun about my daughter. You should let him do his job.'

In fits Tarun absorbed what was going on. And then a frightening thought entered his head. Is Sangeeta dead? Murder or suicide? He looked at Sergeant Rakesh Gupta. The man was sitting impassive, arms folded across the lap, as if he had nothing to say, that he was merely an observer. His uniform was a size too small, the stomach flesh rolling over the trouser belt.

'Do your job sergeant. I order you to arrest him. Take him to the station for questioning,' Mohindra Pal said, his dark face turned purple.

The sergeant uncrossed his arms and shook his head slowly. He appeared so courteous, so upstage in behaviour, he could have come to invite them home for tea and biscuit. This politeness, civility, scared Tarun more than outright rude and rough behaviour that he expected of them.

'Pal sahib, the thing is like this,' the sergeant said, 'there is no evidence to link this man to any crime until we find your daughter. I cannot arrest someone on a whim. But if you give me time, I will speak to him to see if he can help us with our enquiries. But it must be in private.'

Surprised, Tarun scrutinised the sergeant's face, looking for evidence of double speak. But he appeared sincere.

The sergeant turned to Savitri. 'Is there anywhere in the house I can talk in privacy.'

Tarun's heartbeat picked up again. He didn't want to be alone with the sergeant, fearing he might say or do something incriminating. The only safe way, he thought, was to come out with it in public. A voice in the head shouted caution. If they don't know, why tell them anything and complicate matters.

'No, he will only talk in the presence of a lawyer,' Dev interjected, 'I let you in the house purely as a polite gesture. You do not have an arrest warrant...'

Pabiji, who was silent so far, erupted with rage. 'We are a decent family, Pal-ji, never in our entire life have we had any dealings with the police. There has never been any need for them to come to our house. What have you done? This is so shameful. My son is a simple person. He has never done anything immoral or illegal in his life. He is not capable of it, I tell you.'

'*Hanh*, Mataji, I agree with you,' Mohindra Pal replied, 'you all are decent folks. I have no quarrel with you. And your son Tarun. When he was working for me, I had no problem with his work, even though he was slow to learn. Outwardly, he looks so innocent. But who can tell what goes on inside somebody's head? How could I have known that he was scheming something so evil.'

'What evil has he done? You haven't told me.'

The front door opened. No one noticed Mrs. Sharma as she stood at the threshold, inquisitive searching eyes, observing the drama. Savitri shot her a warning signal: go away, now is not the time. Mrs Sharma raised a hand, feigned surprise, hitched the sari above her ankles and left.

'What evil deeds my brother has done? Your daughter has run away from home, and you are accusing him of her disappearance. Is he hiding your daughter in his pocket?

What will he gain by it? Have you considered that she may have been unhappy at home? No, instead you accuse him of abducting her without any proof....' Savitri said it all in one breath, and then gasped for air.

Mohindra Pal had pushed his head back and shut his eyes while she was speaking.

'This is outrageous,' he said, 'no, it is nothing like that. My daughter was happy at home. She had everything she wanted, our love, money, and freedom.'

'Then why has she run away?' Savitri said, rolling her hand feverishly to make her point.

The room was ablaze, everyone talking about Tarun but not at him as if he were a mere bystander, an uninterested party. He was still standing by the glass cabinet, the shoulder brushing the calendar.

He felt so exasperated and angry, he leapt forward as if he had seen a blinding flash of light. 'Stop it, stop it,' he screamed, 'I will tell you what you want to know.'

The room fell silent.

'No, Tarun, no.' Dev lowered his face on his palms. Mohindra Pal swung around facing Sergeant Rakesh Gupta with a look that said: See, see, he is guilty.

Sergeant gestured to Mohindra Pal to calm down. 'Sit down,' he said to Tarun, 'let's talk.'

Tarun stayed standing.

'Tell me now,' he said in a measured tone like a headmaster to his pupil, 'Have you ever been in contact with Mr Pal's daughter Sangeeta?'

'Yes,' Tarun said, not hesitating, and looked around the room. Pabiji was praying with eyes closed. Savitri was staring murderously at him.

'Where did you meet her?' Rakesh Gupta asked.

'In a bookshop.'

'Good. I am only asking these questions for Palji's satisfaction and for yours. I am confident you won't hide anything. Now tell us what you talked about?'

'What was there to talk about. She was talking about books and her favourite authors. We were there only for ten fifteen minutes. That is all.'

'Did you meet again?'

'Twice more, by the trees on Saket Road.'

'So, you talked about books again?'

'That and other things.'

'What other things?' the sergeant asked.

Tarun did not reply. He did not see why that was relevant.

'Did you touch her at any time?'

Dev yelled, 'you don't have to answer that, you don't have to answer that.'

'No, I never touched her,' Tarun replied, 'we just talked, that's all.'

'Just talked, says he just talked,' Mohindra Pal exploded, 'I don't believe it.'

'You want to hear more? I will tell you. It was her. She sent notes with her brother asking me to meet her. She wanted to apologise for her father's behaviour. She was very unhappy about this and other things.'

Mohindra Pal stood up as though a thousand volts had passed through him. The chair screeched. Like a chained animal he walked a small circle and then sat down again.

The sergeant waved a hand, urging Tarun to keep speaking.

'You want me to tell you more. Then hear this. He is not Sangeeta's father.'

Savitri gasped. 'Tarun what are you saying.'

'They are step brother and sister. Sangeeta's mother was a maid in their house. She was… she was…' He was about to say forced to have sex but could not bring himself to utter the words in the presence of his mother and sister. 'His father did something to the maid, and that's how Sangeeta was born.'

Pabiji stood up and left the room with hands on her ears.

The sergeant nodded. 'Did she indicate at any time she was going to leave the house, or that she was unhappy about anything?'

'She was unhappy all right,' Tarun replied.

'What makes you believe that?'

'She said she was treated badly, kept at home like a prisoner, not allowed to do what she wanted.'

'So, that's why she wanted to leave home?'

'I suppose so. But she never said anything about leaving.'

'Did you ever suspect she might.'

'No.'

Sergeant stood up as if he had heard enough. He brushed the seat of his pants, pulled the fabric free from the crack of his buttock. 'Now we have to be back at the station,' he said to the assistant.

'But… but…' Mohindra Pal ran after them. He looked as if the cogs inside him had broken, and he was slowing to a stop.

They ate dinner in silence. The only sounds were the ladle knocking the pot, scraping spoons on metal plates, gurgle of water going down someone's gullet. Even the escape of steam from a fluffed chapati fresh off the hotplate was audible.

The sacks of wheat and sugar lay forgotten where Tarun had left them and Padma had returned without Kanta's son, the lawyer. He is away in Ghaziabad, not expected back till late, she had said.

Tarun's hands shook horribly. He tore a piece of chapati and dipped it in *matar paneer* curry before transferring it to the mouth. He had felt a level of satisfaction, elation even, for summoning the courage to reveal Pal family secrets to the public. Now remorse had set in. Was it wise to humiliate Mohindra Pal like this? What if he would seek revenge? There was no knowing what he could do.

Tarun could see Pabiji was too shocked to say anything, and Savitri was furious with him, for he had fraternised with the enemy and kept it a secret.

Tarun unrolled the bed in the front yard and lay his head on a pillow. He looked up at the sky lit to a chemical incandescence, the stars appearing too close as if one could pluck them with a hook on a long pole. The green across the road deserted, considered unsafe at night by the residents of this backwater of Malvyanagar. By day men sat in the shade chatting, boys stopped for a game of marbles or *guli danda*.

Early next morning, he rolled up the bedding, changed noiselessly into a fresh shirt and trouser and left home while others were still asleep.

❀

At the crossroad, an old peepal tree stood in derelict splendour, like a forgotten ancient monument. Dusty yellow green leaves. A flock of chirpy parakeets were flitting around in the dense canopy. Chained to its enormous trunk, on which someone had carved a name and obscenities, was an abandoned street hawker cart dotted with bird droppings. A dog was asleep under it, curled up into a ball. At the crossing were giant hoardings of Hindi films and skin lightening creams promising instant results. The moist air, smelling of early morning dew. An old man in night pyjamas appeared from a bye-lane, walking briskly in a straight line. Another man and a woman in salwar-kameez joined him. Tarun recognised them as the early morning walkers headed for the track by the pond. Pyari's house was less than a quarter of a mile away.

Tarun glanced at his watch. The time was fifteen minutes past six. Why is she not here? Is she going to let me down again?

He saw a female figure emerging from a side lane. His heart fluttered. He strode earnestly towards her and smiled.

She did not smile back. 'You should not have come,' she said, stopping a distance from him. He guessed she did not want to appear too intimate should anyone be watching.

'Your grandmother has told me everything.'

'She is not my grandmother. She is an aunt. The old woman talks too much,' she said.

Unlike their earlier meeting, her pretty face appeared sober, betraying a trace of anxiety in the black flickering eyes. Tarun wondered how much trouble she was in. In what way he could help.

'I can't stay long,' she said softly, 'why did you want to see me?'

'Why have you stopped going to Abida Bai,' he said.

She took a sharp breath. 'How do you know?'

'I know... I went there. They said you had not been there for two months. Anyway, I am here because I want to help you.'

'What for *babu*? I do not need help.' She sat down on a boulder under a tree.

'You don't have to pretend. Let me help you.'

'But *babu*, I am happy. I am genuinely happy,' she said and looked away into the field where a farm worker was poking the soil with a hoe.

'He beats you, doesn't he?'

She did not reply.

'You don't have to put up with it. If he troubles you, we can call the police. I know sergeant Rakesh Gupta at the station,' he said, hoping to impress her, that he knew people in high places.

'Police?' she said, 'what are they going to do? They never help us.'

'They will help, trust me, they will. I also know a good lawyer.'

'*Babu*, these police, and lawyers are for big people like you. Not for us poor. There is no justice for us.' She waved a hand at the slum dwellings, one of which was her mothers. 'Police only ever come here to arrest or to harass us.'

'But I am here.'

'O, *babu, babu,*' she said and shook her head and looked into his eyes, 'what are you doing here? Leave me be. And you know my reputation. What will your family say when they find out? Please go home.'

'I don't care what my family will say. I want you. Let us go away together, far away.' He surprised himself for saying it outright. His heart palpitated, overcome by an urge to say: I love you! I love you! I love you!

She placed a hand on the chest. '*Babu*, what are you saying?'

'Don't call me *babu*, I have told you before,' he said, and then the words flew out from quivering lips, 'I love you.'

'Don't do it. Please don't do it. It's not worth it,' she said as if she was terrified.

'I can't help it.' He came closer and placed his fingers on her shoulder. As if the touch was an electric shock, she winced and then began weeping.

Seeing her like this, so vulnerable, so human, so different from the self-assured girl he had met at Abida Bai's house, he felt a pang of guilt, as if it were he who had caused it. 'Stop,' he said urgently, 'don't cry, everything will be alright.'

She nodded, dabbing her eyes with a handkerchief. 'I have to go now,' she said after a while.

'All right, will you meet me here on Saturday?' he said.

'Yes.'

'We can go to the zoo.'

'Zoo.' She looked puzzled. 'Why zoo?'

'No one will know us there. We can see the Bengal tigers too.'

'Whatever you say.'

'Give me a smile.'

She forced a smile and a small chuckle.

'Aah, now you look even more beautiful.'

◆

Whistling, badly but contentedly, behind the municipal offices, Tarun took a shortcut through a narrow lane where monkeys were clambering up lampposts, into thicket of electric wires. A monkey with a baby on the back swung low and made a face at Tarun. 'Shooo, go away,' Tarun said, clapping, and pretended to pick up a stone from the ground.

He turned right into another lane and instantly came upon a barber's shack with a single table and chair. A cracked mirror hanging skewed on the grimy wall.

'Oi, wake up.' He poked the barber in the groin. The man was fast asleep on a mat under the table. 'I want a tattoo done.'

The man sat up with a start, ran two hands over his face as if scrubbing it clean and scrambled to his feet. 'Tattoo? Yes sahib, give me a minute.'

'Hurry up,' Tarun said, settling down on the chair and watching the barber, who also did tattoos, set up the equipment with its sharp needles and black ink.

'What will you like?' the barber asked, handing Tarun a piece of paper and a worn-out pencil only three inches long.

Tarun showed him the back of his right hand, 'I want

alphabets M A N J U engraved, one on each knuckle.' He tapped each of the bone joints of his right hand, and then began scripting the word MANJU on the paper. He had jotted down M and A, with unsteady hands. Halfway through N he put a cross over them and sketched the symbol for OM ॐ. 'I want this on the back of the hand. Just here and make it good.'

'Yes boss.' The barber raised the dangerous looking contraption coated in black ink.

'How long will it last?' Tarun asked, wincing as the sharp needle began prickling the skin.

'Until you wash your hands next.'

'What?' Tarun pulled his hand away. 'I am not paying you for a fake tattoo.'

The barber laughed. 'Babu, you asked a silly question, I gave a silly reply.' He grabbed Tarun's hand. 'You don't have to worry; my ink is permanent. It will be there even when your soul has gone to heaven and the body is lying on the funeral pier.'

'*Oi*, don't talk nonsense about funeral piers,' Tarun said, 'I am still young, not even married yet.'

'*Ohhh*, not married,' the barber cried, giving him a long stare and shook his head, admonishing him.

'Why are you looking at me like that?'

'I don't understand the new generation,' the barber said, 'putting off marrying for longer and longer, like it is fashionable.'

A man in orange kurta, long matted hair, and scraggly beard, came and sat down beside them.

'Oh, Swamiji, welcome, welcome,' the barber said, and

then with a twinkle in the eyes, 'haircut?'

The holy man glared at him making clear he didn't appreciate the joke and then turned to Tarun. 'Look into my eyes.'

Tarun returned the gaze, holding it steady for a moment and then chuckled. 'What kind of game is this?'

The swami kept his gaze firm and intense on Tarun's eyes, going deeper and deeper, as though he was able to penetrate the eyes and read Tarun's brain, the nerves, currents, and pathways, and interpret the signals.

Tarun sat still, uncomfortable, but feeling obliged to play the game.

'I foresee major upheaval coming in your life,' he said. The lips did not move, but the words came out clear, as if he was a ventriloquist.

The barber looked on, in awe of the swamy's enormous powers.

'Do you want to know?' the ventriloquist said.

'Tell, tell, Swamiji,' the barber cried, 'Swamiji is a learned man, he can tell the future.'

Tarun nodded. To say no would be going against the grain, he felt.

'Show me your hand,' Swamiji demanded, getting more assertive.

'Show, show;' the barber said.

Tarun put his palm out.

Swamiji snatched it with both hands, studied it from a distance and then up-close, he rubbed a finger on the crease lines as if checking they were permanent, all the while rocking his head. 'I will need your date, time and place of birth,' he said.

'What for? You are reading my palm only,' Tarun said.

'Then I can't vouch for accuracy.'

'Whatever little you want to tell, it's fine by me,' Tarun said.

Swami yanked Tarun's hand to his bearded face and spat on it, a yellowish blob of spittle. He rubbed his palm over Tarun's, spreading the spittle evenly, and then studied the hand again, deeply, from right and left angles. Finally, he said, 'you come from a good family, you have many brothers and sisters.'

'That is true,' Tarun said.

'You are in love with a girl.'

Tarun blushed. 'Will I be married?'

'I can't say for sure.' Swamiji said and then pressed a finger in the flesh here and there. 'Close your fist and open,' he said.

Tarun obliged.

Swamiji sprang upright and made a face as if he had seen something dark and foreboding.

'What – what do you see,' Tarun asked.

'I see death.'

'Death, whose death.'

'That I cannot say… but I see death.'

Tarun pulled his hand away. 'I don't want to hear anymore.'

The holy man looked at Tarun with wide-eyed horror. 'Death is a serious matter,' he said.

'But you said you can't tell me whose death,' Tarun said.

'It is not like that. I can reveal more but I will need more time and very, very deep concentration.' He swallowed hard and shut his eyes, as if in preparation for going into a trance. He inhaled deeply and released air through the mouth several times and then put his palm out. 'Place ten rupees here, son,' he said softly, as if it was all part of the act.

'Ten rupees,' Tarun cried in horror, 'I don't have that kind of money.'

The holy man came out of the trance and sat back looking the other way.

A long silence followed. A fly's dim whine surfaced on the air, like the sound of distant machinery. Tarun wondered why the holy man was not leaving.

Then the barber said, flicking his shoulders, 'give him something na. He must eat too.'

Tarun took out a few coins from his pocket and pushed them in the holy man's grimy hand. '*Wah, wah* Swamiji,' he said with a mocking chuckle, 'what a performance. I nearly believed you.'

However much his rational mind dismissed the prediction, there was a dark cave hidden away beneath his brain where the monsters slept, fears and nightmares chained up since childhood, but still with a residual power to instil dread.

Days passed. Tarun could not weed out the black seed of doubt which had already begun sprouting in his head.

❀

Baldev glared at him. 'Why do you look so happy?'

'I have reason to be happy.' Tarun replied and handed Baldev a glass of hot tea he had picked up on the way in. 'I want to tell you a secret. Only one other person knows about this.'

'Wait, wait, wait – don't tell me if you want it kept confidential, don't tell me. You know me, I am useless at keeping secrets.'

'I am in love with a girl.'

'*O bale, bale*, tell me more,' Baldev said, 'someone I know.'

Tarun told him about Manju, the meeting at Abida Bai's house.

'Oh, *teri ki*,' Baldev cried, eyes narrowing into a slit, 'you went there.'

'You know the place?'

'Who doesn't. Ask anybody about the *teen manzil* house they will either shut their faces, pretend they know nothing or run like scared rabbits. That is because they are embarrassed to admit they have been there or know someone who has. It's called *teen manzil* because of the three floors. In those days girls used to stand half naked at the windows and balcony. Englishmen used to go there too. Did you know that?'

'No,' Taru said feebly, 'I didn't know anything until Salim took me there.'

'The house belonged to a nawab who had other properties in the area. He left for Pakistan after the partition. But his sister refused to go. She runs the place now and has made it very exclusive. The girls are all high class… anyway tell me about your girl.'

Tarun told him everything, including about Pyari and the old woman.

Baldev made a face as though he could foresee trouble. 'Have you considered the consequences? Your family will never accept such a union.'

'I know all that,' Tarun said, 'but I must take her away to a safe place.'

'What is her caste?'

'They are chamar.'

'Oi *yaee, yaee, yaee*. Not only chamar but also a married woman.'

Tarun did not reply. The gravity of the situation was clear to him. The husband was a violent man according to the old lady. It hit him suddenly. What if the man came to the house in Malviya Nagar and created a scene? Pabiji would be furious. She would order Tarun to leave the house. 'You shameless creature, bringing disrepute to the family. What face will I show to society now? I might as well drown myself in a sip of water.'

The happy feeling, the thumping of the heart when you are in love took a nosedive, replaced with dread and disappointment.

'Do you think *vakeel* sahib will help me?' Tarun asked feebly.

Baldev stopped sketching a wiring diagram on the wall and tapped the pencil on his teeth, as if thinking. 'This is your personal matter. Is it not? What can a lawyer do?' he said.

'But her man beats her,' Tarun said.

'Think about it. How can a lawyer make someone stop

beating his woman? She must go to the police and lodge a complaint. Will she do it?'

She will not call the police Tarun knew, for she had already said so. He picked up the box of tools and started where he had left off the previous day, inserting cables in the channel he had already dug, ready to attach to the consumer unit. But he could not stay his mind. Nor was he able to steady his hands, longing for a potion to calm his nerves, and take away the worries.

He recalled the *holi* festival when he had inadvertently achieved such a state, drifting into carefree oblivion. Local youths were celebrating the festival in the park across their house, singing, dancing, and feasting into the night. The boys cornered him. 'Tarun brother, come, come, have a cold drink.' They handed him a glass of sweet sherbet. He accepted the drink, willingly, joining in the fun. How was he to know of the *bhang* in the milky beverage? Instead of sipping he had downed the whole glass in one go. The boys cheered and egged him to drink more. 'All right I'll have another, it is *holi* after all.'

A song from the film Taxi Driver was blaring from a loudspeaker. '*Jayen to jayen kahan*.' Drifting into the sentiment of the lyrics he began singing aloud, not caring who was listening. The lads were amazed. They had never seen Tarun get sucked into a free-for-all brouhaha. They sang along with him, ready to escort him home should he become too delirious or fall over.

After a while of singing and crooning he drifted to the street, bumping into people as he went. On the steps of a shop, he saw a little girl sitting alone. She was begging. Her small palm outstretched. He noticed she was looking at him. Though he was a short distance away, and there were others walking by, her teary round eyes were watching him, as if he were the only person in the world she could see.

He closed his eyes. When he reopened them, he found the space where the girl was sitting vacant. He looked around the street, desperately searching for the missing girl and then gave a long yowl, like a lovelorn jackal.

'What's up uncle?' The boys surrounded him.

'Where is the girl? I want to give her money,' he said, 'she was there just a minute ago.'

'What girl uncle. There is no girl here.'

He began weeping like a baby. 'Where is she? Where is she?'

The boys led him back to the park, into the eye of the festivity. 'Come on uncle, let's sing.' He drifted into fits of laughter and began miming the song.

Next morning, in the fog of light, a blurred vision, everything from the previous night reappeared as if projected on a movie screen: light, happy, and carefree, explosions, fireworks, drums, shrieks of laughter, feet thumping the ground, the little girl.

That was three years ago. He had never touched sherbet again.

'Pass me the claw hammer and run the cable to the next room,' Baldev said, and after a pause, 'go to the old woman, the aunt. She will tell you everything about the husband.'

'I was thinking the same,' he said. It was a lie. He was in no state to think straight. He held his face in his hands.

Why must a man take injustice lying down, take it hard and quiet. That's no way, no way at all.

He wished someone would hand him a glass of sherbet and not tell him of the added substance.

25

The cart was not there anymore. The dog he had seen previously now had a companion, a sickly brown mongrel with boils on the patchy skin. They were scavenging in the open gutter, flies hovering over them like moths attracted by light. Tarun ran a hand over his head, smoothing the glistening hair, which he had massaged with a generous dollop of Brylcreem. Hope she approves of this, he thought, and looked down at his legs, at Salim's suit trouser, to check the creases were in place. Brown leather shoes, polished with recently acquired tin of Kiwi beeswax. He had stashed fifty rupees in the shirt pocket, enough for entrance to the zoo, and for lunch. Make a day of it and call upon Jaiprakash Puri. The only regret he had; in the excitement he had forgotten to bring the Kodak Brownie camera.

He stepped back as a scooter rickshaw veered towards him, recklessly attempting to overtake a bicyclist with a large bale of cotton strapped to the rear, raising a cloud of dust. As the dust settled, a pleasant sight greeted him. With a start he began walking towards her, smiling. He searched for bangles on her wrists and the heart kicked in the cage catching a glint in the sun. She was wearing all six on the right wrist. Why not three on each? Was that a new trend?

Her walk was a little unsteady. Nerves, he assumed. Who would not be under the circumstances?

He took the final few steps gleefully as if to take her into his arms. But she stood back.

'I have come to tell you I cannot go to the zoo,' she said.

Hah a joke, he thought and threw his head with a chuckle.

'It's not right to meet like this,' she continued without acknowledging the smile or making direct eye contact.

His throat muscles contracted. 'I don't understand,' he said.

'I want you to go back home now,' she said. Her speech slurred, as if she had been crying.

'What's the matter,' he said, wanting to pull her close.

'I want you to go…' she said and raised her eyes to him.

He noticed her eyelids were heavy and her limp hand was searching for something to rest on like someone who has just woken from sleep. And then he saw her lips. They were off colour as if drained of blood.

'Manju,' he cried and grabbed her around the waist and felt her body go limp.

A boy stopped to stare.

'You, come here,' he said, 'do you know Pyari's house? Can you call someone?'

The boy backed away alarmed.

A man stopped his bicycle. 'Accident?'

'No, she has fainted. I need a taxi to take her to hospital. Can you help?' Tarun said, pleading, 'call me a taxi brother. God will be kind to you.'

'All right, wait here.' The man lowered the bike to the ground and ran to the crossing.

Tarun shifted Manju's weight to the other arm. The movement revived her. She opened her eyes, rolled the eyeballs. 'Manju, wake up?' he cried. But the eyes shut again, the head fell back. He didn't know how long they had been standing like this, like husband and wife embracing. It felt wrong, and he began construing scenarios. What if someone passing by recognises him? A neighbour, or even Dev or Pali. He thought of her husband and suddenly she felt unbearably heavy in his arms.

He heard the sound of pebbles crunching and swung his neck around. Is it the husband? A taxi halted on the gravel. The man with the cycle came running. He helped Tarun lay Manju's limp body on the back seat.

'Government hospital. Take the Kutchi Lane. Hurry,' Tarun instructed the driver, 'first stop there, at the brown door by the tree.'

He dashed in through the open door. The aunt was sitting by herself under a washing line.

'Manju is not well; I am taking her to the government hospital,' he said and started to back out.

'Meenju, where is she?'

She rose from the charpoy, laboriously, with a hand on each knee and hurried to the taxi, her bow shaped legs appearing to give in at each step. She saw Manju's prone body on the back seat, sighed and gave Tarun a harsh look, as if accusing him of a deliberate misdeed.

'I didn't do anything. She just fainted.' He protested. 'You very well knew I was meeting her here this morning, didn't you?'

Once on the way to the hospital he patted Manju's cheeks and attempted repeatedly to make her sit up. Her hand slipped to the side of the seat, and the bangles jingled. He brought the hand back up. The taxi's whine in low gear and the rocking motions lulled him into deep thoughts. What is all this about? He had left home optimistic, excited, anticipating a good day. Ever since meeting Jaiprakash Puri he had wanted to see the Bengal tigers. What better way than to take Manju with him, impress her with his knowledge of wild cats. He had discovered recently these animals can climb trees and swim too, a natural ability with which they are born.

'If you do not mind me saying so, she is suffering from dehydration. You should make her drink water,' the taxi driver said, speaking to the rear-view mirror.

Irritated that the driver had been watching him, he said firmly, 'pay attention to the road.'

'I know the signs of dehydration,' the driver said gravely, 'trust me this cannot wait. I can get you water.'

'All right, then get it.'

The driver stopped at a hardware shop and ran into a side lane. Back in two minutes. 'My cousin's house,' he said, passing a glass of water through the open window, 'try to make her drink *sahib*, soak a handkerchief and place it on her face, quickly, quickly.'

It was difficult to tell if water went down her throat, but

quite a bit dribbled down to the neck, as he held the glass to the mouth.

'Keep going, keep going.... now stop.'

Manju coughed feebly.

'Now hold the wet handkerchief to the face,' the driver said, and jumped back into the cab.

'It looks like the whole city has fallen ill,' Tarun said, seeing the number of people crowding the hospital entrance.

The driver chuckled knowingly. 'It's like this only every day, nothing new.'

The pandemonium, the shouts and screams, the harrowing cries of the sick and injured, the high stench of medicines, shook Tarun in the stomach. He too began to feel ill. An hour to register Manju, and then they shifted them to an equally crowded inner chamber, where they let her lie on a bench. Another hour passed. Tarun accosted an officious looking attendant in white shirt and a clipboard in his hand. 'What time the doctor will be here. She needs attention straight away,' he said.

The man glanced fleetingly at Manju. 'I agree with you.'

'Then do something,' Tarun screamed.

'I am just the office boy,' the attendant said irritably and moved on.

'It's no good,' said a man sitting on the bench, shaking his head in sympathy, 'your relative will be seen last.'

'Why? We are not the last to arrive.'

'Yes, but don't you know how the system works.'

'How does it work?'

The man slid his hand in the trouser pocket and jingled

few coins. '*Bhaijan*, give them money for tea and cigarette, *phatafut* your name will go to the top of the list. I came here at the same time as you, my mother is already with the doctor, the top doctor.'

'Who to give money to,' Tarun asked.

'That bald man in the office.'

Tarun walked to the office and hesitated at the door.

'Go in, go in, no need to knock,' the man said.

Tarun opened the door and went in. A round faced, oily skinned man was leaning back on his chair, surrounded by grim looking shelves stacked with tattered manila folders. 'My relative is extremely ill, she needs to be seen by a doctor urgently,' Tarun said and placed a half rupee coin on the table.

The man slammed the table. The coin jumped. 'Get out, get out,' he said, 'I am a hardworking man with twenty years dedicated service – yes twenty years – a wife and five children and mother-in-law to support.'

Tarun shuffled out of the office and returned to the bench.

'What did you offer him?' the man asked,

'Eight annas.'

'See that's the problem.' The man slapped his thigh, annoyed that Tarun had not followed his instruction. 'The going rate is one rupee.'

A woman opposite, regarded Manju's prone figure. 'What's the matter with your wife?' she asked.

'I don't know,' Tarun replied helplessly, 'I am trying to get a doctor to see her.'

'Listen to me now,' she said, like an old aunt giving

advice, 'she doesn't look well at all. Don't just sit there, talk to someone.'

A doctor in white coat, flanked by two nurses, happened to be passing by. 'Go and talk to that doctor. Go, go, go, hurry,' the woman said.

In a spontaneous reaction, he ran to the doctor and blocked his path. 'Sir can you please look at this lady. She is extremely ill,' he said, making his voice loud and firm, and directed the doctor's attention to the bench. 'We have been waiting for hours. Not even a nurse has seen her.'

'But this is not my department. You must wait for your doctor.'

'We have already been waiting. How much longer must we bear this.'

'He will come – he will come – that's all I can say.'

'He will come sometime today. But she needs attention now. It will be pointless after she is dead?' Tarun said firmly, emboldened by the supportive glances he was receiving from fellow relatives.

'All right show me the patient,' the doctor said, flaying his hands in exasperation.

'Here sir.' Tarun said, pointing at Manju who lay listless, foaming at the lips, hair plastered to the forehead. The doctor took Manju's wrist in his hand, studied her pale face. 'Is she your wife?'

Tarun hesitated. 'Err – yes, sir.'

'She should not be here. You should have taken her to the emergency department.' He instructed the nurses to call for a stretcher. 'To resuscitation, immediately, without delay. I will send Dr Biswas.' He touched Tarun's shoulder, a brief reassuring tap and marched off. As Tarun waited, relieved things were starting to move, an incident from the distant past came to the fore. A funfair in their hometown. He was on a wooden horse going around a central axis. Usha, who was about nine-years old, was sitting on another horse next to him. There was a sudden and loud crack, and then he found himself lying on the floor under the collapsing structure while Usha had gone on a little further and landed in the dust headfirst. His first instinct was to save his little sister who was howling, looking at him expectantly, as if he would come to her rescue.

Two porters arrived. With the help of the nurses, they transferred Manju to the stretcher. Tarun followed. Like a funeral procession they made their way silently through warrens of corridors to another part of the building, eventually to a women's ward. Patients lay in beds coughing, groaning, protesting. Others were still and silent, as if shocked by the grotesque display of pain and suffering. Relatives fussing and complaining. Stench of medicines in the air, reminding him of Dr Mallick's pharmacy.

He watched the nurses setting up blood pressure monitoring straps. A young man in white shirt arrived. His boots clicked smartly on the hard floor. He went straight to Manju's bed, lifted her eyelids, inserted a tube in her mouth, listened with a stethoscope, and fired instructions in medical jargon Tarun did not understand.

'Sir, wait outside, we will call you when we have something to report,' the nurse said, manhandling Tarun out of the ward.

Tarun gazed at Manju's very pale face one final time as

if it would be a long parting and returned to the waiting area. He blinked away a tear. An old man in white lungi cleared a space for him on the bench. He sat down, feeling very tired and hot.

He had sat there for an hour or more, dazed. He heard a voice that disconcerted him further. Pyari was shouting at a peon, 'my daughter… Manjula… where is she?'

'How am I to know your daughter? Am I God?'

'Her name is Manjula Dhonda.'

'*Arre wah, wah*, what a lovely name, but it still means nothing to me. I work in the pathology department.'

'Then where to find her,' Pyari screamed.

Tarun shrank further in the seat. He did not want to face Pyari, though she must have known who had brought her daughter to the hospital.

Hours elapsed. He had lost the concept of time, and could not bring himself to leave. He had to know the truth.

'*Babu, o, babu*, wake up.'

Tarun opened his eyes with a start. Pyari was standing over him, offering a glass of water. Her knuckled fingers around the base of the glass. He shot up erect, looked at her face to gauge if she was angry, distressed, or astonished to learn of his involvement with the daughter.

'Here drink this *babu*. It's been such a long day.'

He did not react. Was she blaming him?

'*Babu*, drink this,' she said a little more assertively.

He took it, realising how thirsty he was. 'How is she?' he asked.

She shook her head. 'Not good.'

'Not good?'

She stared at the ground.

'Haven't the doctors told you what's wrong? Why did she faint?'

'Yes *babu*,' she said with her hands placed on the head. The head shrank into the chest as though she had placed a heavy weight on it.

'If you know, why aren't you telling me?'

'Babu, you are a good man,' she said, 'why have you got involved with her.'

He said nothing. How could he say he had been to a brothel? The mere thought made him want to get up and leave. Did she know her daughter was a dancing girl?

'You better go home. You will achieve nothing by waiting here,' she said.

'But how can I go like this? I don't even know how she is.'

'Please listen to me *babu*,' she said, 'go home now. I will not say anything to Pabiji or anyone else.'

It was the way she said it. He knew instinctively she meant it.

'You are a good person, and you come from a respectable family. How can I hurt you or the family? Go home and everything will be alright.'

He nodded. 'But you haven't told me what really has happened to her.'

'What to tell you…' She bunched the fingers of her right hand and placed them on the lips and mouthed the word poison.

He had assumed it was heat stroke or something similar.

But poison? He felt dizzy suddenly as if the poison were in him too. 'Why?'

'What to tell you... that wretched girl...' She waved her hand. 'If that wretched girl dies it will be for the good, I tell you...' her voice turned shrill and loud, 'she has brought nothing but misery... my whole life.'

'*Shhh*, keep the voice down,' he said, 'let us go outside.'

They went and stood by the side entrance, under the shade of an overhanging canopy.

'How is she now?' he asked.

She pointed a finger deep into the throat. 'They inserted a tube in the stomach to suck everything out. She is sleeping now.'

'Then she will be alright.'

'Don't know *babu*. It's up to God.' She joined her hands together and looked up at the sky.

'She will recover. I am sure,' he said, 'where is her husband? Why isn't he here?'

'He will not come.'

'I was told he beats her often.'

She did not respond.

'Why don't you do something about it? She is your daughter.'

'What to tell you. She fights him too. Like cats and dogs. But how could I ask her to leave him.' She sighed deeply. 'She may not listen to me... but still she is my daughter. What life is there for a young woman without a husband in our society? Already my relatives laugh at me. What she needs is a good beating, they say it will straighten her, teach her to respect her husband.'

'That is very wrong,' Tarun said, 'beating never solves anything.'

'You understand these things. To tell you the truth I have suffered too. You can't even imagine how much. My husband was a bad man, a gambler and drunkard. He used to beat me, beat me, beat me. Babu, I have suffered. When Manju was thirteen years old, he died.' She squinted her eyes and looked to the left and right as if blinded by sunlight. 'I had to bring up three girls all by myself. The other two were no trouble, they were very obedient, and always listened to their elders. But Manju was terror from the very beginning, doing as she pleased, she would not listen to me or anyone else.' She wiped her face with the sari. 'There was no man in the house to discipline her. What could I do?'

Tarun looked back to the day he had first met her. She had not come across as a hard, treacherous woman.

Pyari continued. 'When she was seventeen years old, I got her married. I thought married life with children of her own would make her happy and she would settle down. I gave her a good wedding, gold braided saris, jewellery, everything. It made me bankrupt, but I did not care. I did not want to give her reason to complain. But do you know what that wretched girl did? Six months after the wedding she walked out on him. Left the poor boy.... She ran away with the tailor from the village. A *lafanga* who carried himself like a film hero and so much older than her, and like her father a drunkard too, I tell you. Only later I found out they were carrying on even before I arranged the marriage with that poor boy.'

Tarun desperately wanted to say something, to console

her, but no words came to him which appeared appropriate. He was ashamed to admit his spirit was dry and empty too.

She clapped once. '*Baas*, as soon as she went to live with him, he gave up tailoring and started sending her out to work so he could loaf around and get drunk with his *lafanga* friends. If she refuses to work the beatings start. But she refuses to leave him. I don't know what kind of magic he has done on her.'

Tarun wondered if Pyari knew the kind of 'work' her daughter did? There was no way he could tell her. He understood her pain, and of the family. The evidence was on her face, deeply ingrained, as she stared with blank eyes at the floor.

'You look unwell, better go home,' she said.

Tarun nodded, agreeing. The dreams of the past few months thundered down on him all at once, like a torrent from a burst dam, with wrecks and jetsam from various stages of his life jumbled and cascading down along with it – so that he was twelve again and sitting on a bed, first night in the ashram dormitory, inquisitive stare of boys, whispering in each other's ears, someone pocking a finger in his chest, as if checking he was real, 'you want to be my friend?' – and nineteen, father in hospital, missing him so terribly in spite of father's intense disciplinarian attitude – only girls and sassies cry, man up now. Tossing on his bed, Tarun was all these ages at once. He was ten, unable to breath – they said he had asthma, though he did not know what it meant – everything was hazy – lying in bed staring at the curtain or was it in the dormitory – lay awake delirium of terror, memorising every single flower on the wall chart. It was an old cotton sheet nailed to the mustard colour wall, the flowers were hand painted by someone: rose, chameli, raat-ki-rani, lily, marigold, and others. He liked the yellow of marigold, his favourite colour. Once he had planted a marigold in the front yard. Suraj came and placed a foot on it, laughing. Tarun cried for the entire day. It's only a plant, mother said angrily, look around you there are hundreds everywhere, you can have any you want, dig it up and replant where you want it. She was referring to the wild bushes in waste land behind the house. Krishan and Mohan mocking and teasing him, sometimes they beat him if he didn't run an errand for them, and then threaten him with more beating if he told anyone. He felt terrified of girls, and would stutter when a girl tried to befriend him, even though he was fifteen then. The tug of all these contradictory times and places made him forget where he was.

❀

The conductor yelled at him, reminding him he must pay, only children under fourteen can have free bus rides. 'Are you a child,' he said sarcastically. Tarun handed him the bus fare. He considered not going back home. Never. Wished there was a river nearby. He would take off the shoes and walk right in, keep going. He would explore the riverbed, deeper and deeper, until the feelings of worthlessness, failure, shame, and humiliation, would no longer haunt him. Swamiji's bearded face and orange kurta appeared, larger than life. I see death, he had said. His eyes piercing into him like sharp daggers. He did not say whose death. But he saw it for sure. Was it Manju's death he was seeing?

It was already dark by the time he reached home. The house was running at its normal pace. Pabiji was in the back room, saying the evening prayer. She had lit an incense, allowing the smell to diffuse throughout the house.

In the front room Padma was on the floor, with legs folded to the chest. She had taken up yoga yet again. 'Look uncle, I am doing *muktabaya asana*,' she said enthusiastically, 'I can teach you if you want.'

In bed that night he tossed from side to side. Finally, he got up and paced the yard, barefoot so as not to disturb anyone's sleep.

The stillness hung intact and impenetrable. A dog barked nearby. As if it was a relief to hear a sound. He slipped into the sandals and opened the gate. It was an eerie feeling, as if he were alone in the world. He started walking without a purpose. Turned right at the end of the lane and took the path that went all the way to the railway track. He could hear the grit under his feet. Complicated shadows making him wary of what lay ahead. A lapwing gave a startled cry. He arrived at the level crossing. Clouds of insects in the air were blinding him. He could feel them on the skin. A rusting bicycle lay discarded near the gate locked up for the night. He stood in the middle of the track. Parallel rails, narrowing into eternity, moonlight reflecting on the steel. An owl was known to live in the abandoned lookout platform. He stood very still and waited for it to come out. Nothing happened. He walked on, stepping on railway sleepers, ritualistically, as if to miss one would bring bad luck. The air whining with mosquitoes, and silence broken only occasionally by the startling dash of an animal in the undergrowth.

He waded into a field of pampas grass, the blades reaching his neck. He did not want the day to break. By walking on and on the night will stretch to eternity. He had a vision of Salim scolding him. Did I not tell you not to entangle yourself with that girl? You will suffer. Do as I say, not as I do. Do you believe in God? Well, you should. He could almost hear Salim's grating voice telling him he was looking to deify humans because he did not have the stomach for God. Yes, he was in a bid for self-transcendence, projecting onto this small succulent dancing girl to release himself from the solitary carnival of despair. He could not think of anything other than her and the components of her. Her red bangles? He was so primitive mere bangles bewitched him.

He shifted to a beaten track. It was like a thread he must follow to the end. Where is the end? Is there one?

The sky was filling up with a grey light, dissolving the dense blackness. Soon the sun would be up and blazing. Now the silence was beginning to break with the caw of crows.

A voice called from a distance, 'Tarun sahib.'

It was Harjeet. Lungi pulled high to the waist, a *lota* of water in his hand, he was going to the fields to perform the morning ablutions.

Tarun pretended he was deaf and mute.

'Tarun sahib, what are you doing here?'

Still Tarun blundered on, trampling thorny bushes, and raising dust. The sandals caked in dirt, frayed trouser legs. Like an exhausted soldier returning from the battlefield.

Harjeet dropped the lota to the ground and rushed to take Tarun's arm. 'Come, let us go home.'

❁

'At least let me drop you home,' he said, 'even if you won't tell me why you have been trekking around the jungle in the middle of the night. It is not safe around here. Wild animals or dacoits could have attacked you.'

He sipped tea out of a glass tumbler Harjeet's wife had handed him.

In the corner of his eyes tiny explosions popped, flashbulbs firing. Sitting on the rear seat of Harjeet's auto-rickshaw, clutching the support bars, he saw a girl turning into a house. His heart jolted. Is that Manju? He reared up off the seat, leaning forward, like a racehorse jockey. She turned around briefly on hearing the roar of Harjeet's auto. Their eyes met. He sat back with a deep sigh: take control of yourself you fool.

He slipped quietly in through the gate. The bedding lay where he had left it hours earlier. He wondered if anyone had missed him. He rolled everything into a bundle and carried it inside. The limbs stiff and painful, he hesitated at the door to the front room, the heart pounding, expecting to see everyone sitting erect, waiting. He could already feel everyone's eyes on him, weighing him down like a sack of grain. Illogically he expected them to know everything about the stint in the hospital, about Manju and Pyari. He yawned as he stepped inside. Savitri was at the stove boiling water for tea. Pammi was sitting on a stool reading something held to her face. Dev came out of the bathroom. 'Is the tea ready?'

'Another five minutes,' Savitri replied, 'ask Pali to go for his bath.'

'Why? What's the hurry?'

'He has the job interview this morning. Can't afford to be late,' Savitri said, dropping tea leaves on boiling water.

No one paid attention to Tarun as he placed the rolled bedding on the shelf in the hallway. He realised with great relief no one had missed him. He could do with a couple of hours of sleep. But it could not be. He could not afford to displease the boss by not turning up for work.

Pali came out, all flustered. 'Can I borrow Salim's trouser uncle. I haven't got anything suitable to wear for the interview.'

'No, Salim will be mad at me should anything happen to it.'

'I am only going to wear it for two hours. What can go wrong?' Pali pleaded.

'All right, you can wear it if it fits. But I want it back clean and pressed.'

Pali came out of the room with the trouser on, keeping it hooked up with the fingers. It was two inches too loose at the waist and the legs an inch too short.

Pammi giggled. 'You look like Charlie Chaplin.'

'That's good,' Padma said, 'even if you don't get the job, at least you will have entertained them.'

'Yes, they might give him the job for being innovative.'

'Shut up you two,' Pali yelled.

'Take them off,' Savitri said, 'I will fix it.'

With rough stitches at the waist and unfolded turnups she persuaded Pali to wear them. 'Don't be finicky. No one will notice.'

She blessed him profusely, running a hand over the head, ignoring his protests not to disrupt the carefully combed hair, and kissing him on the forehead. She gave him a lump of sugar to suck on the way out and watched him walk down the lane, keeping a vigil long after he had turned a corner. She said to Pammi tearfully, 'I have prayed sooo much to God. I hope He was listening.'

'Don't worry mama, he will pass the interview.'

Tarun was watching from the other side of the room. Tears came to his eyes too. He came over and hugged his older sister, passionately, like a little boy. Something he had not done in years. When they separated both were crying. She wiped his tears with her fingers. 'Why were you born so unlucky little brother? Why, why, why.'

26

The accident happened like this: Barrister Sawhney had made a last-minute request to hang a ceiling fan in the newly furnished office. A powerful commercial fan arrived on the day they were finishing off the project which had overstepped by ten days. Baldev and Tarun, set out installing the three-blades rotary fan with haste. But to hang the contraption at a spot where one did not exist before required more than screwing a metal plate to the concrete and connecting the wires. They had to expose the ceiling entrails to find the joists straddling load bearing walls. The fan needed to be over-pinned for safety and support and to route a fresh electric cable. After an hour of chiselling and drilling they were ready to hang.

'Yes, that spot is perfect,' the barrister said in between puffing a cigarette and studying the ceiling from different angles.

'OK boss, consider it done.' Baldev scrambled up the ladder. After some more hammering, scrapping, creating clouds of dust, he asked Tarun to pass the motor with the spindle attachment, 'unscrew the blades first.'

Tarun started detaching the blades, a little clumsily. All he wanted was sleep and solitude.

'Be careful,' Baldev yelled, 'if you damage it, it's on your bloody head.'

'I will pay, I will pay' Tarun said, pulling his face in irritation and raising the motor above his head.

'This thing is so expensive even your father will not be able to afford it.' Baldev sneered as he leaned forward and accepted the motor from Tarun's hands. He heard a crack and the rung split in two. Tarun reached out to try and save the machinery. The sudden jerk and forward movement shifted the centre of gravity too far out. He fell on his back and the heavy motor landed on his chest.

Tarun felt nothing initially. Only when he tried to sit up, he screamed. The barrister called the doctor, annoyed at the disturbance and damage to his imported GEC fan.

The doctor examined Tarun, shook his head with a smile. 'No fracture, *haddi pasli saab dheek hai*. Only bruises. I recommend cold press. Do it now, without delay,' he said, 'to whom do I send the bill?'

Tarun looked at Baldev. Baldev looked at the barrister. Barrister looked at Tarun. 'I didn't cause the accident,' the barrister said defensively with his hands up in the air.

The doctor made a face as if pained at the outcome. 'Bones will be fractured if I don't get paid,' he said dolefully and then burst into a guffawing laughter at his own humour. 'The way I see it, this is a commercial setup, the company that employs you two should be responsible for your medical expenses. Am I right, barrister sahib?'

'You are absolutely correct,' Bharat Sawhney replied, 'send the bill to Dalal and Company. I will do likewise for damage to my equipment.'

Tarun argued with Baldev, bitterly. 'How is it my fault? You should have been more careful on the ladder.' If Baldev were able to pin the blame on him, Sameer would dock his pay. He may even decide to dispense with him entirely and find a replacement. He would be back to where he was. Jobless, future as black and grim as the underground coal cellar in which he had once trapped himself accidentally while playing with Hardip. Confined for less than ten minutes, but it felt like an eternity to Tarun who had howled and scratched and banged the door believing it was the end. When finally, they released him from the death chamber, instead of sympathising and consoling him, father had pulled his ears and called him a fool and a weakling. 'Look at Hardip,' he had said, 'how smart he is for staying clear of the cellar.'

When Sameer Dalal arrived, he sent for a taxi and ordered Tarun home, 'don't come back until you are fully recovered.'

Pabiji rushed to the door on hearing the idling drone of a car engine. Tarun hobbled, supported by the driver, looking glum and burdened, as if the ghoul of death itself was sitting on his shoulders.

'Don't ask me anything,' he said and clasped his lips firmly shut.

'Have I asked anything? Have I?' she replied, 'I was going to tell you about a letter which arrived this morning.'

'So what?' He brushed past her.

She followed him in, taking his arm and pulling him around. 'Kaka, I have something to tell you.'

'What?'

'You remember the Kapur family from Jaipur,' she said and instantly his heart began weeping again, no, not more shocking news. He placed a hand on the forehead, wishing the world would stop.

Pabiji continued, 'they have written asking to meet again if we are interested. Usha says they are keen now that Mr Kapur has passed away. Now it is up to you Tarun. We will do what you want.'

He lowered himself on a chair, forgetting the aches and bruises.

❋

Back to work a week later. Sameer did not mention the smashed ceiling fan, no recrimination or docked pay. Baldev was his usual self, loud and boisterous. After the day's work, past seven in the evening, he disembarked the bus at Malviya Nagar terminus. The streetlights had already come on. People had come out for a stroll, to take in the cool air. Tarun took a shortcut through Ramdayal Street, past fast food snack stalls on open land. Skinny men with fast hands hawking cut fruit and tangy snacks: *gol gappa and chaats, chevda and dhalmuth*. Children were crowding around toys and balloons sellers. Tarun picked his way through the crowd, past the corn-on-the-cob seller, sidestepping a mountain of husk. He recognised a song blasting on a loudspeaker, a Binaca Geetmala chart topper on Ceylon Radio. Leaving behind the raucous mele Tarun turned on to the home stretch, thinking of the girl, Miss Kapur. What will the meeting be like this time?

A man almost walked into Tarun. He was broad-shouldered with solid nutcracker jaws, Tarun noticed. A boxer? The man gave Tarun a sharp look as if accusing him of blocking his path. Tarun took him for a drunken fool, and moved out of his way. The man blockaded Tarun again. Again, Tarun sidestepped, this time the opposite way. The man made an angry face as if he were insulted. Without warning he punched Tarun in the stomach.

'Oiee,' Tarun screamed, more in surprise than a warning.

The man took that as a challenge. He rained a series of blows with his meaty black hands. With each blow Tarun was stepping backwards. He tripped on the kerbside and fell on his back. 'Who are you? Why are you doing this?' Tarun yelled.

The man began kicking. On the chest and face.

'Stop it, stop it,' Tarun screamed, hoping to attract the attention of people at the food stalls. He saw the shoe coming at his face and rolled over, squelching on a pat of cow dung. Realising the only way to protect himself was by facing him squarely, fight or flee. He scrambled to his feet. 'Stop it,' he screamed and made fists as if threatening to fight back.

'Come on then.' He gestured with his arms, daring Tarun to take him on. 'You can't have what's mine.'

It blew the wits out of Tarun. What does he mean? He felt trapped blood in his chest, as the panic set it. He started running, first towards home and then changed direction. It would be dangerous to show him where he lived. He dashed into a gulley between two houses, which led to open wasteland. A puppy started yelping and giving chase. Tarun tasted a metallic flavour and realised the lips were bleeding. Past the houses he scrambled through open wasteland, raising dust as he ran. He could still hear thumping footsteps behind him. Manju's husband, he thought. They had warned him to be careful, he was a dangerous man.

He saw the man's shadow getting near, only two feet or so away and changing direction ran towards the highway linking Malvyanagar to Kalkaji. Cars and trucks were thundering past oblivious to who came in the path. Seeing a gap between a car and a lorry, he darted in, managing to cross the road in one dash. The man followed. In the haste he clipped his shoulder to the rear of the truck. The vehicle roared on, unaware of the mishap. Tarun looked behind him. The man was stumbling forward, as if propelled by a great force. Their eyes met for a split second. He looked confused, like a cat caught in headlight, before rolling into a ditch good ten feet away. Tarun stopped. There was no movement in the hollowed earth. He went closer. The man was lying face down, blood oozing from a head wound. The arm stretched behind him at an impossible angle. Dislocated shoulder, Tarun assumed. He went closer still, cautiously peered down to memorise the contours of the man's face, in case he encountered it again. His foot slipped. He was scrambling out when he heard voices. A clutch of labourers was on the way home from a construction site.

'What is going on here?'

Tarun stepped back hurriedly.

'You did this?' They were looking at the prone body and at him, alternately.

'No, I didn't do anything,' Tarun replied.

Two men jumped into the ditch and prodded the body. 'Oh, *bahanchoo*t,' one of them yelled, 'this one appears dead.'

Tarun saw a dozen pairs of eyes turn on him, accusingly. He started running. Covered the deserted wasteland in record time. As he turned into the lane, he noticed a kite fly low over his head as if it too were giving chase. Balancing its wings in the breeze, it circled and then disappeared in the darkness. He had never seen a kite out at night. It shook him even more. A bad, bad omen, he thought.

Just before entering the house, he slowed down. No one took notice of his arrival. He took off his shoes and sneaked to the bathroom. Stripped naked, showered, removing all traces of blood and dirt. Rolled the bloodstained shirt into a ball and hid it under a closet.

'What's up with the bruises, uncle,' Prabha said laughing and throwing a mock punch, 'have you been fighting again?'

Tarun nearly choked on a piece of roti. Composing himself quickly, he said, 'it's nothing, I tripped.'

He ate dinner in silence, while others were chattering, excited about the forthcoming republic day parade in Delhi. His brain was spinning like his bicycle wheels, thinking only of the body in the ditch. What if he were to die? Would Manju blame him? What about Pyari and the aunt? He knew they disliked the man. But did they dislike him enough to see him dead? And if the man were to recover from the injury, would he come after him. Tarun feared the worst.

'What?' he said to a question from Savitri.

'I am asking you if you are in pain because of the fall again,' she said irritably, 'have you gone deaf or what.'

He wanted to say yes, yes, he was in pain, in immense pain, but for reasons other than falling off a ladder or an accidental trip. 'I am going to bed early,' he said, 'I am tired.'

It was around midnight when the horizon cleared and the household woke with tremor of voices, shouts, rattling of the gate, as if under invasion by an enemy army. Arms banged on the door; feet stamped the ground with feral intensity. They collected into a whole – half a dozen policemen in the front yard. Tarun pretended to be asleep. Dev opened the front door.

'Are you Tarun?' someone barked.

'No.'

'Where is he? Get him.'

'The murderer!' another spat.

Tarun stood up, trembling, and stood rooted to a spot deep in the backyard. He saw Pabiji rushing out of her room, in dismay. 'What are you people doing?' she said to the lead policeman, 'you can't come in here.'

While she spoke, the boots stamped in, and voices closed in on hers. 'We have orders to arrest him.'

Pali tried to stop them by blocking the path.

'Out of the way, or we will arrest you too.'

'*Arre baba*, listen to me. There must be a mistake, let's

talk it over calmly.' Savitri tried to reason with them. They swept her aside. 'Pali do something,' she yelled.

They saw Tarun standing like a rabbit caught in a floodlight and rushed at him without asking the name or checking identity.

'Please, please, he is innocent, don't take him,' Pabiji was grovelling, almost on her knees.

Tarun looked back a final time. Pammi was weeping. Pabiji had sat down on the floor, clutching the head. Dev scaling the fence to wake up the neighbour who had a working telephone, recently installed.

❁

The next time Tarun came home was four weeks after they took him away, long after his entrance into the new and frightening world of Tihar jail. On the first day, the guards led him through passageways down a long flank of the building. He could hear the shouts and complaints of the inmates. The place was bigger than he could comprehend, expanding inexplicably as he walked. Cell after cell, brick after brick, it culminated in a spacious open yard blocked by high walls. A room opening onto the yard was to be his home. A repulsive smell pervaded his room and the yard, reminding Tarun of the school latrine – the smell of stale shit.

Judge had already refused bail. On brother Mohan's persistence, who had rushed over from Jamshedpur, he had persuaded the judge to allow a home visit to see his mother. Not a bail, they had maintained, but a twenty-four-hour compassionate home visit.

Mohan warned Tarun on the way home in Barrister Sawhney's car, mother had relapsed into a state of shock – afflicted by invisible spiders of grief. Although she wasn't speaking, her every gaze, every movement of her hand contained a thousand words. Tarun sunk in the seat, feeling small and defeated, blamed himself for bringing grief to the family.

Earlier Barrister Sawhney had consoled him with a hand on the shoulder. 'You have done nothing wrong. We will get you out of there. Just be patient and strong.'

The wardens, men in khaki uniforms, had brought him out to meet him, and his team of lawyers. Tarun was surprised, why he needed so many men to fight for him. Wasn't he innocent? He and brother Mohan had come into the small anteroom reserved for visitors, while a junior warden kept a watch, a little man in ill-fitting uniform. He looked even more bored than the inmates Tarun had seen, who for reasons unknown to him never received visitors.

'We will win the case,' Barrister Sawhney was reminding him repeatedly, 'provided witnesses co-operate.' Witnesses? Tarun was surprised. Then why did they not come to save him from the assault. 'They are afraid,' Barrister Sawhney had replied a little solemnly, 'Ramnath Deo has a reputation.'

Brother Suraj from Calcutta was home too. That was another surprise, for Tarun had assumed, having disgraced the family, no one would go out of their way to help. 'When did you arrive?' Tarun asked.

'This morning,' he said while shaking hands with the

barrister, 'this morning.' And then he dropped the bomb. 'We are going to build an extension for you, as you wanted.'

Tarun choked with emotion. Are they saying this to cheer me up?

'You don't worry about anything,' brother Suraj continued, 'we are going to get you out of there. We know you are innocent.'

Tarun could barely get words out, feeling ashamed that they knew everything, the whole affair, told and retold, about Manju and Pyari. He had imagined an earth-shattering uproar at home. But nothing had happened, not even a mention of his secretive activities. The incarceration in Tihar jail was punishment enough, they thought.

'Whatever has happened, has happened. We are not apportioning blame. But first things first. We must get you released,' Suraj said.

Tarun's body went tight, and he could hear himself breathing through the mouth.

Next day Tarun readied to return to the jail, worrying the suitcase handle, furrowed eyebrows, terror writ in the eyes, like a lamb going to the abattoir. One last act by Pabiji, as he was leaving: she gave him a roti thickly coated with her homemade butter, and sprinkled with salt and pepper, his favourite.

Tarun accepted the folded roti, head bowed.

Back at Tihar jail they pushed him into his cell as if he were a dangerous animal and locked the door hurriedly. Alone Tarun fell to the floor and gave a long howl – the howl of a wounded Bengal tiger ready to kill.

Who was to know the legal wranglings, delays due to over-booked courts, sicknesses, absenteeism, cancellations, plain inefficiency, corruption, the trial would take so long to commence? It started two years, six months, and twenty days after he had become the resident of Tihar jail? He was getting regular visits from family members. Now it was they who were feeling the guilt, shame, and frustration, for they were powerless to get him out. Two months previously Bharat Sawhney had visited him accompanied by a big man of strange manners. Waxed moustache, black bowtie, lights reflecting off his smooth skull. This man reminded Tarun of Hindi film villains.

'This is Narindra Sapra,' Barrister Sawhney said, looking into Tarun's eyes, but pointing at his companion, 'from now on you will be seeing him instead of me. He is a well-respected criminal barrister. You remember the famous case of Sinha versus the state, and the case of Baladewi who had killed her husband. It was none else but Mr Sapra who had managed to prove his clients' innocence.'

Tarun nodded blankly.

'I am retiring from the case,' Sawhney said, and explained the procedure prior to the trial and on the day itself. Again, he counselled Tarun on how to conduct himself in the court. Sit or stand erect, look directly into the Judge's or prosecuting lawyer's eyes when spoken to. 'Sameer Dalal is paying your legal bills. He has requested the appointment of my friend here, Narindra Sapra.'

'Sameer,' Tarun cried, astonished. He had heard nothing

from his boss or anyone else from the office, nor was he expecting to. A hard nosed businessman, why would he spend time or money on someone who was of little use to him?

On the day of the trial, brothers Suraj and Mohan sat on a bench near Tarun, Barrister Narindra Sapra was his usual self, sullen and sober with clenched teeth and a solid jaw. The map of emotion splayed over his face was grainy and unintelligible. 'There is no such thing as luck. If you want something you have to go for it,' he said, 'we have worked hard to persuade the witnesses to come to court. They are solid and dependable.'

On the third day Tarun took the stand. Narindra Sapra's thick eyebrows rose sternly, as if reminding him what he must say and do. Tarun answered all the questions fearlessly, feeling he had nothing to hide.

That afternoon he watched with mouth agape as Pyari arrived at the witness stand, hesitant and frightened. She was a different person than the woman he last saw in the hospital. She was lighter in complexion, older with tints of grey in her long hair. She seemed to pause between speeches in the way a driver would slow the vehicle down and ramp up again.

After Pyari stood down Tarun observed a strange transformation in Narindra Sapra. He smiled. This was the first time he had seen the barrister appear satisfied. Instead of a stage villain, he surfaced briefly as a comedian with a large belly, a comical character, again of Bombay films. He took Tarun's hand in his and pumped life into it. 'Relaaaaax, Tarun, relaaaaax.'

The court was emptying when Sapra stood up abruptly and said to his assistant, 'I hope Mankad has scored a century. If not, I don't want to know.'

The assistant, a short man with a heavily starched white shirt and a fountain pen clipped to the breast pocket, did not reply. He continued methodically collecting the folders and making a single heap.

'Well Sharma – have you lost your tongue?'

'Sir, you said you didn't want to know,' the assistant replied, and then added after a pause, 'twenty-six, caught mid-wicket.'

'Bloody fool,' Sapra boomed, 'never mind, my bet is on Farooq Engineer. Now he is a top-class batsman, if there ever was one.'

'Sir.'

'Yes?'

'Engineer... duck.' Sharma said coyly and made a circle with his forefinger and thumb.

'*Aaah*, damn fools,' Sapra scowled, thumping the desk, 'call the driver, time to go home.'

Mohan leaned forward and whispered in Tarun's ears, 'this is a good sign. They will find you innocent... one hundred percent... it's that cleaning woman, Pyari.'

'What about her,' Tarun asked, thoroughly bewildered at what was going on.

'Her testimony has turned the case around in your favour.' He patted Tarun on the back as two court ushers were leading him away.

Tarun was going home. Seated on the back seat of a hired car, flanked by brothers Mohan and Suraj, they spoke little. Since the day he had entered the prison, he had begun avoiding talking to his brothers and the nephews who visited him once or twice a month. He could not bear to face them. The salvation he had hoped – the prospect of a new wedded life violently thrashed – like the washerwoman beating soap spudded garments with a wooden club. He had confided mostly in the barrister, a man whose voice was commanding and who often reassured him, beyond any other person, that he would soon go free, with the refrain, 'in a brief time.'

As they drove home, Tarun looked out the window feeling as if he was in a city he had never visited before, a city in the hysteria of going home too. In the twilight that was now the colour of dust, in the fury of honking cars, stranded buses and scooter rickshaws, women emerging from a municipal building were crossing the road in the crevices where one bumper ended, and another began. Unable to hold back the question that had been throbbing in his head, he said, 'is Pyari's daughter alive or dead?' He could not bring himself to say the name Manju, for that would imply an element of intimacy.

Suraj made a harsh face. 'I don't want to talk about it.'

Mohan cut in. 'You do not worry about her. From now on you are to stay clear of these kinds of people.'

They entered a road that was so beat up and potholed the driver had to veer onto the pavement, cursing under his breath at other road users.

'Hope they did not mistreat you after I complained,'

Mohan said. He indeed had written a letter of complaint about the inadequate quality of food in the prison, after Tarun had caught food poisoning and dysentery which had lasted more than two weeks.

'No, it was all right,' Tarun said.

Though no one had beaten or bullied him, Tarun felt he had lied. There had been threats and verbal abuse. They had called him a bloodlust murderer, a *khooni*, by the wardens. They had put him in an empty cell with just one window, through which he could see inside other cells. His cell had a dirty sheet on the floor, a bucket to defecate in an emergency. In the cell opposite was a very dark-skinned man. Boils, scars, and dirt covered his body. He sat in a corner of his cage staring blankly at the wall, vacant catatonic expression. This man briefly became Tarun's friend.

'We were allowed out of the cells for two hours every morning for fresh air and a wash,' Tarun said. He did not elaborate that there was only one toilet and one water tap for twenty men to share. There was always a scramble to get to the toilet, sometimes even fights broke out. The tap was in the open yard. You had to sit under it to wash yourself. Only the lucky ones had soap, those who received toiletry parcels from families. Salim also used to bring him soaps, toothpaste and dry fruits or nuts. Full of remorse, he blamed himself for everything. If I had not taken you to Abida Bai nothing of this would have happened. He begged Tarun for forgiveness. For eighteen months he was a regular visitor, if he could not visit, he used to send a letter. Everything stopped abruptly after the month of July. In the last letter Salim had written a short touching story, titled The Friendship. Tarun read it sitting alone, missing his friend and human interaction, and it had brought tears to his eyes.

The Friendship

My steps faltered on reaching the bazaar buzzing with brisk trade. People were buying and selling relationships. The heart beating nervously, I walked up to a shopkeeper and asked him what the going rate was. 'Give me your best price,' I said.

'Which one would you like,' asked the shopkeeper, 'a son's relationship... or father's... sister's or brother?'

I was nervous about revealing what I was after.

'Speak up sir,' he said, taking my silence as lack of interest, 'I will give you a good price but tell me what kind of relationship you wish to purchase today... of humanity... or love... or mother's... or' he lowered his voice here and beckoned me closer, as if offering something extremely rare and valuable, 'the ultimate truth?'

Not even the ultimate truth, what I desired was entirely different.

'Speak up sir,' he said, 'say something, anything. Why are you silent?'

With trembling lips, I said, 'I want a friend – I want friendship.'

The shopkeeper's eyes opened wide in horror, and he shook his head. 'Oh babu,' he said, 'don't you know humanity functions on this very relationship. I beg your pardon, but this relationship cannot be bought or sold. For it is impossible to put a price on friendship, it is invaluable… the day we place a price tag on it, that will be the end of humanity.'

Next day Tarun persuaded the man in the opposite cell to come out and wash himself, lending him his bar of Vatni soap. The man spoke a word for the first time in months. 'Sukhdayal,' he said tapping his chest. Tarun gasped. 'Your name is Sukhdayal. My father was also Sukhdayal.'

Sukhdayal accepted Tarun's bar of soap, but then appeared reluctant to leave his room as if it was an act of extreme daring.

'Go, go,' Tarun said, 'you are smelling the sky, and you might become ill.' As if the man was healthy and fit. He looked extremely pale, and his breathing laboured to the extreme. He presented a blank face as if he did not know where he was.

With little more persuasion the man did come out to the yard where people were milling around, brushing teeth, coughing, gargling. Others were chanting morning bhajans while they waited for their turn at the latrine or the tap for a bath. Sukhdayal joined the line at the tap, frequently examining the bar of Vatni soap in his hand as if he did not know why he had it.

People were giving him a wide berth. 'Oi, stand back,' someone hissed, 'you are making me sick.'

When it was his turn, Sukhdayal stripped to the waist exposing his skeletal pallid chest as grimy as a floor mat at a flour mill. He sat down on his haunches on the slippery concrete enclosure layered with soapy scum and raised his bony fingers to turn the tap on.

'Don't touch it,' someone said, 'get out. I am going to bathe.' The voice was steel-rimmed and cold, the kind that draws attention and instils fear

Tarun heard it and turned to look. His heart flipped at the sight of a short man with a long spiky moustache. Naked but for a very brief loincloth covering his waist and genitals. The skin glistened in the sun with massaged mustard oil. Its pungent smell wafted to where Tarun was standing. Tarun recognised him instantly as the notorious gangster Kalu. Even in jail he commanded loyalty. A band of hangers-on were standing around him like moths attracted to light.

'Son of a donkey, I told you to move from here,' he barked at Sukhdayal, 'are you deaf, doesn't your brain work.'

People began shuffling away from the tap while Sukhdayal was looking around, confusion etched on his face. Tarun wanted to shout a warning to his friend: forget about bathing for now, get up and run.

But Sukhdayal, either did not appreciate the gravity of the situation or had decided on reckless defiance, resumed his bathing by turning the tap on.

'Sukhdayal.' Tarun wanted to shout but managed only a weak caw, too afraid to draw gangster Kalu's attention to him. Kalu placed a foot on Sukhdayal's shoulder and pushed him to the floor. What followed next was too quick for anyone to intervene, even if they wanted to.

Sukhdayal jumped to his feet and faced Kalu defiantly, letting his red fiery eyes speak.

'I said out of my face donkey,' Kalu hissed, 'if you know what is good for you.'

Sukhdayal reacted by pushing the soaking bar of soap at Kalu's face, half lodging it in his mouth.

Two of his followers rushed to his assistance.

No one saw it until it was in gangster Kalu's hand. He crooked his arm and pushed the knife in Sukhdayal's chest. Keeping it lodged as his victim sank with a terrifying scream. Once the body was on the floor, he pulled the knife out with a sideway jerk as if slicing a piece of meat.

Sukhdayal tried to raise his head, eyes wide open as if trying to memorise the faces around him. He coughed, fell back, and did not move again.

Tarun felt his knees weaken, and he too sank to the floor like his friend. Blood spurted from the cut and mingled with the falling tap water; a pink flow gushed towards the gutter. Tarun felt sick, bile rising in his stomach. He cried out to the void, to the frightened faces of onlookers standing a safe distance, vowing never to befriend anyone again and inviting death and misery.

Sukhdayal's red mark in his mind's eyes mingled with pink and crimson of flesh in a butcher's shop they were passing. Tarun quickly turned to look the other way. He saw his reflection in the car's window pane and sucked in air with shock, convinced he resembled Sukhdayal. He was like a worn old blanket, face all dry, poked with pores, cheeks gaunt, eyes like dim windows.

'Why is Sameer Dalal paying the barrister's fee?' Tarun asked as they drove past Malvyanagar post office, nearing home.

'You don't worry about that. We have worked it out between us,' Suraj said, 'he wants you back at work as soon as you are ready.'

Tarun swallowed hard. The throat felt as if it was stuffed with cotton pad. How will work colleagues react? He imagined them laughing behind his back or gawking at him as if he were a released prisoner, who indeed he was. But he was not a criminal. That was clear, and they ought to know it. They should know he was the victim, not an aggressor. Whatever had happened to him was a travesty of justice. He felt quite strongly about it and was ready to speak up now, to defend his honour. The time in jail had hardened him, made him more strident. He recognised the change in him, but not why. And in those years, he had not had an epileptic fit, not once, even though he had become lax with the medication, giving it up entirely in the final six months. But he had not quit the childish imaginings, which he used to indulge in lavishly while passing time, staring out the bunch of the window. Always about Sangeeta Pal. She has professed her love for him, a love so vigorous and pure, she refuses to marry anyone else, not even countenance such a thought. I will wait for you Tarun, wait until you have proved your innocence, however long it takes, wait from now to eternity. He chose to believe in the fiction wilfully. Exerting such power that over time he had come to accept it as revealed truth.

He stood with a hand on the metal gate, looked up and down the lane and at the house. Everything appeared as it was two and half years ago. The same sight and sounds, cries of hawkers shuffling from door to door, people on bicycles clinking the bells, children screaming, radio blaring in the neighbour's house. He wondered if Satish Babu was still around. Then he saw a cluster of bright yellow marigolds growing in a corner of the yard, his favourite flower. He knew instantly who had planted them. It had to be Pammi.

But the house was strangely quiet. The front door firmly closed. No one had come out to meet him.

Suraj placed a hand on Tarun's shoulders and turned him around to face him. 'I met Dalal this morning at the Gymkhana Club,' he said, 'he already knew the verdict, innocent of all charges, and that you were going home today. It is an excellent opportunity for a fresh beginning. I suggest you start work from the first of the month. Don't you agree?'

'Yes,' Tarun said.

'Good, you can go in now,' Suraj said and pushed him gently towards the house.

Tarun walked past the unpruned jamun tree, taking in the familiar fragrance of the fruit, feeling its sugary acidic flavour on the tongue. He opened the door with a firm thrust, intending to leave it ajar to allow flow of air throughout the house, as he used to do each morning upon waking. Suddenly he heard a rapturous applause and shouts of, 'surprise, surprise,' and, 'welcome home Tarun.'

Savitri, Pammi, Padma, even Pali, and Usha, sprang from behind the door to give him a surprise welcome. There was a scramble to hug him, ruffle his hair and tug his shirt. The heart brimming with joy, Tarun allowed him to be manhandled any which way they wanted. Then they made way for Pabiji. She pulled his head down and kissed him on the forehead and then handed him a glass of sweet lassi. 'Drink this,' she said as though it was a ceremonial elixir. He saw her hands were weak, and she looked old and frail with thick-lensed glasses covering her eyes. And then he received the biggest shock of all. Standing at the rear was a girl, who up till then had remained shielded by others. He had not expected to see her, ever, even though he was seeing her every day.

'Sangeeta,' he mumbled. She looked leaner, a little worn, but confident, like she had aged overnight. But hell. It was her.

She folded her arms and smiled. 'Yes, it's me,' she said, a twinkle in her eyes as if she was enjoying shocking him. 'How are you?'

A long silence fell over him as he scrambled to pull himself together. His heart inching up the throat till he could hear blood in the ears and the skin, the chest, every part of the body going heavy.

'I am all right,' he said.

Footnote

Dear reader, imagine this: you wake up from a dream, a wild fantasy, and then find the dream is coming true in real life, or you discover lightning has struck the same spot twice, or a miracle has indeed happened.

Yes, you have guessed it right. Tarun and Sangeeta got married. She was the sunlight under which he stood, warmed.

While Tarun was away, Sangeeta had gone back home from the hiding place with a friend. The family had a reconciliation, and she got the freedom she craved, to chart her own life. About marriage, she said she wanted Tarun. Her resolve was steadfast. She said she would wait till the boy, trapped in a poisonous cobweb of other people's covetous behaviour, was freed. Pragmatic Savitri did not spurn Mohindra Pal's approach this time.

They married in the month of Vaisakhi. It was a simple but joyous occasion. Tarun astride a white stallion to claim his bride. The mare supplied by Harjeet. Baldev Singh beat the *dhol* and danced like a demented dervish. All his work colleagues were present. Sameer Dalal, Bharat Sawhney, Narindra Sapra, slopping whiskey and sharing bawdy jokes.

Pabiji, attacked by the monstrous termite of grief and old age died two years later. Sister Savitri had moved out of the house, to live with daughters Padma and Pammi who had procured a flat in nearby Kalkaji. Pali, one morning rent the air with screams of joy, waving a letter of acceptance in people's faces. He went off to Muradabag to start an apprenticeship with an ordnance manufacturing company. Dev too had received an offer of employment from a school in England. Within three months he had waved goodbye to family and friends at Palam airport, boarding a BOAC flight to London. Earlier, friend Salim had met a tragic death, mowed down by a runaway truck on GB Road. All this happened while Tarun was still in Tihar jail, attempting to make friends with a Sukhdayal from Punjab.

Since her appearance at the courthouse Pyari had melted away. Tarun made no attempt to contact her or Manju. Sister Mita continued to come and go as she pleased, commuting between Rishikesh and Malvyanager.

Sangeeta had become a famed author. Her memoirs, turned into a novel, were snapped up by MacMillan. At the age of fifty-six, while the family was celebrating Diwali with lit candles, laughter, and exchange of gifts, exploding fireworks, and ringing temple bells, Tarun lay dying of a sudden heart attack.

After a period of mourning Sangeeta returned to her ancestral home. The house sat empty until brother Mohan moved in with the family.

In 1985, having outlived its useful purpose, the house was set for demolition in favour of a modern three-storey apartment block. While they were carrying away the furniture and knocking down walls an object came in light under the Godrej steel almirah, embedded in ancient cobwebs and layers of dust. It was an old matchbox. Padma recognised it as part of Tarun's collection. This specimen was about seventy years old. Matchsticks still rattled inside the box, though the sulphur had melted and burred. The label was still readable. It read *Bengal Tiger*. At the centre was a crudely sketched image of a tiger with black stripes. Lower down was the writing: *Safety match box, Retail price two paise. Made in India* was printed on the reverse.